A Recipe from Rome

LAURA BOTTEN

ISBN 979-8-9881338-0-3 (paperback)

ISBN 979-8-9881338-1-0 (e-book)

Published by Laura Botten

www.laurabotten.com

To my mother, whose heart and kitchen are always full;
and to anyone who has ever bought me a pizza.

*You just can't argue with it: food is one of life's
greatest pleasures. Take anything else away,
but leave me my food. Food was art, curiosity,
sensual gratification. Food was love.*

— Luca Spaghetti

THE APPLEBY BIRTHDAY cheesecake is a thing of beauty. I don't know who's drooling over it more: me or my friend Simon Becker. He's been staring at it with a greedy hunger in his eyes throughout the entire song right up until I blow out the candles.

A crust of soft cookie crumbles the color of sand, creamy white batter, and, special for today, a top layer of dark red cherries. I can already taste it without even taking a bite: mild and sweet, as comforting as a hug from my mother.

"What'd ya wish for, Appleby?" he asks, head tilted to one side.

"That this was 1974 instead of 2004. We were so born in the wrong decade." I yank the candles from the cake, tossing them on a paper plate.

As catchy as "Happy birthday, dear April" is, my eyes have been glued to the microwave clock counting down the hours until that monotonous melody in my head will be upgraded to that of Creedence Clearwater Revival. But having had the misfortune of being born a few decades too late, it'll have to be without the Fogerty Brothers in the lineup.

"I've heard good things about Creedence Clearwater Revisited," my friend reassures me. "Although I don't think anyone can top Australian Pink Floyd." Knowingly, I nod in agreement.

My mom, her blond hair pulled back into a thick pony tail, slices each of us a generous hunk of cheesecake, the three of us huddled together around the small kitchen table at our humble Appleby household in a quiet suburb of Chicago. Roy Orbison's voice echoes out of the tinny speakers of her old record player that stubbornly persists to keep working all these decades later. When she's at work, Simon and I dig through her hidden collection of cooler artists like the Doors and the Stones, the warm musky scent filling the air, dust under our fingernails.

Simon eyes his slice as it's placed before him. "I've been looking forward to your birthday for months." His laugh sputters out of him, crinkling his brown eyes, sparkling with anticipation.

I slice off a piece on my fork. "Becks, I've been looking forward to it for three-hundred-sixty-four days." The cake feels cool and creamy on my tongue, leaving hints of delicate sweetness amidst bursts of tangy cherries.

Earlier, bowls and bowls filled with the goopy batter were scattered on the stove and countertops, ready for the taking—Mom makes extra because I like the raw batter, eggs be damned. On baking days, the kitchen looks like a movie production set for *Willy Wonka*, littered with sweets on every surface. Sometimes, with every bowl of batter or brownies or chocolate pudding I eat, I feel like I'm slowly mastering the role of an Oompa Loompa. "Have another bowl," Mom says. Consider it done, Ma.

"I can make one for you too, Simon," my mom says, her blue eyes filling with hope as she looks at him. "Isn't your birthday coming up soon?" She's sitting back with a cup of coffee in her hands—her sixth of the day—content to watch the hours she slaved away in the kitchen pay off via two hungry teenagers. "April can bring it to you at school."

"That's okay," Simon says with a mouth full of cake. "I ordered a cheesecake last year for my birthday. I'll probably do that again."

"Didn't you say it was awful?" I ask.

"It wasn't *awful*." He takes a swig of milk. "It was just… different. Not as good as Ms. Appleby's." He looks at her with a sheepish grin before taking another big bite.

"You sure you don't want some?" I ask my mom. "Every year, you go to all this trouble and never take a slice for yourself."

She frowns and shakes her head, tucking a stray strand behind her ear. "You only turn eighteen once. There's plenty." She pushes the cake closer to me and my friend, who despite having just been served a piece, is quite obviously still lusting after the rest with his eyes. Hey, who am I to judge? It takes one to know one.

"One" being a gourmand. How we've both managed to save room for dessert after having not one serving, but two, of my mom's famous spaghetti is mind-boggling.

Earlier this week she had asked me, "What do you want for your birthday dinner? I'm giving you total control over the menu. And don't worry about dessert—I've got that covered." Her secret sparkled in her eyes, two bright oceans of promise.

"Spaghetti okay?"

She feigned shock and pinched my cheeks playfully. "We just had spaghetti two weeks ago."

"By my calculations, it was three weeks ago."

"Oh, how have you survived for three whole weeks without spaghetti?" She'd winked at me before folding the last of the laundry. "Sure you're not tired of it? I can make something else. Spaghetti's so… simple."

"No way, never," I said, grabbing a stack of towels and shoving them in a most untidy way in the narrow linen closet. "No one makes it like you. Tastes like Grandma used to make it."

"Well, she taught me an old trick a long time ago. And one day, I'll teach it to you. Secret's in the sauce." She'd glanced at the picture of the three of us on the wall. I'm three-years-old in it, a dead ringer for my mom in our matching blond hair and blue eyes. She and my grandma are standing on either side of the pony I'm sitting on. I still have the same eyes and hair, only now the former are covered by glasses and the latter is a bit darker and too short to be in pigtails. "She'd be so proud of you, getting ready to go off to college." The pride in her face as she beamed at me, caressing my cheek with her warm hand, had melted me like butter.

❦

With two full tummies, Simon and I pull into a parking garage near the Rialto Square Theater in Joliet. He parks his Honda Civic on the top level, waiting to turn off the car until the last note of "Heroes" by David Bowie fades out: a marker of a true friend—a true *human being*. You don't cut off David Bowie. He thumbs his chest indicating he's the king, then points to me, the queen, all while singing along in his nasal voice. I humor him, playing an incredible virtuoso air guitar solo.

Once inside, underneath the mesmerizing neon lights of the theater, our last hurrah begins before we go off to two different colleges. While he pledges in a fraternity at a big state university to study esoteric theories like politics and philosophy, I'll bunk at the dorms of a small private college in the city—close enough to home that I can eat my mom's cooking every weekend—where I'll "study" radio broadcasting (which really just sounds like a way to earn college credit for listening to more CCR). Simon agrees with me that I already have the perfect radio name: April Appleby.

Based on the twinkle in his eyes and the silly grin on his face, this might be the best concert we've seen in the last four years. "Appleby," he shouts to me over the live music, "this is even better than when we saw Peter Frampton at Summerfest."

"I know! And we were in the front row for that one!"

When they launch into "Down on the Corner," my cheeks start to hurt from smiling so much. What's not to smile about? Tonight's been perfect. Singing along with our favorite band feels like we're taking an oath to stay friends forever, our bond strengthened while the rollicking sounds of the sixties and seventies swirl underneath the glow of the gilded theater. Our bodies never make a dent on the red seats as we stand, dance, and sing like there's no tomorrow.

I can still smell the sauce simmering, taste the creamy batter. And now, as I hear the sounds of my favorite band, all my senses seem to be ushering me into a new trip around the sun, piloted by the two people who are always there for me.

FIFTEEN YEARS LATER

CHAPTER 1

OLD FLAMES

"Ouch!" My toast is burned again, and it feels like two hot rocks between my fingers as I yank them from the toaster, which apparently has only one setting no matter how many times I fiddle with it: charred. They land with a thud on the plate, which still has yesterday's crumbs on it. I sigh. "Now to make this edible."

First, the butter. It melts against the black as the kitchen fills with the sound of scraping. Then raspberry jam from a jar that's nearly empty. I scribble "jam" on an ever-growing grocery list, and head for the dining room table, shoving over my laptop, a pile of unopened mail, and a rainbow of post-it notes with various illegible passwords jotted down on them.

Tater Tot meows at my feet. "I know, hardly an impressive meal to start the day." My teeth crunch into the bread, and Tot meows again. "You're not satisfied with your breakfast either? You barely made a dent." Her little plate of goop sits on the floor, the dining room infused with the odor of fish oil.

"Well, mine ain't much better." I leave a few bites of scorched bread—not because it doesn't taste good, which it doesn't, but because I lost my appetite after receiving that text last night.

"Here, jump up." I lift the blinds just high enough for her to sit on the windowsill, and a hazy square of light barely brightens the room. I set the plate next to my overflowing sink. Dishes: another item on the to-do list. But first, a morning run to clear my head after a night of restless sleep.

The October breeze feels cool against my face, hot with sweat. I run underneath the L tracks, held up by concrete that looks like it could crumble to the streets of Chicago at any second, its colorful murals blurring past me as I propel myself toward Montrose Beach. The rumble of a train above me heads downtown, and it drowns out the sound of my breathing. Adrenaline carries me to the lake as the rays of a ripe tangerine sun ricochet off the choppy waves like a frenzied kaleidoscope. Gravel crunches beneath my feet as I quicken my pace heading north along the rocky shore. The crashing waves sing to me, geese honk overhead, and my breathing flows in a steady rhythm, trying to forget about that perplexing message that lit up my phone.

There was a time when hearing from Ian Zellner would have put the biggest smile on my face. But now, seeing his name triggered a tsunami of jumbled emotions. At first, he was a thorn in my side, seemingly oblivious that his feelings were unrequited. The last thing I needed at that time in my life was a boyfriend. What I needed was a concealer powerful enough to cover the puffy circles underneath my eyes that would not stop crying. But his persistence eventually wore me down. Catching the flu during winter term my freshman year of college was the opportunity he was waiting for to prove his feelings. He knocked on my dorm's door.

"Go away," I grumbled from my bed, the only source of light coming from bright flashes on the television.

"Greetings! It's Ian," he said brightly. "I come bearing gifts." After a beat, he added the enticing detail, "In the form of soup." He said the last word as if it were an offer I couldn't refuse. And, well, for me, it was.

Most college girls would wait until they had a little color in their face and a flattering outfit on before inviting a cute guy in their dorm, but I had no qualms about opening the door in my greasy hair and grubby sweats. For one thing, maybe seeing this version of me would finally do the trick to put him off pursuing me. And two, there was free food at stake, which, as it turned out, was just as appealing to me while nauseous. "What kind of soup?"

"A tried-and-true classic: chicken noodle." He handed me a warm Styrofoam cup. "I know broccoli cheddar's your favorite, but I didn't think that would go over too well right now." He pointed to my stomach, which felt like it was practicing cartwheels.

It was a gesture reminiscent of something my mother would have done for me when I was younger. Heating soup up on the stove and crumbling crackers in the broth and turning classic reruns on the TV as I was tucked underneath a blanket on the couch, perfectly content to have a fever if it meant missing school. Curious, that human nature beckons us to prepare food for someone who needs healing. A bowl of broth: a basic necessity for survival, yet it can be a powerful elixir of compassion and love, too.

"Oh! I nearly forgot!" Ian snapped his fingers, then

reached into his back pocket. "I brought you some other unnecessary-yet-enjoyable items to aid in remedying your current bout of viral discomfort." As he handed me a small paper bag, he adjusted his glasses in what looked like an attempt to hide his appraising eyes taking in my new look: unwell and lamenting. But to my surprise, his assessment of my appearance ended in a genuine smile rather than disgust.

A strawberry-flavored Hi-C juice box and a comic book appeared. While the latter was never my thing, turning him away after his trouble seemed rude. "Wanna come in? My roommate got a ride home for the weekend, so it's just me and my cesspool of germs. Don't say I didn't warn you."

Not a second of hesitation. "Sure!" He stayed close to the door after closing it, nervously running his fingers through his wavy brown hair. "Many believe the misconception that your standard navel orange contains optimum levels of vitamin C, when in fact the almighty strawberry has fourteen percent more per serving." Then he nervously fiddled with his watch, causing it to beep a couple times. "Hence my flavor selection."

It took me a second to follow. "Oh, the juice box. Good to know. Thanks."

"Apologies, I nearly forgot." He reached inside his backpack, for what I hoped was a box of chocolates—I'd need something sweet after the soup. Seconds later though, he presented a modest bouquet of yellow Gerber daisies to round out my get-well-soon kit. Some of the petals were smashed.

"They're so… alive and cheerful." I grabbed them gingerly, fearing the smashed petals might fall off. "Thanks." A vase: not part of the typical dorm accessories checklist. I set them on my desk propping them against a tower of CDs that

I borrowed from the campus radio station, where they wilted each day for a week until finding their fate in the dumpster behind the dorm.

"Shouldn't you water those?" my roommate had asked when she returned the next week.

"What's the point? They're still going to die. Why bother getting attached to something that's just going to disappear on me?"

But I didn't tell Ian that.

The breeze from Lake Michigan blows away the sweet memory of how our relationship began: an honest friendship, one that bloomed at a time when another had disappeared. Pumping my legs harder, I squint in the face of the rising sun as I turn around, heading south, a hazy view of the Chicago skyline in the distance. This new vantage point conjures up the flip side to that memory: how it all ended. All it took was one mortifying phone call nine years later to make it official. It was exactly one week after we mailed save-the-date cards to our closest friends and family. It read "April and Ian are goin' to the chapel on September first," and it had a horrid photo of us holding hands and skipping down a bridge that no one could possibly have believed was candid. Calling my maid of honor to say, "Just kidding! Don't save the date" was quite the shining moment. Torrential waterworks began despite my attempt to deliver the news with the air of a knock-knock joke. I feared the tears would run me dry with the nonstop blubbering that ensued. She was kind enough to call the rest of the guests to break the news for me. No one can understand me when I talk through my tears; my voice hits notes so high they can't even be detected by the FCC if attempted to broadcast.

At first Ian was understanding when I told him I changed

my mind about getting married. "Let's consult the Google calendar," he said calmly, as if we were rescheduling a lunch date. "Have you synced yours up with mine yet? I'm sure a superior date will present itself. Not May though—there's a huge tech conference I must attend—but we probably won't wait *that* long to postpone."

God bless him and his gadgets. His toys. He was a computer geek, and I, a radio nerd. Not quite enough common ground upon which to build a marriage. I never even felt a single butterfly flutter in his presence. We were always better off as friends, but after he'd given me a sense of home and love during the years when I'd needed them the most, it was far too easy to walk right into his open arms and stay there, huddled in safety while my world fell apart. If I had broken things off with him, wouldn't he have felt just as abandoned as I'd felt when I lost my mom? It never seemed like the right time. It was now or never.

"We're not postponing." My voice was quiet, but firm. Somewhere I found the strength to bring my eyes to his. "We're canceling."

He reached out to take my hand. My instinct was to shake it off, but I let him have this one last gesture of intimacy with me. "Whatever's the matter? Have I done something? Have I upset you?" After a few seconds, the tiniest of smiles softened the worry in his face. "Have the latest Android updates made your life a living hell? God knows the latest system upgrade was colossal. I'm happy to move the SIM card into your old phone."

A tired laugh escaped my mouth. "I don't think a SIM card is going to solve this problem." My fingers felt swollen from the heat of his hand, and I slid mine out from underneath. Without looking at him, I removed the ring, struggling a bit around the knuckle. It felt like I might pull my finger out of its socket, but I had to see this through. "Sorry, Ian." I reached my hand over to him, palm up, displaying the ring. "I'm an Appleby, not a Zellner." His face lined with confusion; not pain like I'd expected. That was a small comfort.

Feeling a lump rise in my throat, I push myself to run faster but no matter how quickly I pedal my legs, the heartbreak lurks in my mind's rearview mirror, haunting me every time I glance back at it. The one solace that softened walking away from Ian was our mutually unorthodox decision to remain friends. This has proven extremely effortless, except when it's not, which has, so far, only been the case under one specific circumstance: when one of us is dating someone else. It's too third-wheelish. Which is why I have to wonder why he suddenly texted me last night. He didn't say much, just "Greetings, it's Ian, I trust this is still your number?" Did he and his latest girlfriend split up? Does he want us to pick up where we left off and resume our friendship again? Because that's starting to wear on me a bit. He's either in my past, or my present. All this back and forth is making me more nauseous than when I had that bout of flu in college. How do I tell him that if our friendship has contingencies, then I'd rather it remain ancient history?

All these mixed-up feelings swirl inside me like a Midwestern tornado, driving me to a near sprint, my feet kicking up gravel. Sweat seeps into my shirt despite the cool autumn air. A lock of my hair comes free from my messy bobby-pinned bun, blowing in the breeze. My heart, already racing from running nearly five miles, beats even harder now at the thought of the uncomfortable conversation I'll soon be having with someone who, in vain, once offered to build a life with me.

Leaving the lake behind, I gulp in the fresh air as I run back to my Lincoln Square apartment, my shadow challenging me to a race. I breathe to the rhythm of my pedaling legs. It's meditative—hypnotic almost. Before I know it, I'm racing down the last block, running off the confusion and heartbreak, considering possible responses to text Ian.

"Yep, you've reached your ex-fiancé. 'Sup?"

"Oh, you remembered me? You must be single again."

"Yo, I'm still really sorry for breaking your heart and I kind of miss you but it hurts too much so let's just end this back and forth once and for all, k?"

Slowing to a walk, I'm back at my front door, panting as I climb up the three flights to my apartment, the stuffy air in the stairwell stifling. I unlace my shoes, turn the key, and squeeze in through the door before Tot can escape into the hallway. The smiling faces of me, my mom, and my grandma look back at me from a wood frame on the wall, oblivious to the future's losses we'd endure.

"What should I say to him?" But no words come. My mom's face simply smiles back at me, one hand around my shoulders, the other petting the pony. Her eyes two beautiful blue, shiny marbles.

My fingers are damp as I swap my sunglasses for my regular ones. I squint at the bright screen of my phone, taking a steadying breath. But before I can reply to Ian, an unexpected social media message distracts me:

"Hey, Appleby, what are you doing the week of November fourth? My work's sending me to Rome, and I can bring a guest."

Simon Becker sure knows how to break the silence after fifteen years.

CHAPTER 2

SECRET INGREDIENTS

"**DON'T YOU THINK** you're going to have enough pizza in Italy?" my friend Greg asks as we hustle back to my apartment, the pizza box keeping my hands warm against the October chill.

"You can never have enough pizza." The wind picks up, blowing my hair in my face and threatening to take our bag of bruschetta with it. "Besides, the spaghetti I attempted to make didn't turn out—again. Ugh. I spent so much time messing with the sauce—came out way too sweet—that I overcooked the pasta and it turned to mush."

"Cooking never exactly was your forte." Greg snickers.

"Nope, but eating on the other hand…" I hold up the pizza box and don a cheesy smile, "I'm a pro."

Between my mom's homecooked meals, Ian's attempts at cooking when we lived together, and now living mere blocks from my favorite pizzeria, I've never needed to learn how to cook a proper meal. As for my mom's sauce, she never had a chance to let me in on the secret. So, here I am in my own place, a thirty-three-year-old woman, barely able to boil water. What I lack in cooking skills I more than make up for in regret for never having paid attention to how my mom made any of her dishes. All those after-school suppers and birthday desserts are forever locked in my childhood, and I don't have the key. I'm living under my own roof with an oven that might as well be a shoe rack.

As we scurry underneath the L tracks nearing my building Greg grumbles, "We couldn't have had this delivered?"

I fish the key out of my pocket and let us in, safe from the wind. "It's, like, five blocks."

"This wind makes it feel like five hundred," he says, huffing up the stairs. "I could have helped you with the spaghetti, you know. I've got more fresh basil and tomatoes than I know what do to with."

"In your kitchen slash greenhouse?" I kick off my shoes in the hall outside my door.

"I get buckets of sunlight in my kitchen," he says defensively. "My perennials are pretty much dead 'til spring though. Harry keeps complaining about it every time he comes over."

As the door swings open it shoves my running shoes, caked in dirt, out of the way. "Ever since I found out he's not a greenthumb, I always knew I liked that Harry." The door shuts. "Hey, I thought tomatoes only grow in the summer."

"Outside, yes. But it's toasty in my place. They're just a lot smaller and not as juicy. But still. Homegrown!" He takes off his winter beanie, revealing a mat of light brown waves, the salt and pepper gray patches more noticeable in the golden light of the sunset glowing through the window. "You should get a plant, my God," he gestures to my apartment, completely lacking any greenery whatsoever.

"If I can't pet it or eat it, I don't want to be bothered with it."

"Then get a tomato plant or something. Adding some fresh herbs and spices to a dish? Might help you with brushing up on your cooking skills before Italy."

"Or lack thereof." Cat hair flies off the curtains as I abruptly draw them shut. "Besides, I'll be eating, not cooking."

He waves the flying fur away. "As you should! But you might pick up a few things while you're there."

"Yeah, a few pounds maybe."

"Or a vacuum. God." He coughs, and I'm pretty sure it's for dramatic effect.

Italy is the last place I thought I'd finally reunite with my old chum Simon. The occasional social media "like" was the only connection we had after high school. We never had so much as a friendly beer, let alone a transcontinental vacation. Seeing his name on my phone conjured up images of our teenage years like a Polaroid slideshow. For fifteen years, my concert buddy had been noticeably absent. Our friendship has remained alive only in the past, in a time capsule of teenage zest.

But that's about to change in a few weeks.

I shove my waffle iron out of the way on my kitchen counter to clear room for the pizza. A little dried batter falls off.

"Do you ever clean?"

"Only when people I like come over." My multitasking skills impress as I both reach for a couple plates and stick my tongue out at Greg. "The waffle iron is a bitch to clean so I always put it off. Which is one of the reasons I hardly ever use it."

"And the other?" He grabs two pizza slices.

"It was a housewarming gift from Ian when we moved in together." I exaggerate a smile and give a dorky thumbs-up. "Every waffle comes served with syrup *and* a side of bad memories!"

He makes a face like he's about to lose his lunch. "How can you keep something an ex gave you? I threw all of Rick's stuff in the dumpster."

"I remember." Flicking off more dried batter, I explain, "Well, it's better than that iPod Touch he got me when he was trying to force me to like all of his shiny gadgets and precious technology. Who knows where that old thing ended up?"

Ian had to learn that the fastest way to my heart was through my stomach. That was often the route my mom took, too: loving me and feeding me were synonymous. What my mother and I lacked in financial abundance we more than made up for in groceries. To be full was to be happy, loved. I was always full.

I pat the lid of the waffle iron. "This sucker's the gift that keeps on giving, Greg. And sometimes, you just need a waffle, you know?" The plastic lid on the container of bruschetta snaps loudly as I remove it.

"Oh my God," he looks at me, the green of his eyes vibrant with a good idea, "I know what you need. You should review some restaurants in Italy for the podcast! Maybe befriend a sexy Italian chef." He throws his head back in a laugh, then wiggles his eyebrows at me while reaching for the bruschetta.

I consider his suggestion while I wedge a few pieces on my plate next to my pizza. Expand our reviews across the pond and critique some authentic Italian restaurants in Italy? Color me intrigued. "That's brilliant! Look at you, comin' up with good ideas for a change."

"And a hot chef would finally put Ian out of your mind, too."

"Hey, *he* reached out to *me*. I feel bad that I never responded. Talking to him just feels like—like opening old wounds."

Greg has been my relationship sounding board ever since we met at WRCK, a legendary classic rock station in Chicago that hired me after graduating from Columbia with a degree in radio broadcasting. We both got started behind the scenes—working bar events, running the board, grabbing the boss's coffee—and the only way we could scratch our mutual itch to be on the air was to start our own podcast out of my closet: *Order Up*, a restaurant review show. I still can't believe he actually thought I'd jump ship once WRCK gave me the afternoon slot. Me, give up an excuse to sample all the eateries in Chicago? I don't think so.

After the literal dumpster fire that was Greg's last relationship, he might not be the wisest to give love advice, but he was the one person who didn't judge me when I dumped Ian six months before the wedding. Maybe that's why Greg was so understanding: he understood firsthand how murky the waters of romance can be.

When we're done eating, I throw the leftovers in the fridge, and we head into my windowless closet-turned-studio to record the podcast, the only light coming from my laptop and a few strands of Christmas lights. Tater Tot snores lightly on the shag rug by our feet, unimpressed with my attempt at an Italian accent as I try sprinkling a few key phrases into my review.

"*Era delizioso!*" The strange combination of letters feels unfamiliar on my tongue.

"Hon, you gotta roll your R's more," Greg says. "Like this." He makes an incomprehensible noise that causes Tater Tot to wake up and glare at him.

"Who do I look like? Giada De Laurentiis? *Errrra delizioso!*" I say it with more oomph this time, exaggerating my R's and gesturing wildly with my hands for Greg's benefit.

Heavy on the sarcasm, he retorts with, "Perfect. You'll fit right in."

I adjust the pop shield on my microphone. "Okay, before we get sidetracked, I think we can both agree we're awarding a full apple for taste."

"*Sí, signorina.*"

"And they threw in complimentary *biscotti* cookies—chocolate dipped—so that's another full apple for service." We both agree to award a full apple for each of the two remaining categories, also: atmosphere (they always play Italian music in their dining room which is painted to look like you're eating al fresco in Italy), and price. "Four out of four apples for Trattoria Lucci in Lincoln Square!"

I can count on one hand the number of restaurants that we've awarded fewer than four full apples. The occasional botched takeout order from somewhere might cost them half an apple, but we reserve giving cores for the most extreme cases. In fact, we've only given a core to one establishment that failed the atmosphere category. It looked like it hadn't been cleaned since the second world war. After our visit, they failed a bunch of inspections and closed down. But damn, it tasted incredible.

"Alright, my little apple pie, I'm hittin' the bricks."

"Takin' the brown line?"

"I think I can walk the half-mile."

"Even after all that pizza?"

"All the more reason. I'm dreading tomorrow. I've got so much cleaning to do before Harry comes by. I need the place to be perfect if I'm going to get back on his good side."

"He's still droppin' hints, huh?"

"Shamelessly. And I keep pretending like I don't notice. Hence my plan to rustle him up my famous maple-glazed salmon as a distraction."

I give him an approving nod. "Look at you, Mr. Fancy Pants. But you can't avoid the subject forever; the holidays aren't too far out."

He sighs as he opens the door to leave.

Later, I edit our stumbles from the recording, and add sound effects and Italian music to the mix. Rating a restaurant that I personally eat at every month seems a smidge biased, so I take one for the team before uploading the episode to Spotify, putting the pizza to the ultimate test: The Leftover Test. Grabbing a slice from the fridge, I take a big bite without reheating. "Four out of four even when it's cold." The episode goes live.

While wiping down my kitchen counter, the flyer that's been sitting on top of the microwave for the last month taunts me again. "Cooking: The Basics" is open now for enrollment for spring classes. Maybe, with a little instruction, I could train my palate and figure out what made my mom's spaghetti so different, so special.

Damn it. Greg's a genius. I don't need some community college to teach me the basics of cooking. I'm going to Italy: pasta paradise! In Rome, I'll not only have the opportunity to eat and review authentic Italian cuisine, but I'll be surrounded by talented cooks preparing those dishes. Italian cooks, whose hearts pump spaghetti sauce into their veins. If anyone can help me figure out my mom's special sauce, it's them.

CHAPTER 3

HUSBAND MATERIAL

"Do u like Mexican?"

Looks like Simon already has a place in mind for lunch.

I tap my reply with icicle fingers, silently cursing the decrepit boiler in the bowels of my one-hundred-year-old apartment building.

"Cheese is a big part of Mexican, so yes." And let's not forget the wonder that is guac.

Today's a big day. My old buddy and I are finally getting together in person. Which is a huge relief; a small part of me hasn't allowed myself to believe that any of this is real. I've gotten too comfortable with visiting him only in my memories.

Originally, we planned on discussing trip details while running along Lake Michigan, but today's relentless rain has forced us to move onto Plan B, which involves meeting at a diner in Jefferson Park. I'll probably embarrass myself and overdo it with the guacamole, but if he's anything like he used to be, he probably will too. Accomplices for enacting the exact opposite of Plan A, like in the good ol' days.

I zip up my black raincoat and grab my big purse, a fold-up umbrella sticking out of it. "Later, Tater!" My cat doesn't bother looking up from where she's nestled on a hoodie on my bed, the room a palette of gray shadows thanks to my blinds' broken tilt wand. Not that the room would brighten up on such a dreary day anyway.

Driving over, I crank the heat on full blast. The only sensation I can feel in my nearly frozen body is my stomach flipping around as a result of the nerves that go along with a reunion fifteen years in the making. Will I still get along with Simon? Heck, will he still get along with me? WRCK starts playing Creedence and it instantly calms me down. "Have You Ever Seen the Rain?" Appropriate.

My fingers finally thaw by the time I parallel park into a spot a couple blocks from the restaurant. Accessorizing my outfit is my yellow polka dotted umbrella—it doesn't exactly turn heads the way an itsy-bitsy, teeny-weeny bikini would, but we're nowhere near swimsuit season anyway. It's almost Halloween; it hits me when a creepy clown walks past me. Normally, I'd be hitting the candy sales this time of year, but discounted Reese's cups are the last thing on my mind. What a strange feeling.

A group of young superheroes is just leaving as I walk inside the restaurant. The warm smell of fresh-baked tortillas wraps around me like a blanket. I take off my coat and grab a booth, rain dripping off my umbrella as I fold it closed. I wipe the mist from my glasses with my shirt, and just as I look up, in walks Simon, shattering my nerves into oblivion.

"Appleby!" He spreads his arms and flashes a toothy grin.

I jump up. "Becks!"

He approaches the table tilting his head to the side the way he always did in high school. It's like watching a hologram. The same short brown hair, the same baby face, the same brown eyes that twinkle when he gets excited. But a curious thing happens. Each step brings more detail into focus, namely his five o'clock shadow and rugged hands, and I watch the teenage Simon I used to know become a man before my very eyes.

We hug. Even through his sweatshirt I can feel the muscle definition on his back. That's new. His rock-hard biceps squeeze around me, and he rubs my back with his warm hands. A little trill of excitement surprises me when we let go, our faces mere inches away for a moment. Despite staying loosely in contact online, no amount of Internet selfies could do his rippled physique justice. I'm suddenly very aware of my nerdy rubber rain boots.

"Long time, no see." He even laughs the same way. A fast, high-pitched, nasal chuckle. If I closed my eyes, I'd swear we were watching *Labyrinth* in his parents' basement giggling at David Bowie's tights and wig while we ditched last period. As he sits down, he says, "Now I know how to parallel park my new truck. It's so big it doesn't fit in my garage. Didn't realize that when I bought it." Cue more laughter.

"Minor detail," I tease. When I tell him I'm more than a little skeptical why he's chosen *me* to accompany him on an international trip after fifteen years—there's got to be a catch—he flashes me an insulted look. A small ice cube slides down my throat as I drink some water, the cold descending to the pit of my stomach while I wait for his answer.

He throws his head back in a hearty laugh. "When did

you become such a cynic? No catch, I swear. C'mon, a week in Italy? Who else would love a week of spaghetti more than April Appleby?"

"I guess I did invite you over for a lot of spaghetti dinners in high school."

"I'm *still* working off those calories."

I give him a quick once-over, trying hard to repress a grin. "Looks like you've burned 'em all off by now."

After a few minutes, the waitress comes over to take our order.

"Huevos con tocino," I say in my best Mexican accent, almost as a dress rehearsal for being in a foreign country for a week.

"Skirt steak," Simon says, keeping it simple and meaty.

The waitress comes back with chips and salsa while we wait for our meal. If I were featuring this place on *Order Up*, that would automatically guarantee them a full apple for service. My hand hovers over the crunchy appetizer. "Want some?"

"Eh, I try not to have too many carbs these days." He pushes them toward me.

My friend will starve to his death in Rome.

Filling each other in on what's happened over the last fifteen years over one meal of beans and rice is a tall order, but we make an attempt. But then the conversation hits that sore spot on my heart—that spot with the purplish bruise that no longer makes me wince painfully but never quite fades away completely. He looks down at the table. After a moment, he lifts his eyes to mine and says quietly, "I'm sorry I couldn't make the funeral. I wanted to."

I swish away his apology with my hand. "You had pledges

that week. I know how crazy those frat houses are about that kind of stuff. Would've been ridiculous to fly all the way up here and miss your chance to be an Alpha Apple Pie or whatever."

The truth is that I wouldn't have known he was there even if I was looking him straight in the face. Neighbors, friends, and relatives came up to me—people I'd known for years, if not my whole life—offering condolences and comfort, but I couldn't remember who they were or how I knew them. Names escaped me, and I responded to all their apologies the same way: with a hollow "Thank you for coming" because I couldn't recall who were close to me and who were merely paying their respects.

One woman recognized the blank look on my face, trying hard to clear up my confusion. She prompted me, her voice sounding like she was talking to someone who had just woken up from a coma. "April? It's me. Suzanne. From your mom's book club in Harbor Park?" Each detail a puzzle piece that didn't quite fit, the picture nothing more than a jumbled abstract image riddled with holes.

She'd been a neighbor and a friend for fourteen years, but my mother's absence ruptured all equilibrium, and I no longer recognized the facts of my own life. It was like I was a stunt double, playing a part, trying to remember my lines. It was a kind of psychosis really: recognizing a face but having no idea who the person was. Saying goodbye to my mom meant saying goodbye to my childhood, and if that was what adulthood was going to feel like, I didn't care for it.

"I know," Simon says, bringing me back to the present, "but it seems so—so juvenile and selfish now. I should've been there for you." He reaches across the table for a second.

Is he going to grab my hand? "Hey," he says, tapping the table a couple times before pulling his hands away. "Remember those red velvet cupcakes your mom used to make? I was thinking about those the other day." He leans back and grins, the twinkle returning to his eyes.

"Those were her favorite."

"Mine too. They were so…" He snaps his fingers, alternating hands while searching for the word before landing on: "velvety."

"I wish I knew how to make them. I would have made you some for today."

He pats his stomach—underneath which, thanks to the Internet, I know hides a six-pack—and says, "It's okay. I don't think that would go over too well at the gym tomorrow. CrossFit's hard enough as is."

It doesn't take long for the conversation to steer its way to our preferred topic: music.

"Hey, did I ever tell you about the time I saw Jimmy Buffett at Northerly Island?" Turns out, after living down south after his college days, Simon's been living right around the corner from me for the past few years, heading into the city on a regular basis to catch concerts. After earning his diploma, he'd moved to Oklahoma, then St. Louis, and eventually, back to the Land of Lincoln where, unbeknownst to me, he's been in his Rosemont townhouse thanks to its close proximity to O'Hare. Honestly, I could never keep track of his whereabouts online—he never seemed to stay in one place for very long. I assumed his Chicago-tagged posts were taken during quick visits with his parents. But in reality, our reunion could have happened much sooner.

"Since when are you a Parrothead?" I tease him, crunching

on a tortilla chip. "Jimmy Buffett's a far cry from when we saw Alice Cooper in Milwaukee." What happened to the classic rocker I used to know?

He tells me that after the encore, he looked over to tell his friends that the show was so great, he'd been won over. That's when he realized he was surrounded by total strangers. "Didn't recognize a single person I was with! Turned out I wasn't even in the right section." His eyes crinkle into slits as he cracks up at the memory.

"How did you not know what section you were in?"

"Appleby, when you're eatin' cheeseburgers in paradise all night, you have to prepare for the experience a bit, you know?" He holds two fingers to his lips and inhales. Another giggle, and then the truth slaps me in the face like a sassy soap opera character: "It was the best concert ever."

The teenage boy who'd hung out with me down on the corner has grown up and moved to Margaritaville.

My stomach sinks with petty jealousy and I find myself changing the subject. "Something must be in the air. Not only have I heard from you out of the blue, but also my ex, Ian. He texted me the other day. Haven't talked to him in years."

A look of concern crosses his face for the briefest of seconds. "Uh oh. What did he want?"

I shrug. "I dunno. Never responded."

"In my experience, the only reason an ex reaches out is to get back together with you. Maybe he finally realizes what a prize he lost." He gestures to me with his hand before reaching for his water.

As our waitress sets down our food, I consider this. Up until now, I've assumed Ian wants to reactivate our friendship again—that's usually the pattern when we both happen to be single—but what if Simon's right? What if he wants more? He couldn't possibly want to get back together after all this time, could he? After I canceled our wedding? And, to muddle things up more, does Simon think I'm a prize? What exactly does he mean by that?

"Is, uh, that something you'd want? To get back together with him?"

"Please, he never even gave me butterflies. At best he gave me moths." I scoop up some eggs and change the subject yet again. "So, why exactly is your work sending you—us—to Italy?"

He explains that his company, global trucking carrier Worldswift Transport, offers annual incentives for its sales staff, which, on a technicality, Simon is a part of in the rental division. Not only is there an extravagant annual trip for its best employees, but domestic travel is a part of his day-to-day, which is much of the reason why we haven't hung out despite the fact that we've been living half an hour away from each other.

Friends aren't the only ones left behind thanks to his constant traveling; Esther bunks with his parents every time he has a plane to catch. No longer the spry little puppy he adopted in college, Esther slumps her way up her little pug-sized staircase leading to Simon's king-sized bed every night when he's at home. I practically melt as he shows me a video, his sweet encouragement as she climbs each step a reminder of why I loved spending so much time with him as a teenager. I make a silent vow to myself not to let his travels drive a wedge between our newly rekindled friendship.

"But anyway," he continues, shoving the phone back in his pocket, "all the top salesmen are going on this trip."

"Will you be working while we're there?"

"No, no. This is basically a reward for how many accounts I have. I beat my own record last year."

"Your work gives you a free trip to Italy; my job gives me free donuts once a week. Sounds about right."

"I still can't believe you landed a gig at WRCK," he says, stabbing some more steak. The station was all we listened to in high school. It was on all six of his preset buttons in his car.

"Yeah, eventually." I count on my fingers. "Let's see, three, four, no five years after hiring me, they finally gave me my own show. And all it took was for them to fire the previous host. And another one bites the dust." I lift a forkful of eggs to my mouth.

"Ch-ch-changes," he makes a crude attempt to sing David Bowie. "I miss hearing that Sunday night Doors feature you did at your college station. That was the best."

"You listened to *Psychedelic Sundays*?" I can't repress the smile on my face.

"Every week. Well, almost every week. Whenever we were too hungover from our Saturday night frat house parties, we'd sleep in, wake up in time for dinner and order Mexican food, and then stream your show. I used to brag that I knew you." Embarrassment flashes on his face for a second, and he takes a sip of water.

I often thought of him during those shows; the playlist was right up both of our alleys, reminiscent of simpler times in high school. But without my mom, there was no going home on the weekends like I'd originally planned. My weekend radio shifts became my new home. And, of course, Ian knew my schedule by heart. Had I known that an old friend was listening to me I might not have felt so alone.

Maybe I wouldn't have let things go so far with Ian; his constant presence didn't leave much room for anyone else's companionship.

"Why didn't you ever tell me? I would've given you a shout-out."

He shrugs and looks at me for a moment, as if considering his words carefully, but all he says is, "I dunno."

A quiet beat settles over the table before the conversation resumes with the subject of work.

"Sales is all I've done since college," he explains. "All at this company, too. And all in rentals." Each sentence seems to kill a little more life in his voice.

I cover my mouth, careful not to splatter him with rice while asking, "What happened to philosophy and politics? Isn't that what you studied?"

"Philosophy and politics don't pay the bills. I'm actually thinking of applying for a national position—to move up, you know? It's pretty much guaranteed; they all but offered me the job. The application is basically a formality, I just haven't filled it out yet." He scoops up some grilled veggies. "Problem is, my boss won't be too happy. He'd be lost without me."

"Shouldn't your boss want you to succeed?"

"In a perfect world. But I'm kind of stuck there. I really want a change. Everyone else has been promoted except me, and I've closed more sales than all of 'em!" He leans in and lowers his voice as if there might be a mole among the cooks behind the counter. "I think my boss keeps me where I'm at because I'm his right-hand man."

"That's totally unfair." A thought strikes me, and I can't hold back a smile. "Hey, W-W-J-D. Remember?"

We both say together, "What would John Fogerty do?"

We laugh like we're sixteen again, when the solution to our problems was to scream along to "Fortunate Son" and let the world hear the wrath of our anger about the teenage injustices we'd endured. Like when the cafeteria would run out of Bosco Sticks during lunch. A travesty.

"I'll tell you what Fogerty would do: he would freakin' go for it." I spread some beans and rice on a tortilla. "It sounds like you deserve a step up."

"I'm ready for one. I'd be way busier though, but I'd have a couple assistants. And it'd be more money."

"You could buy another truck. A smaller one!"

His laugh thunders out of him, his muscular chest vibrating. "One that would actually fit in my garage, you mean?"

"Exactly. Then you wouldn't need ten extra minutes to scrape off the ice in the winter."

"Oh, no commute. I'm remote. I've only met my boss in person a handful of times. And some of the other guys on the team I've never met at all. Who knows if they'd even recognize me?" He pushes the tortillas a little closer to me. "So, is there more to your life than rock radio?"

"I do a podcast on the side with a friend. Just for fun." I fill a tortilla with eggs and bacon and take a bite.

"Cool, what about?"

With a full mouth I say, "Food." He laughs.

When we're finished eating, our waitress clears our table and drops off the bill. I'm running out of time to bring up the elephant in the room.

"Is your work comping this trip? If not, that's cool. I have a little dough, but I might have to keep things on the frugal side out there."

"It's all paid."

"You serious? Those three little words are right up there with 'I love you' or 'free cheese pizza.'" Could this get any more perfect? First, my friend whom I've missed for fifteen years invites me to Rome, then I see he's morphed into a hunk of man, and now he tells me it won't cost a dime.

He laughs and picks up the check. But then he utters a phrase that's usually followed by bad news, and I fear my luck has run out. Apparently, there is a catch after all.

"There's just one thing." He says it nonchalantly, pulling out his wallet. My stomach does a small backflip—not the greatest feeling after you've consumed huevos con tocino.

"What's that?" Nervously, I adjust my glasses and tuck my hair behind my ears.

He casually slides his credit card into the bill with the efficiency of someone who has made that move thousands of times. His voice comes out as though he's about to make an insignificant comment about the weather or something when he hits me with:

"You're my wife."

CHAPTER 4

LEARNING TO FLY

"Just call me Mrs. Simon Becker."

Greg had nearly spat out his chicken pot pie over lunch a few days ago when I explained that I'll be playing house with my muscly old friend in Rome. "He asked you to be his *wife*?" He over-enunciated each letter of the last word so that it sounded like two syllables.

"Pretend wife," I corrected him, taking a bite of my own pie. "There's a big difference. It's a work trip for him, and he's only allowed to bring immediate family or a spouse. The latter of which he doesn't have. Which is mind-boggling; he's a sexy, rich dog dad."

"Sounds to me like you have a thing for him." He gasped sharply. "Or maybe he has a thing for you! You told me he has sisters, right? He could have brought family, but instead he wants to share a hotel room with you," he pokes me a little too hard in the chest, "in *Italia*. Did he have a thing for you in high school? Why else would he randomly bring you to

Rome now? I'm telling you: he's making a move. That's what Harry did with me and that trip to New York a couple years ago, remember?"

"And you've yet to repay him with that trip to Nebraska you've been promising him."

"He's not ready to meet my parents."

"Or you're not ready for your parents to, oh, I don't know, be happy for you?"

To shut me up, he dragged me to a thrift store where we selected a not-too-gaudy cubic zirconium ring for me. "We need it to look at least a little convincing," he said, as I tested out how it felt on my ring finger. Strange putting one on so many years after taking Ian's off.

Could Greg be right? Could Simon have had feelings for me back in high school? Sure, we spent a lot of time together, but we liked the same bands and had a bunch of classes together. It was innocent. Right? I considered asking Greg's opinion of another nugget that Simon had shared over lunch: that he'd listened to my college radio show in secret. But I shrugged it off; that was about the music, too.

The notion that Simon has feelings for me is still just as preposterous now at O'Hare, my fake diamond ring not exactly sparkling underneath the florescent lights. Flying isn't my preferred way to travel. Navigating our way through the sixth largest airport in the U.S. feels a lot like being stuck in a really elaborate corn maze. As a lifelong Midwesterner, you'd think I'd love being stuck in a corn maze.

I do not.

But at least corn mazes have caramel apples and candy corn at the finish line; O'Hare just has intimidating security checkpoints and grumpy TSA officers. And not a single caramel apple. No, I'd much prefer driving. There's nothing like the good old American road trip. Once college was behind us, Ian and I took ten days in June for one last hurrah before we had to put our shiny new degrees to work—after all, we had a down payment to save up for if we wanted that townhouse. We set out for the one city in America that was sure to feel like an escape from reality: the mystical land of hippies, peace, and free love. And the thing that was going to get us to San Francisco was my brand-new road atlas of all fifty states. It was amazing, showing every possible route for an epic road trip, like the ultimate maze on the back of a cereal box. We hit the Mother Road in my old Buick—it had been my mom's—stopping to marvel at the quirky oddities of Route 66, then turning north to snake along the California coast to San Francisco. There was just one problem: he had his phone navigate from the passenger seat. Some new app he and a friend were developing.

"Ian, will you please shut that thing off?" I'd barked as I turned up the radio to drown out the computerized woman's voice. "We've got my maps."

"I'm aware, but let's keep the GPS activated just in case."

"In case what? All we have to do is head west until we hit ocean."

"I predict you'll change your tune, April. Now that the app is coded, the next task on the docket is testing it. Steve thinks it'll be even more impactful than we imagined! This thing is going to revolutionize road travel."

"Uh huh. Don't they already have a GPS app?" The red rocks of New Mexico had blurred by outside the car. He would have seen how beautiful it was if he hadn't been staring at his phone.

"Correct, but this one will be so much more advanced. Up-to-the-second updates! Between the satellite feeds and the user-generated data, this'll be a game-changer for not only vacationers like us, but also the average commuter. And think of all the delivery truck personnel!"

"As I so often do." I paused for just enough time to roll my eyes. "Wait, does that include pizza delivery guys?"

"Once we get the configuration to merge the satellite info with the device's existing GPS data, there's no stopping what kind of traffic alerts drivers will get. Construction, accidents, downed traffic signals, potholes…"

"I already have an app for that. It's called my eyes."

"We're thinking of calling it 'Swerge.'" His eyes had lit up behind his glasses. "Get it? 'Swerve' and 'merge' combined?"

No wonder our engagement fell apart; Ian was never fazed by sudden reroutes, relishing surprises that jump out at you when you least expect it. But I needed to know what to expect ahead of time; some surprises are scarring.

Much later, when the two of us signed our life away to buy the townhouse, when he popped the question, when we set a date, all I could hear was the echo of a robotic voice warning me: "In one mile, say 'yes.' In fifty feet, move in together. At the next light, change your name and identity and become someone's wife until you die." How could I pledge my undying love to someone who I knew deep in my heart should have only been a friend? It was my grief that opened the door for his love when I was blinded by sadness, and I buried myself deep within the safety net that was Ian and his incredible ability to show compassion. Before I knew it, we were accelerating straight for the altar. I needed to find an exit from that relationship and just stop driving.

Driving isn't an option for this trip though. My new "other half" and I are finally boarding the plane an hour later than planned thanks to an unidentified delay, but Greg's theory is all I can think about. In a few hours, I'll be parading around Rome as Simon's wife. Does he expect me to kiss him? Did the hotel give us a room with one bed? Should I have packed something a little more appealing than an old T-shirt to sleep in?

"Here we are." Simon interrupts my thoughts as he finds our seats, grabbing my carry-on and stuffing it in the over-head compartment for me. He grunts a little. "Jesus, Appleby, what's in this thing?"

"The usual. A few outfits. My walking shoes—those ancient ruins are gonna be brutal. A few pairs of heels—it sounds like there are a few fancy dinners planned. My good camera, my wireless mic, chargers. Oh, my vitamins—I had to bring them; I'm always low in vitamin D. A few travel guides: a dining one, a historical one, an art one…" I trail off as Simon's face glazes over. "Okay, I put everything I own in the carry-on. What if they lose our luggage?" Heat rushes to my cheeks as I hear how paranoid I sound. He snaps the compartment shut. Thank God he goes to the gym.

"Wait, this is the wrong row." I do a double take as I look at my boarding pass. "We need 'L.'"

Simon checks his own ticket. "No, this is right. See? Row 'F.'" He holds out his ticket for me to see, the veins in his hands popping from the exertion of dealing with my luggage.

As if a delayed takeoff wasn't enough bad news, I'm now facing the distressing reality that our seats are not together. They're not even in the same row. Not a big deal for a VIP frequent flyer like Simon, but for little old April, this is worse than not having the security of a barf bag within reach. Not only am I alone on a romantic level, I'll now be alone on an aviation level. Flying through the sky, over the ocean, with no manly arm to grab onto to calm my nerves. I might be a fully grown woman, but in this moment, I feel like a big, pathetic baby.

"Who cares? Sit here anyway." He points to the seat next to him with an air of nonchalance.

My heart is now beating out of my chest to the rhythm of "Black Betty" by Ram Jam. "What if someone else has that seat?" My voice is a conspiratorial whisper.

He shrugs and teases me by whispering back in an equally conspiratorial whisper. "Maybe it's no one's seat." Well, if the sales thing doesn't work out for him—which it obviously is—he could make a killing teaching a course called "Go with the Flow for Beginners."

I take his advice and sit down next to him anyway, hoping all the other passengers walk by. But it's no use. After a couple minutes, a man stops at our row, claiming the seat I'm in as his. My carry-on nearly topples me over as I yank it from the overhead compartment; just about the only thing I didn't pack in it are my keys which are safely hiding behind a giant jug of protein powder on Simon's kitchen counter. I lug my bag a few rows back, kept company by my own worry and a tiny paper bag that I hope will remain empty.

"Keep an eye peeled for open rows," Simon texts me.

I reply with a bunch of thumbs-up emojis, hoping to conceal the fact that I'm petrified. The last time I was on a plane was seven years ago, but at least then I had some peace of mind knowing that if our plane suddenly lost control, land would break our fall, not an ocean. Which is insane—both scenarios end with me dying a brutal death. But I don't want to crash *and* drown; I'd rather just crash. It was a flight back home from San Francisco with Ian—our first of several visits there. The sunny beaches of California was the perfect setting to celebrate our engagement. The only problem was that I was walking along those sandy shores alone most of the time while he was geeking out at a big tech conference playing with the latest smartphones and gadgets. To him, this trip was a way to kill two birds with one stone. To me, it felt like a manipulative trick; he hadn't told me how much of his time the conference would eat up, and I didn't have a ticket for it. (Not that I'd have wanted to attend if I did.) That was what starting a life together looked like? Spending time apart? The red flags were waving in the wind: we weren't right for each other.

A vibration from my phone snaps me back to the plane. Simon's texting me suggestions to keep the other passengers away. *"Just tell them you have lice."*

I giggle, and my muscles relax a little. But he keeps going for good measure:

"And talk with a lisp. People avoid lispers."

A laugh blurts out and I cover my mouth with my hand, rolling my eyes. Before I know it, my heartbeat slows down and my anxiety crisis subsides. And, hey, maybe it's actually better not to be sitting next to him on this nerve-wracking seven-hour flight. What if I really do throw up? Me vomiting up the airport wine I'd hoped would calm my nerves doesn't need to be our first vivid memory together in fifteen years.

Once boarding is complete, he looks back and sees that I'm still neighbor-free. He wastes no time grabbing his backpack—a *reasonably* sized carry-on—and walks back to my row, head tilted to the side, and plops down next to me, grinning.

"Together again," he says, patting my knee a couple times.

I let out a sigh of relief that I hope he doesn't notice, and the last of my tense muscles relax. Has he always had this effect on me? Or does this have to do with the fact that he's aged like a fine wine?

✎

"Here, I brought an extra pair for you." Simon hands me some earbuds. "The airplane ones suck."

"Thanks," I say. "This movie needs good quality audio." Cued up on my tiny screen is the Queen biopic *Bohemian Rhapsody*, a perfectly loud distraction from our oncoming ascent into the stratosphere.

"And if you need some melatonin to help you sleep later…" He holds up a bottle of supplements. If I had any skepticism about how often he travels by plane, I don't now. He really thought of everything, didn't he?

While the melatonin is tempting, sleep is the last thing on my mind. The rumbling plane engines have caused my heart beat to rumble again, too. All my muscles tighten and I take a deep breath: It's time for takeoff.

Phase one: the plane lurches forward, barreling down the runway at speeds strong enough to shift all my internal organs. This is my least favorite part: when we're still on the ground, but we're moving so fast that it feels like a drag race on steroids. Ignoring the window, I concentrate on the tiny screen before me, turning up the volume, pretending the world isn't rushing by. The synthy guitar plays over the film's opening credits. *Deep breath in.* The piano of "Somebody to Love" begins. *Slowly exhale.*

We've now begun phase two of takeoff: when we leave the ground and the Earth's surface isn't horizontal anymore, but sharply angled. I feel dizzy, weak. Morbid curiosity tempts me to peek out the window, but I resist. Instead, I focus on the tiny screen and Rami Malek's Oscar-winning portrayal of Freddie Mercury, dressed in a flamboyant red and yellow robe in the opening scene, strutting past his cats eating their breakfast buffet like feline royalty. Instantly, Tater Tot's grumpy face appears in my mind's eye, guilt sitting heavily in my gut. I wonder if Simon feels guilty for leaving Esther behind. I want to ask him this, but my body is so tense that the words don't come.

Phase three: elevation adjustments. My ears pop. My muscles tighten. I reach over and grab Simon's buff arm—an old habit from flights taken with Ian. *Ian.* His unanswered text is like a toothache I can't ignore. At some point, I'll have to address it. Is he single and ready to mingle again? The thought fizzles away as the plane soars higher. My adrenaline kicks in, and all I can think about now is that I'm about to fly over a deep, cold ocean.

My grip tightens on Simon's arm until my knuckles turn white. I can feel him looking at me, probably with concern—maybe pain?—but I can't meet his gaze. I'm lightheaded, and for a second, I think I might pass out. My heartbeat pounds in my ears. As much as I hate this feeling, knowing that Simon is next to me makes it all worth it. Having my old friend back has made everything feel right again. He's a happy part of my past, brightening up my current days.

As we ascend higher, my stomach drops again. Soon, an

entire ocean will separate me from those who love me—and from those whose love has expired. Something about that feels liberating, and I remove my hands from his bicep, ready to see the world.

In this moment, suspended somewhere between outer space and Earth, excitement sparks in my veins. And with every drum beat, every guitar strum that finds its way to my eardrums, that excitement swells until it squashes the last of my anxiety. I don't even notice my nerves anymore. This trip won't change the world, but it just might change my life.

I'm on my way to Rome.

⌀

"Did you know Bob Seger wrote 'Like a Rock' while on an airplane?" Simon sets his fork down on the tiny rectangular tray and takes a swig of water.

"Really?" I look over at him in surprise. "Cool! No, I didn't know that." Just before I can express my amazement at his stumping a radio supernerd with music trivia, he quips:

"It was about the seats." He laughs at his own joke.

We're finishing up an airborne meatball dinner: Simon sees this as a protein-heavy meal, whereas I consider this a preview of the Italian culinary coming attractions.

"For airplane food, this actually isn't bad," I say, nodding my approval.

"Surprising, right?" He takes his last bite, swiftly changing the subject. "You know, 'Bohemian Rhapsody' is kind of overrated," he says, pointing his plastic fork to my screen, the movie's closing credits now rolling. "The song, I mean."

"No way! That's one of the greatest songs ever recorded!

If we really were married, that statement would be grounds for divorce." As I give him a playful shove, I recall last week's ticket giveaway at WRCK for Queen's tour next year. I let Simon give me crap about Adam Lambert being their new singer, but manage to convince him to be my plus-one since my request for a pair of tickets was already approved. Digging into my carry-on, I find the notebook I'll be using for my restaurant reviews, and on the back page, jot down "Concerts 2020," and underneath that, "Queen." "I'm telling you, when you hear that song live, you'll change your tune."

"Okay, you're on." His eyes twinkle, and I can't believe how easily we've gotten our friendship back on track. The proverbial band is really back together!

The flight attendant comes through the aisle and clears our trays and plasticware.

"Oh, I'll keep this for later," I say, grabbing the roll and stuffing it in my bag before it's thrown in the trash.

"Here, take mine, too," says Simon, handing me his unwanted carbs. I wish all my friends were so anti-bread.

Once the trays are clear he brings up the trip. "I signed us up for a cooking class. It's at a winery."

"No way." I briefly squeeze his arm again, this time from anticipation. "Becks, that sounds amazing." My regrets for not having signed up for the community college class shrivel. Fate had something better in store for me. What better place to learn to cook than in the culinary capital of the world?

"Yep. It's on our last full day." He scrolls through the movies on the screen before him. "It was either that or another guided tour."

"You made the right choice. I could use all the help I can get in the kitchen."

"C'mon, you mean your mom didn't teach you a thing or two about cooking?"

"I think she just liked cooking for me so much that she never thought about teaching me how to do it. Then she wouldn't have had a reason to cook for me anymore. I wish I'd asked though." A melancholy settles in for a moment, and he gives me a sympathetic smile.

I certainly was around her during the meal prep stages though. When I'd tag along at the grocery store, I'd grab whatever she had put in the cart and start eating it, like a little supermarket tapeworm. By the time we made it to the checkout line, we were littering the conveyor belt with empty boxes, thoroughly confusing the cashier. "Can you make sure these invisible Pop Tarts ring up for the sale price?" For most people, grocery shopping can be a chore, but my mom always seemed so happy combing the aisles, buying different ingredients if there was a sale. We'd hit up the sample tables multiple times, too. "We can't let it go to waste," she'd say.

Simon pops in his ear buds, cuing up another movie, and I do the same. We're not very far into our next selections when the flight attendants are wheeling snacks past us, offering more rolls, yogurt, ice cream, crackers, and pop. Despite having just eaten a full meal a short time ago, I take an ice cream and save some crackers in my bag for later. The familiar comfort of being provided for, being fed, fills me up—literally. It's as though my mom trained them for the job. *Make sure they eat enough! Offer them food every hour, on the hour!* A smile spreads on my face, feeling the warmth of my mother in this stuffy plane.

CHAPTER 5

BENVENUTI A ROMA

TWELVE HOURS AND one missed connecting flight later, we stumble into Fiumicino International Airport, Rome beckoning just beyond the terminal.

Two large motion-censored doors part. Walking through them feels like entering another world. On a white wall, royal blue letters elegantly spell out "Welcome to Rome." The Roman skyline sprawls out on either side of the greeting. The silhouette of St. Peter's Basilica on the left; the outline of the Colosseum on the right. A handful of painted "V's" transform into birds flying over the city.

We made it. We're really in Rome.

Simon, on airport auto-pilot, leads the way to baggage claim; I follow, my carry-on rolling behind me like a heavy caboose.

"Surprise, surprise. Our luggage wasn't lost," he says with a wink in his eye, grabbing both of our suitcases off the belt.

Our relief is temporary. We're now in a massive crowd of tired travelers searching for transportation.

"See our ride anywhere?" he asks desperately.

I scan for a sign that reads "Becker" in vain. "Shiitake mushrooms. I don't think they're here anymore."

Missing our connecting flight has put us back a few hours, which means we've also missed the last of the pre-arranged airport shuttles. Being lost at an airport in a foreign country with zero hours of sleep isn't high on my wish list of new experiences. The two of us, unsure of where to go or who to call, are like two desperate, lost puppies. With jet lag.

A man approaches. "Need cab?" A strong Italian accent drips over his words like olive oil.

Simon's eyes widen. "Yes." He practically shouts with surprise, like he's just won Bingo.

Outside, a cool drizzle falls, creating tiny foggy speckles on my glasses. After inhaling recirculated airplane air for half a day, I drink in what feels like the freshest autumn breeze that's ever filled my lungs.

The man throws our luggage in the back, stacking them carefully like Jenga blocks. He reaches for my big one first as my smaller yet heavier carry-on waits in the wings.

"You bring empty suitcase?" He asks me. "This so light!" He tosses it in the van and turns back to me with a playful smile. "Ah, you gonna do some shopping, huh?"

My Italian dictionary doesn't have the phrase "I'm paranoid and don't travel much," so I play along. "Exactly."

◆

"Where are you from?" The Italian woman sitting next to the van's driver has taken an interest in us. I want to say something in Italian to show that I've made an effort, but my jet-lagged brain can't recall any of the phrases I learned before the flight.

"Chicago." After a brief pause, I add, "America." This is the most hilarious thing Simon's ever heard, and he spews laughter next to me.

"As opposed to those other Chicago's," he teases. My cheeks blush.

I pull out my phone to text Greg to let him know we've made it to Rome in one piece. And to remind him that Tater Tot prefers filtered water from the Brita. But my phone has other plans.

Cannot connect to network. Will send when connection resumes.

Alternatively, I call, but instead of hearing the phone ring on the other end, I hear a recording of a very Italian woman speaking in very fluent Italian, probably telling me that I have no service and can't make any calls. Do I have to punch in an international code or something? I'd called the cell phone company a couple weeks ago, and texted the number the representative had given me. "You're all set," she'd told me. My phone was supposedly set up to make international calls and texts. After another failed attempt to make a call, I conclude that my phone is clearly not all set.

"Is your phone working?"

"Seems to be." Simon sounds unconcerned.

"I guess I'll have to wait to connect to the hotel's wi-fi and email my friend instead." Having an ocean between you and home is one thing, but a useless cell phone? I've never felt so unreachable and far away. I might as well be on Mars.

The rain splatters against the van's windows. I look between the wet drops, taking in my first sights of Italy as unfamiliar looking trees blur by the expressway. They're tall, with thin sturdy trunks that break off into lots of smaller branches at the top, densely covered in lush green leaves. They look like perfectly-shaped giant broccoli florets.

"I like your trees," I say to the driver and woman in front while snapping my first photos of Italy.

Through his nasal giggles Simon says, "There's way cooler things to take pictures of."

For a second, I consider saving some space on my phone for the attractions we'll see in the days ahead, but then the woman hits me with:

"That's how we get our pesto."

Oh my God. *Pesto trees.* Sprouting all around from the depths of the earth welcoming praise and awe from onlookers hungry for the green goddess of sauces. I flip to page twelve of *Eating Italy: The Foodie's Guide to Rome* and find a list of sauces. "They're called stone pine trees?" The woman nods, and I continue. "It says here they produce the pine nuts needed for the sauce. You know, I don't think I ever realized there could be any type of nut in a sauce." When Simon and the woman giggle, I briefly worry that trying to recreate my mom's sauce is too ambitious. I clearly know nothing about concocting a delicious sauce. Am I out of my league? "I love pesto…" The words leave my mouth quiet enough for only me to hear.

It was the summer after high school graduation. My mom and I went out for lunch every weekend, vowing to try one of everything on the menu at Noodles and Company. Usually, we each got something different, sharing half of our plates with each other. But on our last visit, the weekend before I moved into my dorm, we both ordered a large plate of pesto cavatappi. We delighted in its green freshness, the way the sauce stuck to the grooves of the textured corkscrew pasta. "I think this one's my favorite," she declared, the blues of her eyes sparkling as the sun washed over her face. She said that after she tried every new dish there, but that time she really meant it. Pulling her hair back into a straw-colored pony tail, she then scraped the plate with the side of her fork, leaving as little sauce behind as possible. This was normally my move, and up until that point, I never saw my mom do that. We never had a chance to make a return trip to have it again. She would have loved these trees.

The roads begin to narrow now and wind around as we get closer to downtown Rome. We drive past gorgeously ornamented buildings and statues. Elaborate fountains splash on every corner. Spirited murals of graffiti are sprayed every-where: on cars, buildings, newsstands. Motorized scooters zip past our van. Compact cars in every color zoom along the road, while others are parked haphazardly in the middle of the street or on sidewalks. A curious smile creeps over my face upon witnessing this urbanized chaos—it feels a little bit like home. Not exactly the quaint Italian rolling green hills I'd pictured before departure.

We come to a grand-looking staircase. "Are those the Spanish steps?" I can't help but hope for a glimpse of what we missed on the walking tour we didn't make.

Man, I'm hilarious today. Simon has another good giggle with the Italian woman, who eventually composes herself. "No." She clears her throat. "The Spanish Steps are farther west."

I close the camera app on my phone. "Oh."

⌁

We spin inside through the revolving door and step onto gleaming black-and-white tiles. It's magnificent. The Westin Excelsior will be our home for the next five days, and it's quite a step up from a vintage apartment with inconsistent heat. Gorgeous chandeliers line the gilded ceiling. A swanky bar and a posh lounge are opposite an ornate event space. Rose-colored marble walls hold up artwork and mirrors framed in black and gold. In the center of the room sit breathtaking purple orchids atop a table that has golden winged lions for legs.

Damn. Italians know how to decorate.

I feel like I'm Cinderella, dressed in rags, walking through her stepmother's palace. The gray sweat pants and gym shoes I've been sporting for nearly a whole day now can't possibly smell Febreze fresh, and my ratty Rolling Stones t-shirt is so worn that I'm pretty sure it's see-through in the right light. I don't exactly exude European elegance.

We find the special check-in booth for Worldswift employees and their guests.

"You're the two we've been waiting for," the woman behind the table says cheerily. Her smile is blinding as she squeals, "You're the last ones!" with enough enthusiasm to fuel an entire cheer squad. I wouldn't be surprised if she presented us with a trophy for coming in last P-L-A-C-E place!

Simon signs us in, and the bubbly woman hands us nametags to wear to Villa Miani, the mansion where tonight's welcome shindig takes place. Nametags seem tacky for such a lavish event, but I only know one person here and he barely knows his own coworkers—nametags might come in handy. My stomach drops when our differing last names present themselves in black and white. Did the woman notice? Obviously, brides can keep their own names—I seriously considered it during my truncated engagement, much to Ian's chagrin. Still, I shove the nametag in my hoodie's pocket where our marital lie is safely out of sight, relieved that our cover hasn't been blown. She also hands over an envelope stuffed with two-hundred euros for spending cash, to be split between me and my "husband." How many scoops of gelato can a hundred euros buy?

We head up to our room via classy wood-paneled elevators adorned with mirrors, our reflections staring back at us.

"Wouldn't your coworkers know if you got married? How are we gonna pull this off?" My tired, bespectacled eyes are surrounded by a web of bloodshot veins. My flat, greasy hair has never lived up to being "dirty blond" more than at this very moment.

Simon, with his brown well-rested eyes and not a single hair out of place, reassures me that no one's the wiser. "Nah, we all work remotely. I've only met my boss in person twice. Most of these guys don't know me outside of emails and conference calls. I'll tell them we eloped if I have to." He chuckles at the thought.

The doors open and Simon holds out his arm, letting me off first. We zig zag down a corridor adorned with paintings in gold frames and candelabras until we find our room. In a word: plush. A sigh of relief escapes me at the sight of two giant queen beds. Their bright white comforters greet us with a temptation to sleep that's stronger than free cupcakes at a bakery. A chandelier glows from the ceiling while the windows are dressed in gold and plum drapes, cinched at the middle with tasseled gold ropes.

Simon promptly makes himself at home, hanging clothes in the closet. He scatters protein bars and phone chargers all over the desk. His laptop's light blinks as it charges.

"I'm gonna hop in the shower," I say. My blinks are heavy and often, and I try hard to ignore all the big white pillows stacked like jumbo marshmallows.

"Cool," Simon says, kicking off his shoes and crawling into the bed by the windows.

It could be sleep deprivation that sparks a pang of irritation, but I can't help it. First, we miss our connecting flight and, subsequently, the walking orientation tour of the surrounding area, then my phone decides to turn into a paperweight, and now this?

"What the hell are you doing, Becks?"

He gives me a look. "Churning butter."

"You're breaking the rule."

He laughs. "What?"

I point at him with my toothbrush. "You said, and I quote, 'Whatever you do when we land, do not take a nap.'"

More giggles. "Oh yeah. Hey, rules were meant to be broken, Appleby." He gestures to the second bed. "Feel free to hop in, but this ain't my first rodeo. You, however, are an international travel newbie. Newbies must always follow the rules. Too risky, otherwise." He winks, then plops his head back on the pillow.

"Fine, but after tonight's dinner, I will sleep like I'm comatose until the sun rises." I resist the urge to bellyflop into the second bed, an open pool of luxurious five-star comfort. Instead, I step into the shower, letting the warm water wash away the grime and the hours of disorienting travel.

A little later, after I look like myself again with clean hair—moussed and blow-dried—and a fresh dress for tonight, Simon wakes up and brings his phone into the bathroom.

"Refreshed?" My words are iced with a hint of bitter jealousy.

He yawns, stretching his arms in a big Y. "Oh yeah. I feel great." The little grin he gives me is met with a playful glare. The bathroom door shuts, the water turns on, and the distinct sound of drums begins to play. Then, the bass line. The guitar. And finally: the vocals.

Echoes of John Fogerty's hollering voice mingle with Simon's nasal one as the unmistakable music of CCR seeps beneath the bathroom door like an incantation, magically charming away his irritating nap and the nerves I feel about pretending to be his wife in a sea of strangers. I don't know if he's playing air guitar in there, but I'm definitely tapping my feet out here.

❧

To: gregorystorms@wrck.fm

Subject: Ciao from Rome!

We're here!!!!! My phone is useless. I can't call or text, so if you don't hear from me at all, that's why. I'll try to email you a lot though! Our hotel is niiiiiice. Okay, gotta finish getting ready for dinner tonight. Going to a mansion. No biggie. Wish you were here!!

April

CHAPTER 6

WHEN THE MOON
HITS YOUR EYE

WE'RE GREETED IN the foyer by a band of five lively Italian men in red vests blending the sounds of guitar, accordion, trombone, tambourine, and saxophone like a musical ragú sauce. Quite the first impression of Villa Miani, a gorgeous neoclassical mansion which, according to page ninety-three of *Rome Day by Day: 31 Essential Ways to See the Eternal City*, was built in 1873 atop the hill of Monte Mario overlooking the Eternal City, which is now twinkling in the moonlight.

As Simon covers a yawn with his hand, I tease him. "What, was that a diet Red Bull or something? Or did Baby not get a long enough nap?"

"It just hasn't kicked in yet. You did bring that extra one right? There's room in there with all your *Rome for Dummies* books?"

I pat the side of my purse. "It's in here. Don't worry,

sleepyhead." My blue heels click to the beat as I dance my way toward the coat check, my pink and blue dress whirling, my hair swishing from side to side. Simon heads inside toward the bar while I listen to the band a little longer. The accordion player notices me watching. He has thick dark eyebrows and wears a smile on his face so genuine that his eyes are smiling, too—he's totally pulling off what I couldn't in my awkward passport photo. He glances at my nametag and shouts my name over the music as if I'm an old friend he hasn't seen in years, but with his accent it sounds like "Ah-pree-lay!" I've never loved the sound of my own name more. With a twinkle in his eyes, he steps over to me with the beat, showing off his accordion skills. As if one personal serenade isn't enough, now the guitarist trots over, not missing a single strum of his strings. The two of them duel for my attention with not only their musical mastery but their Italian charm, outplaying each other and hamming it up. These guys are giving the Fogerty brothers a run for their money. Before I even make it to the bar, I'm already intoxicated; drunk on the irresistible spirit of the music, buzzed on the glamour of the mansion, high on the thrill of a week in Rome just beginning.

The ballroom is stunning. "Fancy" multiplied by infinity. Chandeliers sparkle like jewels, casting a warm glow over a mass of smiling faces. The walls, covered in ivory flowered wallpaper, shimmer with hues of pink, gold, and silver. Shiny, gold frames hug intricate tapestries and paintings. White statues guard the estate from the corners of the ballroom. Olive-green drapes frame the arched windows looking out onto Rome, the dome of St. Peter's Basilica lit up against an indigo sky. My guidebook mentions that this mansion is a popular spot for weddings, and it's easy to see why so many couples pledge their undying love here: it's overflowing with romance.

"When's y'all's wedding anniversary?"

I've taken no more than a couple sips of my champagne when this question zaps me from my romantic daydream. It's an interesting feeling when a complete stranger poses this question when you are, in fact, depressingly single. Daphne Hartsmith, a lively, frizzy blond-haired woman of about forty wearing dangly earrings, a black top, and patterned leggings, is accompanying one of Simon's co-workers on this trip. I can't explain it, but I feel like I've known her for decades, not seconds. Is it the friendly charm of her southern accent?

She sees me appraising her, and smiles.

No, it's her blond hair and blue eyes. She could be a long-lost aunt.

"Um," I pause briefly and glance at my not-so-other-half who's now gulping down the last of his champagne as if avoiding having to answer. Is it just me, or does it seem like the top button on his white pinstriped shirt is starting to strangle him?

"We've known each other a long time," I say vaguely, now focusing on my own flute filled with bubbly. Did she notice we don't have the same last name on our nametags? Should I take mine off before someone else notices?

Daphne, without breaking eye contact, places her hand over her husband's chest. He's a little stocky with warm chestnut-brown eyes, short dark brown hair, and his immense salt-and-pepper stubble indicates that he could have a full beard by the time dessert is served.

"This here's Chuck. We just tied the knot three months ago."

"Howdy," he says with a head nod. Both of their faces are swallowed up by the biggest smiles I've ever seen as they rub noses. The two of them hail from South Carolina. They have warm drawls and bright smiles that sparkle like the ones you see in toothpaste commercials.

I guess it's my turn. "Simon and I met in high school…" I trail off, trying to buy some time. "It's kind of hard to keep track of dates after so many years." I have to shout a little over the band and hundreds of conversations going on around us. Irrationally, I hope the noise will defer her pressing the issue.

But Daphne's eyes widen with peaked curiosity, eager to know when Simon and I never said "I do." I once again look to Hubby, searching his face for clues to indicate whether or not I should blatantly lie. But his silence goes on for a spell too long. The moment of truth is upon us, and it got here much quicker than anticipated. I brush some imaginary cat fur off my dress, then fiddle with the gold zipper in the back. Anything to avoid having to lie to this nice woman's face.

"Y'all *are* married, right?" Daphne presses, her jangly bracelets clanking together as she takes a sip of her drink. I notice a tattoo on the side of her wrist; it reads "trust" in black letters.

Before we can answer, Simon's boss Rob and his wife Vicki drift into our conversation.

"Of all our sitters, you hired Donna?" Rob sounds exasperated, his voice hitting a frequency twinged with mild panic. "She's going to let the kids stay up late all week."

"And *she'll* have to be the one to deal with the grumpy little monsters the next day." Vicki takes a long sip of champagne. "Besides, she was the only one available for the whole week." The three Thompson boys, back home in Florida, are rather pleased that Donna's in charge, Vicki explains. They couldn't care less that their parents are spending a week in the world's most fascinating city. "They're more excited that Bad Cop isn't there to enforce all the rules." She pats Rob's chest, covered in a conservative gray button-up shirt. He's clean shaven with so much gel in his short brown hair it's glistening. As if being Simon's boss wasn't enough reason not to pull any funny business, now I learn that he's the stricter parent, which only intensifies this little game of *To Tell the Truth*. Will Simon's real wife please stand up?

Daphne's eyes are now staring into the depths of my soul, perplexed that I can't seem to answer such a simple question. Is it hot in here? Amusing as I thought it would be to pretend to be Simon's doting wife, this is about as comfortable as getting a pap smear with salad tongs. The both of us are let off the hook, however, when someone announces that dinner is being served in the main ballroom. The crowd, now a hungry herd, swallows up Daphne's unanswered question.

⁓

Two glistening spheres of mozzarella paired with juicy tomato slices, thick tubes of saucy pasta, fresh, crispy greens adorned with flavorful black olives, and tender chicken cover every inch of my plate. This is a buffet fit for famished kings. Or jet-lagged tourists.

I discreetly remove my nametag and shove it in my purse before diving into my dinner, taking inventory of my choices. "Where do I start?"

Simon, having already made a dent, now slices off a piece of chicken. "The buffalo mozzarella. It's the best."

"As in mozzarella from buffalo? You can milk those guys?"

He nods, chewing his chicken while slicing off another hunk of cheese. Giving a quick scan of the room, he leans over to me. "Red Bull me."

I hand it to him under the table, and soon a loud pop hits my ears. Clearly, discreet is not going to happen. He shrugs and chugs.

While the wait staff pours red wine into our glasses, Chuck and Daphne, unquestionably still in the newlywed phase, are nauseatingly cute as each feeds the other.

Surprisingly, instead of bitterness poisoning me at the sight of true love, a smile finds its way to my face. Not only because the Hartsmiths are obviously soul mates, but because their adorableness brings to mind a sweet memory of my own. Lake Michigan. Chicago's skyline beaming in the background. It was a sunny April day, but the winds still had an arctic bite to them. My hand had been keeping warm inside Ian's as we walked along the shore in comfortable silence. When he abruptly stopped and turned to face me, I bumped into him, knocking both of our glasses askew. He reached over to fix mine before fixing his own. And then he reached into his pocket and knelt down. Sometimes I find myself wondering what it would have been like if I embraced the relationship we had and said "I do." Would we be like the Hartsmiths, shamelessly feeding each other in public like they're the only two people in the room?

"Hope you're hungry, pumpkin," Chuck says. He stabs a cherry tomato and brings it to Daphne's lips.

She giggles, then as if forgetting where she was for a second, clears her throat and starts telling us about their life in South Carolina. "We have three kitty cats back home. Bo,

Luke, and Daisy. Sure hope they're not giving the neighbors a hard time." She flashes Chuck a glance before adding, "Oh, and Chuck's got two boys."

"*We've* got two boys," he corrects her.

She lowers her head and muffles her voice slightly. "Not yet."

Breaking the tension, I blurt out, "I have a cat too! I mean, *we*. We have a cat. And a dog. A pug. Tater Tot and Esther." I'm babbling and feel my face get warm. "Who needs more wine?" I top off Simon's and my glasses before passing the bottle to Vicki, who drains it, promptly asking a passing waiter for another bottle.

"Great year you've had, Simon," Rob says from across the table. "This is the third year in a row now that you've topped your sales, right?"

"Fourth," Simon corrects him.

Rob addresses the whole table with a proud look on his face. "Simon is the only sales rep in the rental department to have ever beaten his own record for four consecutive years." He turns to look right at Simon now. "I can't wait to see if you can lock in Sandersons." He quickly clarifies for half the table. "Biggest grocery chain in the entire upper peninsula. We've been trying to nab them for years. Simon's the only one to get them to even peruse a contract. Multi-year deal." He grins as he picks up his wine glass. "Just waiting for them to sign on the dotted line."

Simon gives a humble smile before finishing his wine. The waiter comes back with another bottle of red, which is consumed in record time. In celebratory anticipation for some, perhaps to relieve anxiety for others.

"No pressure or anything," I say under my breath to Simon, clinking my glass with his.

A nasal laugh bleats out of him. After he takes another sip, he starts drumming the table with his fingers. Looks like someone got his wings.

The band begins to serenade individual tables, and as they approach ours, a familiar melody rings through the dining room, but I can't put my finger on it. I put my fork down and concentrate on the notes. Then it hits me.

"YMCA" by the Village People. "An Italian classic," I joke.

Everyone at our table cheers. Simon raises his glass commending the band's musical prowess. One of the band members hands Daphne a red tambourine which she gleefully smacks against her hand in the air, her blond waves bouncing to the beat. Another band member gives Vicki a blue tambourine, matching her blue blazer and glimmering earrings. The rest of us giddily clap along, proud that two of our own are now honorary band members.

Friends don't let friends dance the "YMCA" alone, so in an effort to dilute how ridiculous Simon looks forming his arms to the letters, I do the same. But it dilutes nothing, and now we're the only two dancing to the Village People in the ballroom. So much for not attracting attention to ourselves.

By the time dessert is served, our table has emptied several bottles of wine, largely due to Vicki taking advantage of being kid-free for a week. Rings of rich mousse topped with whipped cream and drizzles of red raspberry sit like thrones of sugar atop rose gold platters. But none of the sweet treats interest Vicki.

"Signore, ancora vino, per favore?" She speaks with

confidence, perfecting the Italian accent. Her sleek, black hair shines under the chandelier lights. Her eyes are like dark chocolate, and freckles of cinnamon sprinkle across her light brown nose and cheeks.

"Take it easy there, tiger," says Rob.

"I'm on vacation," Vicki's words slur, "cupcake."

"It's still a work function for me, honey."

"And for me, darling, it's a vacation from your mother telling me how to raise three boys. Who can't ever sit still."

"Yeah, and thanks to her we were able to get away." He takes the glass out of her hand and sets it down. "Just… slow down, okay?"

The waiters return with what we've all already had too much of, one of them rolling his eyes as he sets the wine on the table. Typical Americans, he must be thinking. Getting drunk off the wine that's supposed to compliment the meal. Mercifully, the waiters also provide an alternate beverage.

"Caffé?" one asks.

"'Caffé' invariably means 'espresso' in Italy, April, just so you know," Simon warns me discreetly. Ah. Now, coffee to the millionth power isn't normally something I'd voluntary drink. Unless, of course, it's been doused with a pound of sugar and a gallon of cream. But at that point, I might as well drink a milkshake. I've always loved the smell of coffee though. It reminds me of being home with my mom. She was constantly brewing coffee, Styrofoam cups stacked next to the coffee pot like the Leaning Tower of Pisa. Morning, noon, and night, she was never without a mug of freshly-brewed hot coffee.

Ian, too, was a coffee-holic. When it came time to register for wedding gifts, one item caused controversy: the coffee pot. Should we get a single-serve machine? An old-fashioned machine with a big decanter? A French press? These were questions he, a man with coffee in his veins, posed to me, a life-long non-coffee drinker. Why he wanted my opinion on an appliance I'd never use was beyond me, but I gave him mine anyway: old-fashioned machine with a big decanter. Better for the environment than a single-serve machine, more bang for your buck, and it reminded me of my mom's coffee pot. What a waste of breath; he ended up scanning a trendy single-serve machine. Of course: how could he resist the latest in coffee technology?

Maybe it's because I'm feeling nostalgic. Or maybe it's the waiter's accent, his dark wavy hair, the way his white smile contrasts against his olive skin. In any case, I surprise myself by eagerly responding, *"Sì!"*

"I'll get in on some of that action, too," adds Simon.

When the waiter sets down two tiny cups of coffee that looks dark as night and smells strong as stone, I feel different—braver somehow. Instead of opting for the safe choice of water, I'm boldly going where my taste buds have never gone.

"Grazie," I say with a smile.

"What she said!"

A spoonful of sugar absorbs into the dark liquid, rings of chandelier light reflecting in it. We clink mugs, and I take a cautious sip, the warm wetness barely grazing my lips. Hot but not scalding. The sweetness of the sugar compliments the espresso's rich flavor. Has coffee always been this tasty? Simon tosses his back like a shot, and I follow suit, gulping the rest of mine down thirstily. Vicki, however, is still on *vino* patrol, and is now requesting two bottles.

It's flowers, however, not excessive wine, that encourages

mischief. Sitting at the center of our table is a square glass vase holding a graceful arrangement of coral lilies. When Simon reaches over to feel the petals his eyes widen as if he's just uncovered a well-hidden secret. "They're real." There's that twinkle again. His next question comes out sounding conspiratorial. "You know you can eat these?"

"Come again?!" Chuck's eyes crinkle at the corners. Even his laugh has a southern accent.

Simon tears off one of the lily petals. "Dare me to eat it?" His eyes are now gleaming, challenging everyone at our table as if we're goofing off in our high school cafeteria.

"Don't eat that thing!" Rob says, sounding very much like the responsible supervisor he must be when these guys are on the clock. His body language, however, says something entirely different. A smile creeps across his face from ear to ear, silently goading on his number one employee.

Daphne, on the other hand, eggs him on much more directly. "Hoover it!" she shouts, her curls coming loose from behind her ears.

Relishing in the attention, Simon opens his mouth and tosses in the petal, swallowing it whole like a pill. He picks up his glass of water and chugs it, rapidly blinking back tears. "That burns a little," he says through a spurt of coughs. The whites of his eyes turn red as they tear up.

"Have some more water," I say, falling into my wifely role, refilling his glass. His Adam's apple bobs up and down as he gulps it. "Are you okay?" I'm now legitimately concerned. I imagine having to call 911, only the call wouldn't go through because my phone is Italy-incompatible. I'd interrupt the band, running up to the bushy-eyebrowed accordion player yelling, "We need an ambulance!" In would rush a team of paramedics shouting in Italian, wheeling Simon out on a stretcher.

My fantasy starts unfolding before my eyes when Simon reaches for his neck, his eyes wide with panic. He starts gagging, his face scrunching up uncomfortably.

"Simon! Oh my God! Are you okay?" He's choking on a damn *flower petal*. I stand up, adrenaline preparing me to perform the Heimlich. "Get up!"

Chuck and Rob begin to laugh. "What's your problem?" I shout at them. "Help me. Help *him*!" More laughter from the table. To my relief, Simon is laughing, too, pleased with his moving performance.

"You jerk." Sitting back down, my legs feel like jelly. I'm not sure which is the cause of my face turning such a vibrant shade of crimson: my humiliation, or my anger.

He coughs through his laughter, reaching for more water. "I was just messing with you."

"Grow up."

"Eat another one!" Daphne shouts.

Once all the coffee has been consumed—and no more lilies are—Vicki wastes no time to request our billionth bottle of wine. This time, it's all hers, as she shamelessly stashes it away in her purse.

Out on the veranda, the cool night air feels refreshing against my flushed skin, warm from all the food, wine, and urgently sipped hot espresso.

"This is amazing…" The words leave my mouth slowly and quietly, almost in a whisper, hypnotized by the view.

"Isn't it great?" Simon asks, though he's looking at me and not the lights of the Eternal City glittering under the stars. In the distance is the illuminated dome of St. Peter's Basilica. Straight above it glows a breathtaking bright white half-moon.

"You know," I say, "I don't think I've seen you look this fancy since prom. Do you remember that we switched dates?"

He throws his head back, and a laugh escapes into the night air. "That's right! We really had some moves." Our dates didn't want to dance, so we swapped, and Simon and I tore up the dance floor in all of our awkward teenage glory.

"Nothing like tonight though." My arms begin to form into a Y, but he pulls them down, laughing.

"New rule," he says, pulling me toward him, his hands warm on mine, "no more Red Bull on the trip."

"Now, I thought an experienced traveler like yourself would know not to mix Red Bull, espresso, champagne, and wine. That's called the Cocktail of Bad Decisions."

He smiles, tilts his head, and for a second looks into my eyes with a look I've never seen from him before. Just as I get lost in his gaze, Rob and Vicki walk over to us, Daphne and Chuck trailing behind. Do they ever stop holding hands?

"Damn, this place sure is gorgeous." Daphne sighs and takes in the view. "Hey, y'all never told me when your anniversary is. When was the big day?"

Simon's eyes flicker briefly to Rob before giving an answer which I am wildly unprepared for. "*Every* day is our anniversary." In a flash, he grabs my face in both of his hands, planting a kiss on me with so much enthusiasm he nearly knocks my glasses off.

To: gregorystorms@wrck.fm

Subject: OMG

Soooo, he kissed me tonight? In a super fancy mansion. We were pretty blitzed. I think he wanted to make sure his boss wasn't skeptical, but still. There was tongue. Any words of wisdom? We're back at the hotel now. He sleeps shirtless. How did I forget to pack breath mints?

How's my little Tater queen?

Here's a pic of our dessert. And me with the accordion player of the band that was there. And Simon and I lookin' all fancy. We clean up pretty good right?

By the way, I didn't tell you before because it kind of sounded crazy, but I'm going to try to figure out the secret ingredient to my mom's spaghetti sauce. This place is magical, and I feel like anything could happen.

Miss you.

April

CHAPTER 7

HEDONISTIC BARBARISM

TWO THINGS SURPRISE me as I wake up this morning. The first is seeing a missed call from Ian when I turn off the alarm on my phone. Apparently, my phone isn't totally useless—it can still receive incoming calls. The second is that, instead of CCR, Simon is crooning along to Dean Martin from the shower. Hearing his nasal voice butcher the lyrics to "Volare" is a pleasant—albeit tone-deaf—reminder that I don't have to deal with exes at the moment. I'm still in Italy. With my fake husband.

Who kissed me last night.

I open my email on my phone and find a response from Greg:

To: aprilappleby@wrck.fm

Subject: Re: OMG

WHAT DID I TELL YOU? He wants a taste of your apples! You both look hot. If he asks you to be in an open relationship, trust me, RUN. I don't want you to go through what I did. But if this is some Roman fling thing, Harry and I both think you should DO IT.

That accordion player is my hero.

Tot shat on the floor. Right between both litter boxes. Get back here soon—these hands weren't made to palm cat turds.

Don't forget to review some places while you go on your secret ingredient scavenger hunt!

Miss you moreee.

Greg

I'm not wired to handle fling things, so I guess I'd better find out what Simon's intentions are before I make any moves of my own—if I make a move. Wait, do I want to make a move on my old friend?

Simon pops out of the bathroom. "All yours." He rubs a towel all over his hair before tossing it on his bed. Not a trace of body fat is to be found on his torso.

Make a move, I shall.

But we should probably talk about last night first. Was his kiss merely a side effect of his Cocktail of Bad Decisions? Or was it his underlying feelings bubbling to the surface after his inhibitions were lowered?

"And make it snappy, Appleby, we gotta grab breakfast first," he adds, throwing a shirt on. "Oh, and if you're dragging me to see Adam Lambert—"

"It's Queen *with* Adam Lambert."

"—then I'm taking you see the best damn Rat Pack tribute show you'll ever see."

I raise a skeptical eyebrow as I pencil in another concert.

"Okay, but you're paying." Secretly, I'm ecstatic: our concerts for next year have already doubled. He could have suggested seeing Herb Alpert; I'm just happy to see the list growing.

After his shower, the state of our hotel's once pristine bathroom is appalling. The marble sink looks like it could have sprung a leak with the amount of puddles everywhere. Toothpaste is gooping out of the tube. Wet towels are tossed into the bidet as if it's a hamper. And I thought living with Ian was messy. (We implemented his-and-her bathrooms after I witnessed men's cleaning standards.) I run a fresh towel over everything and hop in the shower.

At breakfast, fluffy eggs, fresh fruit, and flaky pastries offer a hearty meal to start our day. It's always been my favorite meal, especially when I was a kid. My mom practically lived in the kitchen. On school days she'd throw a tube of Pillsbury cinnamon rolls in the oven for a fast breakfast, the warm aroma the only thing strong enough to get me out of bed. The best part was licking the icing off the plate. I had no shame. Still don't, sometimes. On weekends when we weren't so pressed for time, she'd make bacon. The sizzling and popping were torture as we waited for it to get so crispy it was nearly black. We liked our bacon to crumble at our touch. I'd fashion a BLT, but I'd alter the recipe, omitting the lettuce and tomato to free up precious real estate for the real star of that sandwich.

Simon notices my full plate: eggs, breakfast potatoes, bacon, fruit of every color. "Here, make some room for one of these." He pushes over some melon chunks with an iced *cornetto*. "That's how the Italians do it."

᷉

"Everything okay?" Simon asks me as we grab two seats on the bus. "You were pretty quiet at breakfast."

Of all the feelings swirling around inside me lately, the only one I feel strong enough to bring up at the moment is Ian's phone call.

"Yeah. Except that my ex called me last night." And, um, you kissed me. After pretending to choke on a lily.

He unzips his hoodie. "I take it that's not normal?"

"Well, there was that text he sent right before the trip—which I still never responded to." I turn to look out the window, the clouds darkening above us, before facing Simon again. "And I can't call or text him back now." I hold up my phone that's little more than a camera in this time zone.

"Tellin' ya, I think there might be a little reunion brewing on the horizon for you two." His brows lift, but his face remains serious, his brown eyes darkening under the overcast skies.

Daphne and Chuck board, walking back toward us. Her cowboy boots prove that not everyone opted for practical footwear today. "I fried my hair this morning," she blurts out, the pair of them sitting directly behind us. "Look at this." She taps my shoulder, and I turn around to see her grabbing a fistful of her frizzy hair.

"It looks good to me," I say, trying to hide my confusion. Her hair looks exactly as it did last night: blond and big.

"Did y'all know they have different electrical outlets here?" She asks, sounding peeved as if she was the last to find out. "I nearly set my head on fire."

"I told you that on the plane," Chuck says. "That's why I brought one o' them converters."

"Yeah, well, I've been a bit distracted," she replies tersely, her voice now coming out in an agitated whisper. "Why haven't we heard anything yet? Nothin' but crickets with this new lawyer."

"No news is good news," Chuck says, his voice soothing. "Adoption paperwork takes time."

Feeling like I'm intruding on a private conversation, I flip through the pages of *Passport to History: The Eternal Guide to Ancient Rome* while we wait for the bus to fill up, and tap Simon on the shoulder. "Hey, listen to this: 'The Colosseum was a hedonistic site of organized barbarism.' Is this what your old fraternity was modeled after?"

"Almost. Our gladiator battles didn't involve animals, just kegs."

The bus roars to life, and I immediately snap photos of the pine trees, graffiti, and miniature European cars. We're on the road for no more than a few minutes before fat raindrops splatter against the windows. The scooter drivers on the streets of Rome seem to be fearless in the rain; one drives on the wrong side of the road to pass up an entire line of cars.

A friendly, wide-awake woman's voice booms out of the bus's speakers. "*Buongiorno!*" She exquisitely rolls her "r" like it's a rolling pin flattening raw dough.

Simon cheerily responds, "*Buongiorno!*" His nasal, unrolled "r" is so not Italian. It's not even Little Caesars Italian. I keep my head turned toward the window trying to conceal a laugh.

As the woman gives an overview of what we'll be seeing today, gorgeous sites blur past us. An elegant fountain adorned with statues spouts water up toward the clouds. Even on a rainy day, Rome is beautiful. After passing a stretch of graffiti-covered newsstands and enduring traffic so congested it would test even the Pope's patience, the Colosseum manifests into view. Even from the bus it looks gargantuan. This iconic structure is the image that has always come to mind when I hear the phrase "ancient Rome." It doesn't get much more ancient than something that's been standing for almost two thousand years.

By the time we park and vacate the bus, the clouds of charcoal have puffed up into fluffy white cotton balls against a bright blue sky. I squint at Daphne's oversized sunglasses with envy. The street is lined with tall pine trees, and scooters zip past us at the speed of light. We pause at the Arch of Constantine, admiring the battle scenes sculpted in it. "Erected in 315 A.D." I announce, snapping the guidebook shut. "And still standing."

"You know, we already have a tour guide, April," teases Simon.

In the distance, the Colosseum, the color of sand, stretches out atop a field of grass as green as fresh basil. Crowds of people swarm the piazza. Some aim camera lenses at it that are as big as telescopes. Young couples snap selfies with the gladiator stomping grounds in the background. And others simply look in awe at what was once the largest amphitheater ever built. From this distance, the people lined up around the Colosseum look like tiny ants against the mammoth structure. We march over to line up, joining the army of ants, ready to walk back thousands of years into history.

Our tour guide holds up a flag of cornflower and violet, standing out among the throes of tourists. She leads us to the end of the line, her short brown hair bobbing along with each step. *"Mamma mia,"* she says with an exasperated sigh, "this line is long."

As we inch forward, we get glimpses through the various entry points into the pit of the amphitheater. What is now excited tourist chatter used to be an eruption of shouting and cheering in its heyday of ancient savage brutality.

"The opening event lasted a hundred days," our guide explains. "Gladiators battling each other, some pitted against animals, while 50,000 daily spectators watched."

"Not exactly a rock concert," Simon says to me out of the corner of his mouth before chuckling.

Once officially inside one of the most popular tourist attractions in the entire world, Mamma Mia, clutching her colorful flag as it waves in the wind, leads us up some very rustic, steep, and uneven steps. After snaking around a few twists and turns, we find ourselves walking on the main concourse, overlooking the maze-like pit below. Surrounding us are walls and columns made of travertine limestone, volcanic rock, and brick, massive enough to hold up the sky. I crane my neck upwards as if I'm in the front row at a movie theater. The clay-colored arched walls, imperfect with chunks missing, stand unwaveringly strong as the clouds darken again, now thick and gray, swirling around the amphitheater in the wind. Being inside the Colosseum feels like wearing a suit of armor—like the sturdiness of the stone can protect us from anything, even from Mother Nature's moods, her angry clouds hovering above.

Looking over the edge and down into the pit, I visualize the gladiators, imagining the deafening roar of the spectators. Being here feels completely foreign, and not because we're in another country, but because we've walked into another time. The seasons keep changing but the Colosseum still sits here, blatantly occupying the same six acres it has for centuries, propelling history forward into each new year. We're inside the world's biggest time capsule, transported back to an age gone but not forgotten. It's as if Ancient Rome is proving we can go back in time, challenging us to keep our most cherished memories alive somehow. I have quite a list of moments I'd like to revive.

It's a very recent memory, however, that's consuming all my thoughts: last night's kiss. Simon's been so quiet, he must be thinking about it, too, right? I look over to him, trying to gauge his mood, see where his mind is at. He turns to look at me and smiles, waving me over as he leans against a rail. What if Greg was right? What if he has feelings for me? Wouldn't that complicate our friendship? If only we could stray from the crowd, then maybe we'd have a chance to talk about it—about us. If there is an "us."

I pose my question as nonchalantly as possible. "You know what we should do tonight?"

"Actually, I already have an idea for what we should do."

"Oh? Because I was thinking it might be fun to grab a drink somewhere maybe? And catch up?"

"April," he says, grabbing my shoulders. "We should watch *Gladiator* tonight." He lets go of me and gestures around the arena. His smile takes over his face as he laughs at his brilliant suggestion. "Great movie! You've seen it, right?"

"Can't say I have."

Instead of addressing last night, we remain in ancient history, stopping at the heart of the Roman Empire: the Roman Forum. Our tour guide leads us to the end of another lengthy line of tourists, once again crying, *"Mamma mia!"*

The Roman Forum feels almost like a national park, but instead of lush green trees and bright flowers everywhere, all the greenery is covered with rubble, bricks, and parts of ancient buildings. Despite being in pieces, its powerful majesty shines marvelously. With the clouds still lurking, it almost looks like the aftermath of a recent tornado, as if the Roman Empire could have met here just yesterday before a storm hit. Impressive architecture, now splintered into pieces. Sculptures scattered and detached. Bits of ornamentation adorn what's left standing. Columns that once lead to the entryways of government buildings now lead nowhere.

A seagull with a round white belly and gray wings sits atop a single column that held up a roof thousands of years ago. Now it stands in isolation, its former surrounding structure long since crumbled to the earth. In the distance are two statues of the Roman goddess Victoria, wings spread wide, like they're ready to take flight at the first flap of the seagull's wings. The bird turns his head this way and that, as if taking in the view of the Roman ruins from above, marveling that all this has lasted through generations of humanity. Ancient ruins that once signified power and intelligence, entertainment and activity, now remain lifeless, occupying space as nothing more than a physical manifestation of the past. But within the still existence of these ruins lives an integrity. An identity that newness would erase.

The bird remains perched on his column, glancing around and puffing out his chest as if impressed by what he sees. But nothing lasts forever. Empires fall. Dynasties disappear. Companies fail. Relationships crumble. Friendships fade. People depart.

The stillness of the ruins comforts me. They might be lifeless, but their memory is preserved. Simon sits on a stone ledge intently listening to Mamma Mia talk about what used to be the all-powerful Roman Forum, now a hollow shell, a snapshot that safeguards the memory of what it used to be. A blue patch of sky finds its way through the swirling silver clouds. The seagull flies off, perhaps fluttering toward a ray of sun, while the statues of Victoria remain, along with all the other ruins, unchanged. Ancient Rome might be history, but it's still here, just with a different objective. And Simon and I are here too, perhaps trying to find another patch of blue sky where we can discover a new purpose for our own former glory days of hedonistic barbarism.

CHAPTER 8

EASY BREEZY CAPRESE

IT'S OVER LUNCH that I finally see the uphill mountain I've set out to climb in search of my mom's secret spaghetti sauce ingredient. I don't know what was more foolish: thinking the Italian chef at every restaurant would send each dish out with step-by-step instructions, or limiting myself to finding the special ingredient in only one of my mom's dishes. Her spaghetti dinners were delightful, but there was another dish, one we only had once a year, that was her pinnacle culinary achievement. Its rare appearance on the Appleby menu makes it an even more challenging quest.

Lasagna. How could I have overlooked my mom's lasagna? It was the stuff of legends, and it only made an appearance once a year: on Christmas. She'd make a huge pan, and we'd eat a slice every day until New Year's. Just think: in less than two months, I could have a big pan of lasagna sitting on the table between me and Greg after we've exchanged our annual white elephant gifts. I stifle a laugh picturing me in an apron layering a lasagna. But stranger things have happened. I'd need lasagna sheets, probably ground beef, tomato sauce (which, if I force myself to think positively, I'm well on my way of figuring out), and the cheese. Ah. It's within the layers of cheese where this mystery lies.

Who might know how she concocted the cheese mixture? Not Ian. After I'd moved in with him, he'd cook for me, initially making many of the dishes my mom used to upon my request. After a few weeks though, my half-eaten dinners must have tipped him off: his versions just didn't cut it. He began experimenting with other meals like teriyaki chicken and grilling more red meat than I cared to stomach. Most of the time, his cooking didn't taste half bad, but I missed my mom's cooking something fierce. And now, in the country known for so many of the dishes that nestled into my heart while growing up, my yearning to find one needle in the haystack has doubled.

I'll start at *La Bruschetta,* a quaint wood-paneled restaurant with murals of lemon trees on the walls. In the dimly-lit basement, rows of wooden tables sit underneath a ceiling made of arched bricks. A painting at the head of the room depicts a group of people dining while a gray cat enviously watches them. Tater Tot glared at me similarly when I left our apartment two days ago. She tolerates Greg during his weekly Sunday visits, but having him as her houseguest for a week is asking a lot from such a grumpy feline.

Simon and I sit across from Rob and Vicki at a cozy, rustic table, our pupils enlarging in the dim lighting. Daphne and Chuck sit on the other end whispering sweet nothings to each other.

"What do you have your heart set on?" Simon asks, scooting his chair closer to the table.

Perusing an Italian menu while my stomach is grumbling as loudly as a stadium full of European soccer fans makes it almost impossible to choose only one dish. While I'd love to begin my spaghetti search, we're in for a multi-course dinner tonight. "I think I'll choose something light. Leaning towards the *pasta e fagioli* soup."

"Since when are beans and pasta considered light?" he asks with a laugh.

"I mean, it's soup."

"A hearty one with carbs and protein. You always could pack it in." He winks at me and folds his menu shut. "Think I'll get the same actually."

"Copycat." I reach over and grab a slice of bread. It's soft in the middle hugged by a crunchy crust, and I dip it into oil and parmesan cheese.

"Um," Simon starts, glancing at Rob who's watching our exchange, "*darling*, you know you're breaking one of the rules by doing that, right?" He points to the cheese.

"*Honey*, that rule was made to be broken. You should know something about that. Besides, cheese makes everything better. We did a whole episode on a cheese shop a few months back."

"Episode?" Vicki asks, setting down a glass of red wine that's serving as her appetizer.

"I host a podcast about food with a friend of mine," I explain while pouring more oil on my bread plate. "We review restaurants, but we're not exactly the toughest critics."

"Gonna review this place when you get back?" Simon

points to my bread, soaking up the oil. "Lots of good food here."

"Which is why I'm pretty sure everywhere we go out here is going to earn four apples." At Rob's and Vicki's confused expressions, I explain, "Apples as in Appleby, my last name—er, maiden name. Anyway, that's the highest rating. Oh, look, our salads are here."

And not a moment too soon. The buffalo mozzarella sits in a big ball, waiting for me to sink my teeth into it, leaving no room for my foot in my mouth.

When Rob, his hair slightly less gelled than last night, makes a bathroom run, Chuck notices we're one salad short. Somehow it must have been lost in translation when we ordered. He points to the unattended salad. "Hand me the boss's plate, would ya? I'm starvin'."

Without question, Simon obliges and passes the unguarded salad down to Chuck, who scoops half of it onto his bread plate.

"You animal, just ask the waitress," says Daphne. "She obviously forgot yours."

Chuck slices off a chunk of mozzarella before handing the plate back to Simon. "No, no, don't bother her. She's plenty busy. This'll do. Rob won't notice."

"You're stress eating your boss's food, hon. I'm sure we'll hear something soon." She takes a sip of white wine. "And I thought *I* needed to relax."

A couple minutes later, Rob comes back to the table and looks at his mutilated salad in confusion. Chuck smiles at him, basil leaves hanging from his lips. "The southern gentleman I thought I could trust. It was this one," Rob says, half-grinning and pointing to Simon, "that I was worried about." He picks up his fork and digs in to what's left.

It's not long before our main course arrives. Simon and I enjoy our matching bowls of *pasta e fagioli*, cannellini beans and flat Italian pasta pieces swimming in a light brown creamy broth.

"*Bravo*," Simon says, "this is good." His head is mere inches from the bowl. He's practically drinking it. I guess a stroll through ancient ruins can give a CrossFit workout a run for its money.

"It's *really* good," I correct him, grabbing another hunk of bread. I break off a few soft parts and toss them into the warm pool of pulses, letting them soak up the broth. "This is the kind of thing that I feel like I should be able to cook. My mom could have pulled this off in an instant, you know? She'd throw whatever ingredients into a pot and in minutes there'd be an immaculate stew steaming on the stove."

"You like to cook?" Vicki asks.

"I'm not sure—I don't really know how." My laugh is a crude attempt at covering up my embarrassment.

"You two don't need to know how to cook in Chicago," Rob says. "Great food there. Florida's restaurants are hit or miss. But Vicki likes to cook."

"For three kids…" She takes a sip of wine, already back at drinking away her parental responsibilities awaiting her back home.

Between the married couple with kids and the newlyweds who've done nothing but whisper into each other's ears—even more charming in their southern accents—I'm careful to steer this conversation away from children. I could only imagine the kiss Simon would plant on me if someone asks us when we're going to start making babies. "Well, I really want to learn to cook. Are you and Rob taking the cooking class?"

She looks to her husband. Rob finishes his bite of spaghetti and says matter-of-factly, "Yep. There was no way we were doing another walking tour. Signed us up for the class in a heartbeat."

"That's what I said!" Simon chimes in.

"We see eye to eye on everything," Rob says. "That's my guy!"

"We're doing the cooking class, too!" Daphne finally breaks her gaze with Chuck, the two of them huddled over a pizza like they're the only two people in all of Rome. This might as well be their honeymoon. "And it's at a winery!" She sings the last word and picks up her glass in a toast.

"That might make it a bit more challengin'," Chuck adds with a grunt.

"Challenge accepted," Simon says, his nasal laugh sputtering out of him.

"Speaking of challenges," Rob turns the conversation back to work. "Any news on the Sandersons account?"

"Not yet. I've been watching my email though." Simon reaches for his phone.

"No emails at lunch," Vicki says, holding up her hand. She gives her husband a stern look. "You work these guys too hard." Under her breath she adds, "Your mother was right about one thing: you're a workaholic."

Rob attempts a whisper, but fails. "And look where it's got us."

"This trip is supposed to be a reward, not a work conference."

"This is a huge account we're talking about—"

"Not. At. Lunch." She holds up her dish, ending their squabble. And it's at this moment that my quest, like my stomach during this meal, expands. "Would anyone like to try some lasagna? I think they served me the whole pan."

Far be it from me to leave a sister in such dire straits. I cut off a forkful, cupping my hand beneath it to protect my clothes. "It's so *cheesy*..." Could that be mozzarella?

"April, do you like it? You're a million miles away." Vicki's noticed my pensive expression.

"It's—it's wonderful."

But it's not my mom's.

When our meal reaches the grand finale, Rob is quick to pass on dessert. "Just the check," he says.

My eyes narrow, and a look somewhere between disappointment and suspicion lines my face. He's skipping dessert. For the whole table. I bite my tongue—still tastes like cannellini beans—and decide to give him a free pass. After all, he's Simon's boss, the guy we're lying to about our relationship. The guy who might soon lose his all-star employee.

As we walk back to our hotel, we pass a woman in a window who's wrapping blocks of cheese in plastic. I watch her for a moment, mesmerized by the wedges of yellow, the spheres of white, the hunks of pale orange. She sets them behind a glass counter with a rhythm. She could probably do this in her sleep. She looks up. Her dark eyes meet mine with a look that says "I know something you don't know" before she turns her attention back to the last bricks of cheeses. Everywhere we look, the locals all seem to have a natural knowledge of food. But there's a barrier preventing their knowledge from spilling over to me. "Do you really think we'll learn anything at that cooking class?" I ask, hoping I don't sound as desperate as I feel.

Simon's answer doesn't surprise me. "I think we'll learn a lot about *wine*." Normally, his nasal giggle would make me feel better, but right now I'm unsatisfied with that response. To everyone else, this cooking class is a fun romp at a winery. But to me, it feels like a real chance to learn about cheeses, Italian herbs and spices, the secrets to making a good sauce. This cooking class is my chance to recreate my mom's famous Italian dinners. How incredible would this Christmas be with a pan of her lasagna with her own special cheese blend baking in the oven, the tantalizing tomato scent filling my kitchen?

La Bruschetta: Four Shiny Apples.

Taste: It looked like I licked my plate clean and Chuck literally stole food from his boss it was so good. The aroma of the *pasta e fagioli* soup teased my senses, wafting warm savory scents into the air. With my first spoonful I was careful to get a little of everything on it. Bordering perfectly on the line that separates warm from hot, it was the ideal temperature. The beans were soft and filling, while the buttery pasta added texture, the salty broth rounding out the flavors. And the broth was perfect for bread-soaking. It wasn't long before my spoon made beautiful music with the bottom of the bowl. One full apple.

Service: If a waitress is going to forget something, it might as well be a salad. Besides, she left a free basket of bread on the table. One full apple.

Atmosphere: Paintings of lemons and cats. One full apple.

Price: Someone else paid. One full apple.

CHAPTER 9

BLOTTO ON GELATO

"I need to go back to *La Bruschetta*." The door to our hotel room hasn't even shut yet before the words fly out of my mouth.

"Did you forget something?" Concern lines Simon's face.

"No, I need—I just need to…" Barge into the chef's kitchen and yell, "Cheese! Start talkin'!?" Taste all his tomato sauces? Raid his spice rack scanning for a label with my mom's name on it? "I need dessert."

Simon chuckles and kicks off his shoes. "I'm sure we'll have dessert at dinner tonight. They're pulling out all the stops, from what I hear."

"Oh. Tonight's dinner, that's right. Well, do you want to roam around instead? We have some free time." If I can't get answers about cheese and sauce this afternoon, I might as well take advantage of some rare one-on-one time with Simon to clear the air about last night's kiss.

He plops down on the bed by the windows. "Appleby,"

he says, sounding exhausted, "I'm way too tired." His head hits the pillow like a heavy sack of flour.

Mamma mia, he's going to take a Goddamn nap again, isn't he?

I glance out the window, where the sun is shining on the Eternal City, its culinary secrets begging to be discovered. "C'mon, Becks! You're just going to sleep when we could be exploring Italy?" My voice betrays a slight irritation: a side effect of dessert deficiency.

"We've still got a long night ahead of us," he reasons, pulling the covers over him, effectively ending this soon-to-be squabble.

I roll my eyes at his hypocritical nonstop quest for naps, which he doesn't see because his eyes are already shut. My, how we're giving quite the Oscar-worthy performance of the nagging wife badgering her curmudgeon husband. Too bad there's no audience to this scene—no one would question our marital status after witnessing our bickering. Our first full day in Rome seems too early in the trip for me to suffocate my friend with all the pillows he's trying to nap on, so instead, I take a deep breath. He does have a point—tonight we'll be touring the Vatican museums, followed by another late dinner. A nap isn't the worst idea.

But… there's still so much to see. To eat.

"Okay," I say agreeably, not letting this escalate into a petty argument. Maybe it's better this way. If I'm alone, I'll have no one to embarrass but myself. I'll start with the woman at the cheese shop. And if she can't help me, I'll go back to the restaurant. They wouldn't turn me away if I want to, say, give my compliments to the chef, would they? "Well, I'm not tired, and I don't want to keep you up, so I'm going to find some gelato anyway." I turn to my purse, digging to make sure my map is still in it. "I'll be back soon."

A little thrill flickers inside me as I step into the elevator. Exploring a foreign country alone with extremely limited language skills, hardly any euros, and absolutely no cell phone service is either a magical memory in the making, or a recipe for disaster.

The elevator doors open, nudging me into the spotless lobby. The bellhop is having an intense conversation with the concierge, about what, I don't know. The Italian words cease when they notice me walk by, each looking over with a polite smile. I nod at them and push through the revolving door like a lone wolf. Which is something I've gotten used to after losing my mother, breaking off an engagement, and moving into my own apartment. I step onto the sunbaked Roman sidewalk, heading back toward the cheese shop.

It's not long before I encounter my first hurdle. The woman is gone. The cheese sits behind the glass counter in darkness. I try the door, but it's locked. I can still picture her dark eyes meeting mine for the briefest of moments, her lips curled into the slightest grin as she sorted cheeses I've probably never even heard of. Surely, she would she have been able to narrow down what my mom might have used in her lasagna, or at the very least, point me in the direction of an authentic Italian recipe. This isn't a job for Google—it is a job for a professional cheese expert. I circle the block a few times, hoping she'll return, but after ten minutes the lights remain off. She couldn't have gone far. I walk the nearby streets, scanning for her white shirt and dark hair, but it's as if she fell through a black hole. The restaurant will have to do.

Another hurdle: after my impromptu search for a random

cheese goddess, I've knocked myself off course. Retracing my steps is proving to be impossible for this little American tourist. Desperately, I open the map app on my phone, but, not surprisingly, it refuses to load. Without a wi-fi connection, the GPS is useless. Opening the paper map proves just as fruitless; without the address for *La Bruschetta*, how can I determine the route to get there? The map fills with new creases as I fold it April-style and shove it back into my purse. Time for Plan C: finding another restaurant or deli. All of Rome is at my fingertips with no tour guide to dictate the route, no friends or fiancés or fake husbands to clutter up the itinerary. I'm free to roam Rome as I please. Giving up in the face of all this freedom would be a waste.

The sun is shining, and the breeze is cool, and once I embrace the spontaneity of my journey, my stress melts away. In fact, it feels like I'm melting away under the white-hot sun. When I round a corner and see a gelateria, I can't resist. A modest selection of twelve flavors beckons me to lick them all up. An older man with slightly graying hair greets me.

"*Buonasera, signorina,*" he says in very fluid Italian. "*Cosa vorresti?*" The foreign words pour out of him like wine.

I'm a deer in headlights. *What did he say?* Obviously, I spent too much time stuffing things into my carry-on and not enough time stuffing Italian translations into my brain. But pulling out my dictionary right now would be mortifying. Stupidly, I just speak English, but louder and slower than I normally would, foolishly hoping this will be the key to overcoming our language hurdle.

"Hi… I'd… like… some… gelato?" I'm borderline shouting.

Oh my God, April, he's Italian, not taking his new Miracle Ear for a spin.

The man effortlessly switches to English. My cheeks flush with embarrassment. He smiles and asks, "Which flavor?"

This would never happen back home. If a foreign tourist asked me for ice cream, there's no way I'd be able to so effortlessly switch languages the way this man can, with such a good attitude to boot.

Still full from lunch and anticipating a big dinner tonight, I opt for a fruity flavor, irrationally hoping I'll get the indulgence of a dessert with the feeling of a juice cleanse.

"Strawberry please."

"Just one?!" His brows furrow, as if selecting only one flavor is absurd. And, you know what?

It is.

"And lemon please."

For the longest time, I believed that lemon juice was the secret to the cheesecakes my mom baked for me on my birthday every year, but every time I've experimented with the juice and zest of those little yellow orbs, I'm always left disappointed. I'm now wondering if she even used any lemon at all. I've done such a stellar job sniffing out two secret ingredients, cracking a third one is the next logical step to take.

The man scoops strawberry into the little cup first, then tops it off with a perfectly spherical scoop of lemon so light in color it's nearly white.

I summon the courage to say at least one thing in Italian to this man, mumbling quietly in case my accent is horrible. "*Grazie.*"

Only two other people have opted to enjoy their ice cream outside. Two men who look like they might be on a lunch break from work are dressed nicely and appear to be talking about matters of great importance, passing folders and papers back and forth. I've got matters of great importance on my mind as well: should I taste the strawberry first, or the lemon? I grab the tiny blue plastic spoon and dig into them both, anxiously anticipating their flavors on my taste buds.

Delizioso.

Spoonful by spoonful, my mini mountain of gelato shrinks underneath a canopy of shade as the people of Rome pass me by. Soon I start to shiver, my teeth chattering, so I get on with my search for my mom's secret ingredients.

In the sun, the lemon gelato glistens. The cool citrus goes down easily as I walk down the narrow, winding streets. Dozens of parked scooters are neatly lined up like precariously placed rows of Dominoes, threatening to topple over should one get bumped into. Mini compact cars are maneuvered into parallel parking spots so close their bumpers practically touch. Both flavors are now stacked on my spoon, like two pink and yellow Vespas wedged together on the street. I swallow the fruity mouthful.

Faces and fruit and frilly shapes ornament the façades of the buildings, all painted in hues of fresh-churned butter, juicy clementine, and rhubarb, each building a different flavor. Heavy brass door knockers dangle from dark wooden doors like a pair of anchors holding down a boat. Another building is made of gleaming bricks that shine like honey in the sun. I dig for strawberry, licks of pink fruit leaving my tongue zinging.

I'm in a gelato trance, wandering the winding streets of Rome taking in the architecture. Shutters of teal and lava red are cast open. My face bathes in the sun's rays. When I reach the bottom of the cup, there's little left to distract me from the fact that I am most certainly lost. But the real problem is that I'm short on time and have absolutely no plan for how to get the answers I'm seeking. Heading back to the hotel is the best option for now. Which leaves me with my paper map.

Or…

He's tapping at his phone in frustration while leaning against a pizzeria called Antonelli's, his bushy brown hair rustled by the breeze.

"*Mi scusi?*" My voice comes out timid as I approach him, getting a closer look at the dark stubble along his jawline, his chic dark gray blazer miles above the dress code bar set by a pizzeria. He puts his foot against the building and mutters something in Italian, eyes fixated on his phone.

"*Mi scusi.*" I say it louder this time, phrasing it more like a statement than a question. He's either going to wave off this helpless tourist or help her. "*Parla inglese?*" I can't believe my brain is finding these phrases. If I can manage to speak another language, surely I can whip up a decent pasta sauce. Maybe there's hope for me after all.

His smoky gray eyes meet mine. "Lost?" He can read me like the map that's stuffed in my bag.

"Yes. I know I'm not far, but I wasn't really paying attention to where I was going. Do you know where the Westin Excelsior is? By the *Villa Borghese?*"

He looks at me for a beat, as if assessing whether I'm worth his time. "*Sí, sí*, not far. One kilometer maybe." He's soft-spoken, and I lean in a bit closer to hear him better. He adds a vowel to the end of each sentence, giving his words a mesmerizing musical rhythm. "At end of this street, turn left. Then, go right. The street, uh, it is curvy. Stay on left. At *Via Leonida Bissolati*, turn right. Keep going, yes?" He gestures forward with his hands. "And then you arrive at hotel."

Not only am I lost in Rome, but I'm lost in this man's beautiful accent. I know I should pick up my jaw from the ground, but every single, sexy word he just said flew over my head.

"Understand?" He lifts his brows. His bushy, beautiful brows.

"I'm so sorry, could you repeat that a little slower please?" I clasp my hands as if in prayer. To this attractive Roman god who stands before me.

He obliges, and this time I repeat each step out loud to drill it into my memory. As I start to walk away, I thank him, ready to repeat the steps aloud again before I forget the directions, but he surprises me with, "Where are you from?"

I stop walking and face him. He slips his phone into his pants pocket and pushes off the pizzeria with his foot so that he's standing upright. His nose is slightly crooked, and there's a tiny dark spot right underneath one of his eyes. His lashes, dark and long. "Chicago. I'm here for the week. My first time."

"*Americana*." He flashes a smile that melts me faster than gelato in the sun. He doesn't seem to be in much of a hurry, so I keep talking, hoping I don't blunder and paint "Americana" in a bad light. I tell him about this morning's amazing tour of the Colosseum.

"Ah, yes. It is amazing. But more to see in *Roma*. What is your name?"

I step closer to him. Dark hair peeks out of the top of his white button-up and on his hands. "April."

"Like the month?" Confusion never looked so irresistible. "We say it '*Aprile*.'"

"Yes! I learned how to say all the months in *Fast Talk*

Italian! My pocket dictionary!" An embarrassed laugh sneaks out, and I attempt to tone down my excitement at the thought of speaking in calendar vocabulary with my new Italian boyfriend. "I was actually trying to find this—this cheese shop. I walked by it earlier, but didn't catch the name, and now I think it's closed. Don't places close up in the afternoon in Italy? That's a thing right? I read something about that on the plane."

"*Riposo.*"

My face scrunches up. "I'm sorry?"

"A break in the afternoon. Usually small towns, small shops." His phone dings, and he retrieves it from his pocket, tapping again in frustration. "*Mannaggia*! This app… not working! I hate this phone." He says the words slowly and passionately. I hate his phone, too, dammit.

"I'm not much better with technology, but what are you having trouble with?"

"To park?" He points to an adorable baby blue Fiat that's barely squeezed into a spot on the corner. "I need to pay. I wait for cousin." He looks up, stuffing his phone in the inside pocket of his blazer, waving his hands around. "Why no meters? All gone. Everything is app now." He rolls his eyes. After a moment of bonding over our mutual resentment of technology, he asks how else I'll be filling my time in Rome. The first thing that pops into my mind is the winery cooking class.

A sparkle of silver brightens his eyes at this news. "You cook?"

Shrugging my shoulders, I explain, "Well, I hope to be able to after Friday."

He gestures to Antonelli's Pizzeria behind him. "This

is my *papà*'s restaurant. Forty years in my family. We need another cook." His eyebrows dance playfully.

"You don't want me as a cook. I'm lucky if I don't burn toast."

"*Aprile*," he says, adding a vowel to the end of my name again, like the accordion player did last night. Who knew vowels could get my motor running so hot? "Come back here tonight. Dinner. I will be here. No burning toast. I promise."

Of all the things to resent in this life, I never thought a tour of the Sistine Chapel and a multi-course Italian dinner would be among them, but I explain that time is ticking, and I have to get a move on if I'm going to stick to the schedule. But gorgeous Italian men have their own gravitational pull, so I continue the conversation anyway. "Tomorrow I'll be at Piazza Navona. Any suggestions for lunch?"

But my question goes unanswered when he runs toward his Fiat which I now see has two tires resting on the curb of the sidewalk. A police officer leaves a citation on the car, and Mr. Can-I-Buy-a-Vowel shouts something in Italian. The officer responds in kind before driving off, leaving my new friend to snatch the ticket off the car and stuff it into his pocket, giving me a defeated look.

I walk over to him. "Finding an open parking spot out here seems about as rare as enjoying a blind date."

He rattles something in Italian, fiery irritation amplifying his otherwise quiet voice. Upon glancing at my confused face, he sprinkles in some English for my benefit. "I park here, five minutes." More Italian. Something about *famiglia*. He gestures toward the street, cars lined up on both sides.

"Parking's horrible where I live, too. I'm so sorry—what did you say your name was?"

He sighs, and his face softens a bit. "Giovanni."

Another eyeful of those dark waves and swanky suit threatens to take my breath away, but I manage to say, "Your car's really cute."

CHAPTER 10

THE POPE'S DRESS CODE

BACK IN THE hotel room, a messy bed with sheets astray reveals Simon's dirty little secret: while I was out enjoying an innocent gelato, he's had a little afternoon delight… with work. On his belly, he's sprawled out on the bed, laptop open, zealously typing away. A couple protein bar wrappers litter the rumpled comforter.

"Becks." I toss my empty gelato cup in the trash bin. "You're working?!" What a horrifying thought: inviting stress into a perfect week in the most beautiful city on Earth.

"Yeah, catching up on emails," he says without looking up from his screen, his fingers moving in a flurry of keystrokes. "With the time difference I've got to check whenever I can."

Spoken like a true all-star employee. I've only known one other person to check email while on vacation: Ian. Eventually I learned to tune out all the dings and buzzes of his various notifications; despite all my protests, he could never fully unplug. Sometimes I find myself smiling when I hear the same sounds dinging on my phone. It's weird how we can miss the things that used to annoy us. Meanwhile, I couldn't check in with work—or anyone else back home—even if I wanted to. It's amazing how fast one adjusts to the freedom of not having a working cell phone. It's the perfect excuse to completely detach from reality, and fully immerse myself in my temporary Italian surroundings. Which, as recently as this afternoon, have become even more attractive.

The bed poofs out as I plop down on it, kicking off my sneakers. "Sandersons account?"

"They finally signed." He clicks the trackpad's mouse a few times. "Which means now I'll have some good news to sprinkle in with the bad."

"What do you mean?"

He taps what must be the "enter" key with exaggerated finality and looks up at me. "W-W-J-D. I just submitted my application."

"That's great! So, you're officially going for the job then?"

Simon closes his laptop and sits up, breathing what sounds like a sigh of relief. "Yep. Now I just need to tell Rob. But at least I can soften the blow with the Sandersons."

"Fogerty would be proud. And I'm sure your boss will understand." Pulling my suitcase toward me, I unzip it, digging for an appropriate outfit for tonight's tour of the Vatican museums. "I'm going to get changed," I say, heading for the bathroom. "We should celebrate tonight."

My pink dress with black polka dots and low-heeled boots isn't exactly a party outfit, but it's cute nonetheless. "Is this okay?" I spread my arms wide so he can take a look. He looks me over with a one-second assessment, nodding his approval. "It's not too short right? I don't want to offend any nuns."

He simply laughs, touching the small of my back as he heads for the bathroom. "It's fine. You worry too much." No more than fifteen seconds pass before I hear Dean Martin singing "Volare."

I croon along with Simon and Dean as I touch up my makeup, happier than any person should be to hear that nasal off-key harmony. My hair is much flatter than it was this morning after being fluffed out with the hotel's electrically-compliant blow dryer. I spruce it back to life, rhythmically swishing my head side to side to get my bangs just right. After a few more minutes the water stops and Simon walks into the room in nothing but his boxer briefs.

His snug, sexy, and inviting boxer briefs.

I make myself busy brushing my hair but can't help side-eyeing my old buddy and his chiseled abs, arms, and legs as he walks over to his suitcase. There's something weirdly startling about seeing a friend from youth who has transitioned from the scrawny high school kid who went go-karting with you after prom into an eligible rock-hard hunk of man.

"These or these?" he asks, holding up two pairs of pants.

"The darker ones. They look a little dressier." I look from the pants to his face. Our eyes lock, and neither one of us looks away. The room's dim, with only the ambient light from Rome filtering in through the window.

"You sure?" His voice is softer now, not as nasal. Is this an invitation?

I walk over, reaching for the pants. My hands grasp the darker ones, and my eyes stay fixed on his. "These bring out your eyes."

He stares back. Has the room always been this quiet? I wonder if he can hear my heart beating, which has suddenly picked up as though I'm back in the Midwest running along Lake Michigan. He reaches over to take the pants back, but not before his hands graze mine.

"Darker it is then." He grins. His forearm flexes a little as pulls on the pants. And everything goes black.

Except for his torso.

Still shirtless, he walks to the closet underneath a spotlight, his back gleaming with grooves in all the right places and no trace of even a single ounce of body fat. *Look at those muscle ripples…* As he reaches for a gray button-up, the annoyances of his naps and emails and unexplained kiss all melt away. He starts buttoning from the bottom, his shirt slowly covering his gladiator-like physique.

He is so forgiven for not having gelato with me.

CHAPTER 11

GOIN' TO THE CHAPEL

IT HAD WHITE siding and a single steeple shooting out from the chapel's roof as it flirted with a sky of cornflower. Pink and lavender blooms lined the walkway leading to two white doors. Inside, wooden pews were lined up in perfect little rows as the sun streamed in through stained-glass windows. It was cozy, with just enough space for immediate family and a few close friends. At first, I thought it was cheesy getting married in a little white chapel in a quiet town in the suburbs, but as soon as I'd stepped inside, I knew it was the perfect place to start a life with Ian.

"No photos in the Sistine Chapel." Our tour guide interrupts my thoughts, and not a moment too soon. Dwelling about my failed engagement isn't exactly how I want to spend my time in Rome, but any time the word "chapel" pops up that's where my brain goes. I can't even listen to that sixties song by the Dixie Cups without feeling the tiniest bit of humiliation.

As we walk through a stairwell making our way to the Chapel, I feel giddy, as if I'm about to meet a celebrity. Stepping through an unassuming doorway, I take each step slowly and deliberately, savoring my entrance inside one of the most celebrated places on Earth. My black boots click on the marble and stone floor, which swirls out before us in patterned circles. The Chapel is a big, open rectangle, and it's filled with Simon's co-workers, who are all ignoring the "no photos" rule, holding their phones up toward the famous ceiling, relentlessly tapping the screens in a feeble attempt to capture its beauty. Pictures that will never be able to replicate the feeling of standing in this room and seeing it with our own eyes.

The Vatican decorating team clearly didn't settle for basic "ceiling white" paint. Instead, they hired Michelangelo, who, according to our tour guide, spent four years painting the entire ceiling of the Sistine Chapel, completing it in 1512. The most famous part in the center is stunning to see: The Creation of Adam, depicting God giving life to the first man. The white-bearded God, wearing a flowing white cloak, is reaching out his arm, his finger almost touching that of Adam's. The two are looking right at each other, nearly touching hands. It's almost as if to say that we humans can get close to God, maybe even see or sense him in some way, but not quite reach him completely. Kind of like my engagement: close, but no cigar.

My gown hung in my closet for three years. Not for sentimental reasons; I simply couldn't resell the damn thing. Brides would rather invite their in-laws on their honeymoon than wear a used wedding gown, even ones that still have the tags on. I only wore mine for about fifteen minutes at the boutique, Greg and I giggling as I practiced what would be my "aisle walk." So, on a mere technicality, my ivory gown with pearls along the neckline and lace sleeves that was in its protective bag was considered "used goods." Eventually, I'd had enough, and Greg and I took a pair of scissors and tie-dye to it, made a rudimentary punk rock minidress, and had a fun weekend at Lollapalooza. It was a proper sendoff for a dress whose fate was originally going to be worn during the chicken dance.

"Look at the arches," our tour guide says. Around the perimeter of the ceiling, arches and columns appear to be jutting out from the ceiling, but, as she points out, they're actually flat. Michelangelo painted shadows on the flat surface so perfectly that it looks three dimensional. Even the royal looking drapes that appear to be hanging from the walls are painted on. They look as though I could walk over and feel the velvety softness of the gold fabric with my fingers.

"I thought those were real too when I came here five years ago." Simon notices me marveling at, of all the meaningful frescoes surrounding us, the painted drapes. "Would look great in my townhouse."

"New goal in life: painted drapes. I'd never have to vacuum off any cat fur. Not that I do that anyway."

But like so many other things in life that take on a misleading guise, these curtains, too, are illusions. My friendship with Ian was real, but our romance was a fantasy. What I needed was not to be alone, and he was ever present. During college, he gave me four years of no expectations; a safe, commitment-free friendship was his gift to me during my time of grieving. And, despite the fact that he wore his feelings for me on his sleeve in blinding, neon colors, he knew that I needed time. He waited to make his move until my fear of losing someone else I loved no longer barricaded my heart, and as soon as college ended, our relationship officially began. How does that poem go—or is it a prayer—that you hear at weddings? Love is patient, love is kind? He was the embodiment of that. Sure, it might have been cliché to hear those words at the wedding we almost had, but at least it would have been fitting. So what if he wasn't perfect? Everyone has their little ticks that drive their partner crazy. What if all we really needed was a little more time? Maybe postponing the wedding—not canceling it—is what we should have done. But instead, I ran away. I ran because I didn't want our friendship to dissolve inside a marriage to someone who never tickled my butterflies. All these years, I've felt guilty for canceling our wedding and ultimately ending our relationship, but now I see that I was actually trying to preserve it. Preserve our friendship. Because, he really did mean something to me. Would giving it another shot with Ian really be so bad? Strangely, I can see that happening. If one guy can paint a church that generations marvel at for centuries, then the thought of a new chapter with Ian seems not so crazy.

"Earth to April." Simon snaps his fingers. "Trying to remember the Hail Mary?" His laugh echoes.

"It *has* been ages since my days of memorizing prayers in Catholic school." A quick glance around tells me that none of our friends are within earshot, and I safely explain where my head was at. "I'm starting to wonder if…"

"If you should get back together with Ian?"

"Is that crazy? I mean, I don't even know if that's why he's been calling."

He puts an arm around me and gives me a squeeze. "You should find out first before torturing yourself." A sincerity in his eyes calms me.

"Well, speaking of torture, that's how my neck is starting to feel." I rub the back of my neck as our tour guide mercifully instructs us to look downward to the wall where we entered the Chapel. She explains that it features another masterpiece from Michelangelo: The Last Judgment, painted decades after the famous ceiling, and completed in 1541. With a sky-blue backdrop, this painting displays the second coming of Jesus Christ, surrounded by saints. Below and to the left are the dead, rising from their graves awaiting their final judgment. And over to the right are those who have been condemned to Hell, falling to a doomed eternity with Satan. I can almost hear their screams. Interestingly, Hell appears right above the doorway through which we entered. Was that Michelangelo's subtle way of insinuating that lowly humans are, at our core, sinners, living in line closer with Satan than with God?

"There y'all are," Daphne shuffles over in her cowgirl boots with a dazzling smile. "Can I take your photo if you take ours?" She holds her hand out for my phone, anticipating my answer.

"Yeah, that'd be great, thanks," I say while opening the camera app. "So much for the 'no photo' rule, right?"

She snaps a few pictures, then rotates the phone so that it's horizontal and takes a couple more, all the while saying in a lowered voice, "They done lost their marbles if they think we ain't gonna snap a few photos in here. Am I right?" Daphne hands me back my phone along with hers.

"Let hope breakin' that rule ain't a one-way ticket to

Hell." Chuck pinches his new bride's rear giving her a wink, and the two of them smile for the camera.

"We're all going to Hell anyway." Simon doesn't hold back his laughter.

"These look great." Daphne beams, while swiping back through her photo reel. "You framed this one perfectly!" She holds up the screen, she and her husband smiling back at us. Then she hits the home button and I see a group shot set as her phone's wallpaper. She and Chuck standing on either side of two young boys, their dimples and pearly smiles the spitting image of their father. "Who'd walk away from these boys?" she asks to no one in particular, her gaze not leaving the screen. "Some mother they had."

Chuck takes the phone from her and pulls her in an embrace. "Daph, would ya cut it out? You're their mama now." From over her shoulder, he squeezes his eyes shut, and I can't tell if he's holding back his frustration or begging a silent prayer. When they pull apart, Daphne gives Chuck an incredulous look. "Babe," Chuck pleads, "enough with the lawyer talk, the adoption talk. Hon, you're drivin' me nuts." He smiles at this, an exhausted laugh tumbling out.

"Chuck's right," I add. "I just mean that DNA isn't the only thing a mom gives her kids. Just love them. That's all that really counts."

CHAPTER 12

BITING OFF MORE
THAN I CAN CHEW

AT HOME, 8:24 p.m. is a great time to be on my third bowl of post-dinner ice cream topped with shame-flavored hot fudge, but here in Rome, however, not an ounce of shame occupies my mental state as dinner is just getting started. The meal begins with the *antipasto* course. Platters of prosciutto, salami, olives, quiche, and—my new favorite thing about Italy—buffalo mozzarella adorn our table at the most Italian sounding restaurant in the history of food: *Girarrosto Fiorentino.*

Sexy, right?

It's a quaint, wood-paneled restaurant specializing in Tuscan wine and cuisine, with wooden crates of fresh oranges and grapes next to the entrance. Covering the windows are sheer white drapes with lacy embroidery, and hanging from the walls are paintings of the Colosseum and St. Peter's Basilica.

Bottles of Tuscan Chianti Classico wait to be poured into our wine glasses—but the wait is rather short-lived. Vicki does the honors right away, emptying a bottle among the six of us. I pick up my glass by the stem, swish around the *vino*, sniff it, and take a sip, reflecting in complete awe of the incredible sites we've seen in a single day. The guys, on the other hand, have different matters in mind.

"I'm tellin' ya," Chuck says through a grin, "y'all haven't lived 'til you've had a pedicure." His stubble is growing in thicker by the hour, and I giggle quietly while picturing him in a leather chair soaking his manly feet at a salon.

Simon's boisterous laugh thunders out of him. He pops some salami into his mouth as he heckles, "Did they paint your toenails pink to match your panties?"

Daphne, using a pair of glasses as a headband to hold back her blond waves, chimes in to defend her man. "It ain't about the polish. It's about the exfoliation. Chuck and I get couple pedis all the time now. And I think I'm gonna need one soon if we don't get that damn adoption decree." She turns to Chuck. "I don't get it—we're already a family living under one roof! Your kids love me." After a beat, she asks tentatively, "Right?"

A dimple appears from deep within her husband's stubble as he flashes her a reassuring grin, draping his arm around her shoulders. "Of course, they do. Don't go inventin' crazy theories again."

"This should've been all buttoned up before the wedding. I can't figure why Gerry is taking his sweet time finalizing that decree. Tomorrow mornin', I'm givin' him a buzz to see what the hold-up is." She abruptly stops talking, her eyes darting around at our watchful gazes. Then, leaning into Chuck and lowering her voice, adds, "What if he found out what I did?"

A manly, veined hand that's probably seen its fair share of dirt under its nails covers Chuck's face. He sighs and says, "First, we ain't botherin' the man with another phone call. He'll call us. Second, you gotta stop worryin' about that. Extenuatin' circumstances." Now, turning to the rest of the table, he slaps on a forced smile. "Tonight, no worries allowed. No past ghosts allowed. Let's just enjoy ourselves." With that, he tastes the wine.

To break the tension, I proposition my own "husband." "What do you think? Partner pedicures when we get back home? Maybe find a two-for-one deal?"

An airy nasal laugh escapes his nose as he holds up his glass of Chianti. "Ask me after I have a few more of these."

I slice off some prosciutto. "You don't know what you're missing. It's quite a pleasurable sensation."

"Is that so? Maybe you'll have to show me some time."

Vicki, who instead of laughing has steadily kept an eye on our table's Chianti levels, tops off everyone's glasses, emptying another bottle. As a server walks by, she asks, "*Signore?*" The empty bottle rises in the air, a wordless request for a full one.

Half an hour later, our waiters serve the *primo piatto*: pasta *amatriciana* with *pancetta* and tomato sauce. As a bowl of cheese makes the rounds, I shamelessly announce that I'll be breaking the no-parmesan rule again.

"Actually," Simon is quick to correct me, "that's Pecorino. And you must absolutely add it to this dish."

"Are you sure?" I yank my foodie guide *Eating Italy* out of my purse, scanning the index for "Pecorino."

Simon laughs. "You don't need to consult the experts; I wouldn't lie about cheese."

"I don't know, you studied politics in college. Doesn't hurt to do a little fact-checking." A minute later I learn that Pecorino Romano is a hard cheese from sheep's milk and is a necessity for making a flavorful *amatriciana* sauce. I quote aloud from the book, "Pasta *all'amatriciana* is a staple of Roman restaurants and can be traced back to the sixteen-hundreds. The condiment sauce for this dish has three basic ingredients: *guanciale*, tomato sauce, and Pecorino."

Wait, cheese *in* the sauce? Sprinkling extra on top, sure. But now I think back to my mom's spaghetti sauce. It's not only the flavor that's been hard to replicate, but the texture. Could she have added cheese to her tomato sauce? That's so simple, yet so genius. Why have I never thought of that?

Vicki stabs a couple tubes and says in a breathy voice, "*Al dente*. Magnificent."

"A rare feat for some," I say. "There's a fine line between *al dente* and overcooked mush in my kitchen."

"Come Friday, that'll change." Vicki's diamond ring dings against the wine glass as she picks it up, putting my impostor ring to shame.

"So, April, you were pretty much raised by nuns at Catholic school," Simon starts with a chuckle, "Did the Vatican live up to its potential?"

"Well, the Sistine Chapel was amazing," I finish chewing my food before continuing, "but I really loved the Gallery of Maps."

"*La galleria della carte geografiche*" Vicki supplies, her accent getting stronger with each sip.

"Yeah, that." My mind's eye pictures the long corridor

displaying forty immensely sized topographical maps of Italy on either side. Each one displayed a different region of Italy, with detailed insets of that region's most prominent city. At the hotel last night, while Simon zonked out in record time but I was a victim of jet lag, I'd read in *Passport to History* that Ignazio Danti spent three years creating the maps, finishing in the year 1583.

The wine is making me warm, and I feel a little fuzzy when I say, "There was something so magical about seeing the enormous space we're living in shrunken down into a single frame. And then the realization that we're just a tiny speck sets in, you know? Puts everything into perspective."

"You sound like my old philosophy professor." Simon blurts out a nasal laugh.

"Yeah, yeah, yeah."

"Don't worry, you *sound* like him, but you don't look like him." He winks and squeezes my knee under the table.

Heat surges in my cheeks. "They just reminded me of an old trip I took, that's all."

"Care to elaborate?" Simon asks, lifting *maccheroni* to my lips.

"Oh… just an old road trip." My mouth opens and I bite it, a smile hiding the bitter memory.

Only in Italy do they bring out pasta as a way of preparing you to eat more pasta. Vicki spins her fork in a fresh plate full of fettuccine topped with porcini mushrooms. "Hm, I'm sensing egg in this sauce."

"You can pick out an ingredient after one bite? That your superpower or something?"

"Oh, it's simple really. The sauce is thicker—it's quite rich." She takes another bite, her face in contemplation.

"Actually, it might be cream—or butter—that I'm tasting. Yes, butter."

"You wouldn't happen to venture any guesses as to how to sweeten a tomato-based sauce a bit, would you? Besides basil and sugar, of course."

"Well, those would be the obvious choices. But using certain types of wine could sweeten up a sauce, too." She grins as she empties another bottle of her favorite beverage, as if remembering her voluntary duty to keep everyone shnockered. It's amazing how quickly a bottle empties at a table of hungry—or should I say thirsty—Americans. All it takes is a graceful wave of her hand, and the waiter tolerates her request, bringing another.

"I'd like to make a toast." Rob, who's kept quiet until now, stands up holding his wine glass. To snatch everyone's attention he taps his glass with a knife. *Ding ding ding!*

"Rob, really?" Vicki says. "You're tapping much too hard."

He stands before us scowling like a high school English teacher waiting for his students to calm down before starting his lesson. Harder and harder he taps the glass until *clink clink CRASH*. Shards of glass fly across our table. Vicki takes the brunt of it, her face a cross between embarrassment and annoyance. Simon and Chuck laugh as if somebody has just told a hilarious joke. And I'm sending up a prayer that glass didn't land in my fettuccine—I'm not done eating. A few pointy pieces sparkle around my place setting, daring me to find out.

At the sound of the clatter, the wait staff rushes over to survey the damage.

"I'm so sorry. Can we have another glass?" Rob asks,

carefully handing the waiter what could now pass for a ruthlessly effective sword.

The waiter looks at us rowdy Americans through narrowed eyes, carefully takes the obliterated glass by the stem, and walks away without a word. I can't say that I blame him for hating us. We're drinking them dry, we're loud, and now we're shattering their fine crystal.

With a new glass, Rob makes his toast, thanking all the hardworking employees that make Worldswift excel with greatness. "I'd be remiss if I didn't single out one particular member of the Midwest rental division." He turns to Simon, whose cheeks quickly flush with color. "Four years of topping his own record looks like nothing in comparison to his latest accomplishment."

Simon and I share a glance. Does Rob already know?

"Today, after decades of trying to partner with the biggest grocery chain in Michigan, Worldswift Transport is now the official carrier of everything in the aisles of all Sandersons grocery stores, thanks to Simon Becker who has sealed a multi-year deal!"

Our table erupts in applause. I clap quietly while Simon's face now goes pale.

"Simon," Rob continues, smile lines etching his face, "Worldswift hasn't seen this kind of growth in years, and much of it is due to your diligence, patience, and work ethic. Here's to another successful year in the Midwest rental division!" Chuck is now standing, too, cheering for his coworker. Daphne clinks her glass with a fork in celebration. After the noise settles a bit, Rob says, "Don't be shy; stand up and say a few words."

After drinking some liquid courage, Simon stands.

"Thank you, Rob." He clears his throat and holds up his glass in a toast to his boss. "I learned from the best. Uh, what can I say? I wasn't expecting to gain a client while in Italy. When in Rome, I guess." Light laughter ruffles through our table. "These past ten years in Rentals at Worldswift have been amazing. I couldn't imagine hounding new clients into signing a contract anywhere else." He pauses for a moment, glancing down at me. "But all good things come to an end—"

I kick him under the table. He shoots me a look, and I mouth "not now." Thankfully, he takes the hint, quickly changing course.

"Which, in the case of the Sandersons' contract, won't be for at least five years." He holds his glass up higher. "To new clients."

A smattering of clinks rings out as we toast to his accomplishment. As Simon sits down, he leans over to me. "Um, *ow*. Thanks for that."

"You can't tell him here," I say just above a whisper.

"I've got to be the one to tell him." He keeps his voice low and controlled. "He knew about Sandersons before I even told him. What if my new boss gets to him first? Mason could be trying to call him right now to check my references."

I pick up my fork, attempting to look as though we're not having a conversation rife with nervous tension. "Rob hasn't looked at his phone all night. Vicki must've finally gotten through to him. And he'll probably come with us if we head to a bar after this. You can tell him there, one on one."

Vicki, as if she needs another reason to ask, flags down a waiter. "We'd love another bottle of red, *per favore*, when you get a moment. We're celebrating."

By ten o'clock, we're treated to our *secondo piatto*:

Chateaubriand steak, lemon chicken breast, and veal with marsala wine. (For anybody paying attention, that means we'll now be drinking *and* eating wine.) Vicki shocks no one when she asks for yet another bottle of red wine.

"Oh my God, I'm losing brain cells left and right with her," I whisper to Simon. My hair feels warm as I tuck it behind an ear.

"When in Rome!" His eyes twinkle with laughter, and he reaches over to tuck my hair behind my other ear.

A buzzy warmth flows through me as I sip from a freshly poured glass. "I feel like a wife would kiss you after that speech you gave."

"Oh yeah? Is this a W-W-J-D moment here?"

"I mean," I keep my voice low and flirty, "we have to look convincing, right? John Fogerty wouldn't let his performance flop halfway through the show."

"My blushing bride, April," he says, not bothering to finish the bite of steak speared on his fork. It makes a loud clank as he sets it down on his plate. "How could we have overlooked the CCR frontman? Maybe we should add another date next year." He leans in, his hands warm on my cheeks.

"A date?"

"The concerts."

The wine has relaxed every muscle in my body, and my lips willingly meet his, forgetting the watching eyes surrounding us, completely absorbed in the magic of the present. Tonight's kiss feels different from last night's. It's not a spontaneous last resort, but a mutual attraction that can't be stopped.

It's only when I finally realize that the ringing that I've been hearing for the past ten seconds is coming from my purse that my racing heartbeat practically stops.

Simon's hands are still on my cheeks as I pull away. "What's wrong?"

The name on the screen isn't exactly who I want to talk to at the moment. "It's Ian again."

CHAPTER 13

A BITTER BELLINI

Is that jealousy I see on Simon's face? Or just surprise?

Daphne sees me looking at my phone. "Everything okay?"

While it's still ringing, I drop my phone back in my purse. "Yup."

"Ain't you gonna pick that up?" Daphne sounds shocked. "Someone calls me, I always pick up."

"That's 'cause you're always hopin' it's our lawyer." Chuck says through a grin.

The wine is making everything fuzzy, and I announce, "It's my ex-fiancé. I'm not answering him." Mercifully, the ringing stops.

"You were gonna marry someone else besides Simon?!" Daphne's eyes bulge out like two overinflated blue beach balls. "Girl, we got some catchin' up to do."

Chuck's knife, cutting off a hunk of steak, freezes as he asks, "He's still callin' ya?"

"We… sort of… friends."

"Call him back!" Daphne blurts out. "I wanna know what he wants from a happily married woman."

"My phone can't make calls out here," I explain, "but apparently, it can receive calls from exes. Remind me to opt out of that feature with my next mobile provider."

"Why didn't you take the plunge with this fella?"

I take a deep breath and hold it, searching for a way not to make myself look like the villain in this story. I mean, I'm with the guy for years—living with him for part of that time—and then I just want to be friends? Awful with a capital A. Of course, understanding the context of how our relationship began might make me seem less evil, but that's not a story I'd like to dive into with a table of people I've known for one day.

"Uh, hello?" Simon says with jest in his voice. "Have you seen me?" He gestures to his own body, his laughter smoothly transitioning us into a much-needed distraction. "Hey, I have an idea." He grabs the bottle of wine to top off everyone's glasses. "Truth or dare. I'll even take one for the team and go first. Dare, baby. Let's do this." A mischievous grin forms on his face.

"Shocking," I say.

"C'mon, dare me. Double dog dare me, April." He takes a bite of steak. "C'mon, lay it on me."

"What does one dare someone who voluntarily eats flowers?"

Chuck's suggestion doesn't disappoint. "I got it: I dare you to get a pedicure!"

Simon stands, holding out his wine glass declaring, "I'll do it. I'll get a pedicure. Polish and all!"

"With glitter!" shouts Daphne. "And we want photos."

As he sits down, I put my hand on his arm. "Thank you."

He leans over to kiss me on the cheek then whispers, "What's a fake husband for?"

Finally. *Dolce.* The real main course. If I served myself a slice of tiramisu and a bowl of ice cream at 10:30 p.m. at home, it would be in the dark with the shades drawn: my little secret. But here, this late-night indulgence makes me feel like a damn queen. I start with the tiramisu, the bold flavor of espresso preparing me for the strong coffee the waiter now serves for me. I can feel my pants getting tighter with each course, but it would be a sin not to finish these coffee-soaked ladyfingers in their country of origin. This is a dish worth relishing leisurely. This dessert is downright sexy.

Literally. "Tiramisu's an aphrodisiac," Simon says, lifting a slice of the indulgent cake to his mouth.

"You don't say." I lift an eyebrow. "And have you tested out this theory?" The wine has now obliterated any and all verbal filters.

"Not personally. At least not yet." His eyes are two swirling chocolates, inviting me in for a sweet treat. But the echoes from Ian's phone call are still ringing in my ear, and I don't seize the moment. He looks away from me, clearing his throat. "It was used in a lot of brothels. That's how they would reinvigorate exhausted clients."

"You should have tried that with Sandersons. They would have signed so much faster." Hell, maybe that's how I can catch a real husband: bait him with tiramisu.

Two more bottles of wine and an hour later, the wait staff is wearing their impatience on their sleeves. One checks his watch, another taps his foot. But it's not until Simon cues up Dean Martin's "Volare" on his phone, our whole table crooning along, that the waiters clear every last dish on our table: an indisputable nonverbal way of saying "you don't have to go home, but you can't stay here."

⁓

Girarrosto Fiorentino: Four juicy, crispy apples.

Taste: Pretty sure the entire food pyramid was presented multiple times, and not a single item wasn't bursting with flavor. The *pasta all'amatriciana* was incredibly flavorful. Freshly grated Pecorino cheese softened into the red sauce like early fall snowflakes melting on wet grass. The pasta itself, big and hollow, was textured so that the sauce, rich with a flavorful zing, stuck to it. The lemon chicken breast: tender and juicy. A slice of lemon sat on my plate like a beaming sun of citrus adding a zing of flavor. For dessert: vanilla ice cream topped with fresh blackberries and raspberries; and tiramisu with extra cocoa powder sprinkles resting on the edge of the plate. It was light and fluffy, and begged to be indulged in slowly. I savored all the layers in every bite. The cream: fluffy and subtly sweet. The layers of cookies: wet but not soaked, and they melted on my tongue. One full apple.

Service: It was a million-course meal with nonstop wine. A big, hearty apple.

Atmosphere: Wood paneling and paintings of ancient Rome made me feel like I was in old-world Italy. It was oozing romance. The most charming apple on the tree.

Price: Someone else paid. Another full apple.

᠅

We make our way to Harry's, a famous American bar decked out in 1960s glamour featured in the film *La Dolce Vita* and known for their peach-infused Bellini cocktails.

Inside, it's wood-paneled, a golden glow emitting from the light fixtures covered in lamp shades. The bar curves, and we all squeeze in at the end. Daphne and Chuck steal kisses while sharing a cushioned stool, while the rest of us stand.

With a sip of my Bellini, sweet and thick like a Prosecco-laced smoothie, I whisper to Simon, "Are you going to tell Rob?"

He whispers back. "Tell him what?"

"About the new job! He's in a good mood; now's your moment." I grab his shoulder and give him a playful shake. "I *dare* you."

He downs the rest of his old-fashioned and sets the empty glass on the bar. "Right. Yes." After clearing his throat, he says, "Rob? Got some news." Boy, he really cuts to the chase.

With a greedy smile, Rob jokes, "Sandersons signed at double the rate?"

"I wish." Simon chuckles. "But, no. Though the commission on this one is mighty fine." More chuckles.

A light kick of his foot should keep him on track. "Tell him."

"Tell me what?" Rob's brows furrow with concern while Vicki nurses a fresh glass of red wine. How is she still standing?

Simon looks at me while he says, "Mason Sampson approached me a few weeks ago about a national position." He turns to look at Rob now. "And I'm going to take it." After a beat of silence he adds, "It's a huge step up, and it's not like I'm leaving the company altogether, I just need," he stammers a bit while searching for the right words, "something… more. It's been ten years, and I've been in Rentals this whole time. I want to try this. I haven't told anyone yet. Except April."

Rob's face doesn't betray any emotion. It looks almost as though he hasn't heard a thing Simon has said. Worry creases Simon's forehead, but before long Rob pulls him into an embrace, patting his back in congratulations. "That's great! You'll be an all-star in Nationals. And Mason… Man, he's lucky. You're going to love working with him."

I feel lighter for Simon, the relieved smile on his face a reassuring sight. After another round of celebratory drinks, the seconds fly away from us, making time speed up without our awareness. The music seems to get louder, the lights dimmer, and everything seems perfect right now. In my drunken happiness, I almost feel capable of making time stop, to live forever in the warm haze of Italian bliss. To stay here forever with my old friend and never have to say goodbye.

"I can't believe we're together again. In *Rome*." By my third Bellini, the famous drink tastes frothier somehow, sweeter, and it makes the moment feel special. "It's, like, the most romantic place on Earth. My friend thought—well, never mind." The bubbles of the Prosecco seem to be popping away my ability to keep certain thoughts to myself.

"Thought what?" Simon says. His head tilts, and I ache

for our old friendship, hoping whatever this new chapter is, is real and not some momentary vacation from reality.

"It's nothing."

"I *dare* you to tell me." He laughs, and even in the dim lighting I can see that twinkle in his eye.

"I think I'm all dared out. And I think we should be cut off." I set down my half-empty glass, feeling warm and light, like a feather, the room spinning slowly like we're on a rotating stage.

"It's way too late for that." He sips from another old-fashioned. "What did this friend of yours think?"

Daphne and Chuck are in another world kissing at the bar, while Rob and Vicki have moved safely out of earshot to a small table in the corner, chatting over a couple glasses of wine. The moment has finally arrived, and I'm calmer than I thought I'd be bringing up the subject of there possibly being more than friendship between us. A blessing from the relaxing effect of too many Italian cocktails, I suppose. "He thought you…" I roll my eyes and laugh through the words, in case he finds them as preposterous as I once had, "…*liked* me or something. Asking me to come here—Rome, of all places—out of the blue after so many years. He thought it seemed like you were—like it was a little more than friendly, I guess." I finally meet his gaze, dying to hear if Greg's theory is right. Surprisingly, I find myself hoping it is. I could do worse than Simon. I have.

A laugh blurts out and he takes a sip of his drink. "I was gonna fly solo, I was running out of people. You were a shot in the dark." He laughs again, but I don't get it.

"Wait, what do you mean?"

"Well, Cassandra couldn't make it—"

"Who's Cassandra?" I interrupt.

"A girl from my gym. She's a beast on the bench, you should see. And then I asked a couple friends from college, but they couldn't take the time off. I tried Brenda and Kristie—you remember them, right? From high school? I saw them last summer."

I hold up my hands to tell him to stop. "Whoa, you invited B.O. Brenda? How many people did you ask before you got to me?"

He looks confused and sounds defensive. "It's not like I kept count. I was putting feelers out everywhere. I'm just glad I didn't have to ask my sisters—I was gonna try them next. Either one of them would have driven me crazy." His continuous laughter has never irritated me as much as it is right now.

My stomach drops. "Hold on. You didn't want me to come?"

He looks at me like I'm speaking another language. He shrugs and gestures around. "What? We're here, aren't we?" He gives another laugh, though this time it's a bit uneasy.

"We're here, but it sounds like you'd rather be here with, like, *anyone* else. Except your *sisters*, my God. Gee, thanks, I'm one step above your annoying sisters now."

The last of his smile fades from his face. "No, no, that's not what I said. I just meant that taking a whole week off from work with only a few weeks' notice… Going to another country… I didn't know who'd be able to make it, if anyone. And, you said yourself, it was so long since we'd seen each other. I didn't know how to—how to ask you to come to *Italy*, I mean…"

In other words, I was replaceable. I was Cassandra's and

Brenda's and Kristie's and God-knows-who-else's understudy to play Simon's wife. He didn't want to rekindle our old teenage friendship any more than I wanted to marry Ian all those years ago. And he sure as hell wasn't acting on any old feelings. I was nearly his last resort. "You asked all those people before me? I feel like you wish I wasn't here."

"Whoa, hang on." He sets his drink down, jostling Chuck in his haste. He exhales a frustrated breath that's somewhere between a sigh and a laugh. His words come slowly as he looks me in the eyes. "I wouldn't have asked you here if I didn't want you here."

"All those other people though—I feel like I'm your consolation prize." I wasn't his first choice. I wasn't even his second or third choice. Did our friendship mean anything to him? Or was his invitation an act of desperation? I feel my face get hot and I squeeze my arm between Daphne and Chuck to grab my Bellini, the rest of which I probably shouldn't finish, but do, given my current emotional state. "Sorry, Daph." She and Chuck turn to look at us, concern replacing their usual happy dimples.

Simon's voice comes out calm and steady. "April, it's no big deal. All those other people don't matter. I asked a bunch of people I thought I'd have fun with, and you were one of them. It's not about first choice or second choice; I just asked anyone I could think of who might be game. It wasn't some competition. And I was glad you said yes, believe me. You're making a big deal out of nothing."

"It's a big deal that you didn't want me to come with you. You wanted someone else. Whoever else you asked before me."

Chuck starts to say something, but his words are drowned out by Simon's.

"No, you're not listening. Why are you getting so mad? We were having a good time, I thought."

"Yeah, so did I. But, I dunno, out of the blue I hear from you… fifteen years! My God, I've missed you for *fifteen years*. You have no idea how much I've missed you," I say, my voice shaking now as I reach over to grab his shoulders, giving them a quick shake as if to wake him up. "How happy I was that you wanted me to come with you on this trip. That you came back into my life—I thought I'd lost you forever. People don't just come back, you know? Not once they're gone. And, then I get a passport expedited, I fly over an ocean, I'm in a foreign country, and then you—you keep *kissing* me," I practically shout the word, laced with hysterical laughter, "while simultaneously telling me to get back together with Ian…"

Rob is now walking toward us.

My voice starts to get squeaky, and it takes everything in me to keep my voice at a frequency which human ears can still register. "…and now you basically admit that you'd rather be here with someone else." I'm so hot with anger that I start to sweat. I yank off my cardigan clutching it in a fist. The lump in my throat threatens to choke me. "I need to get out of here."

"What's the problem?" Rob asks.

"April, wait," Simon pleads, walking after me. "I never said to get back together with Ian; I said that's probably what *he* wants." He reaches for my shoulder. "Where are you going?"

I shove off his hand. "Somewhere else. Don't follow me." My vision goes blurry as tears start to well up, and all I can think about is running through that door before one falls down my cheek. I nearly topple over a tray of drinks when I cross paths with a waiter I don't see coming.

The night air slaps me with an unforgiving cold, but I don't bother putting my sweater back on. The air shocks me awake, sobering me up. How stupid to have thought that he had feelings, that he wanted this trip to be anything more than a drunken no-strings romp. Let him wonder, let him think I'm going to find some trouble to get into. A part of me wishes that was in my nature, but I end up back at the hotel, grateful the restaurant was only a couple blocks away.

And immediately, in the silence and stillness of our room, the two neatly made beds staring back at me, I feel so incredibly alone. Rejected. I crack open the mini bar without hesitation. "Thank you, Worldswift." My voice tastes bitter. The mini bottle of wine I empty leaves a better taste on my tongue. A bag of Simon's protein bars is on the desk, staring at me in judgment. *Have you no shame? You're in Rome. With Simon. You won. And this is how you repay him? By pouting? By running away from another person you care about when the situation isn't perfect?*

God, those protein bars are wise. But it hurts less if I'm the one who leaves. If I leave before they do, I'm in control. Right?

Wrong. Right now, Simon isn't the one hurting me. It's my own damn pride. Which is also preventing me from returning to Harry's after such a scene; I have a better place in mind.

Despite the cool night air, my knuckles have expanded with an angry heat, and I nearly yank off my finger as I remove my stupid fake ring, setting it on the nightstand. I've really got to stop removing rings in fits of rage. I spruce up my hair and makeup, connect to the hotel's wi-fi, and tap out an email to Greg. I'll never admit it to Ian, but his beloved apps are coming in handy just when I need them. Once the map loads, I jot down on my hand the route that the GPS calculates after I type in "Antonelli's."

❧

To: gregorystorms@wrck.fm

Subject: We were way off

Just stormed out of a bar on Simon. Apparently, he asked nine million other people to come to Rome before asking me. I guess our friendship meant more to me than him. I feel like a huge idiot. Oh, and Ian keeps calling. I'm not answering. Also, I'm getting nowhere with my mom's sauce recipe, and yet I've decided to crack the code for two more of her recipes while I'm at it: lasagna and cheesecake. Please reserve me a spot at the nuthouse upon my homecoming, because I am obviously insane.

Other than that, today was amazing. This selfie in front of the Colosseum doesn't do it justice. We weren't supposed to take pics in the Sistine Chapel, but I'm pretty sure God would want me to have something to remember it by. I've also learned that I can eat caprese salads for every meal and not tire of them. There are tomatoes and mozzarella everywhere out here and it's still not enough.

Give Tot a hug for me. Sorry she left her own little tots on the bathroom floor, but LOL I needed a good laugh right now. She obviously misses me. Every turd on the tile, a desperate plea: Bring back my human!

April

P.S. Fun fact for you to share with Harry (just please not at my place): Tiramisu is an aphrodisiac. Good thing I had some earlier because now I'm going to find a hot Italian guy named Giovanni who helped me when I was lost earlier. Ciao!

CHAPTER 14

HOLY CANNOLI

I DON'T KNOW what cures a hangover, but I'm pretty sure it's not listening to the voicemail your ex-fiancé left you.

Dean Martin croons from the shower again, but it sounds strange without Simon's nasal harmonies. My head is pounding and my stomach is in knots, and as if that's not enough, there isn't a hole deep enough to crawl into after I embarrassed myself last night. It was always a fine line between drunken bliss and emotional tidal wave with me. The first time I got really drunk with Greg—it was our company Christmas party at the radio station—he complimented my hair, and I sobbed for an hour. Still under the covers, I open my email, tapping on his response.

To: aprilappleby@wrck.fm

Subject: Re: We were way off

Um, talk about burying the lead. WHO IS GIOVANNI? And why isn't there a pic of HIM?

Oh my God. Giovanni. My late-night visit to his father's pizzeria comes crashing to the forefront of my memory.

I stumbled my way to Antonelli's. I remember seeing a group of people at a table inside, laughing and talking. But the doorknob was jammed—or at least I thought it was. I turned it again, this time grunting while pushing the door with my shoulder, but it wouldn't budge. One of the guys at the table noticed what must have looked like a pizza bandit breaking in. A flabbergasted smile appeared on his face, and that's when I realized who it was, though his stylish gray blazer from earlier was replaced with a humble apron, complete with tomato stains.

"Giovanni! You're still here!" I shouted the words a little so that he could hear them through the glass.

He turned the lock and opened the door, standing in the doorway leaning on the frame. "*Aprile?*" he said in an accent that made me forget all my earlier troubles. "Too late for the dinner. We are closed."

"Oh, dinner, yeah, already had it. And the best tiramisu ever. Of. My. Life. Didja know it's an aphra—an abracadabra—an Adirondack?" I winked at him, then looked to the group at the table.

"*Benissimo.* I am with my family. Finishing the bread and wine. Are you okay?"

"I'm great." I made the last word three syllables.

He looked around on the deserted, dark street. "Your friends? You are here with other people, no?"

"*Sì!*" A hiccup interrupted my giggling. "They're prolly still at Harry's. They make a mean Bellini, Giovanni." My shoulders danced with each word. I never loved the sound of the letter "n" more.

"Ah. You were served well. Want to sit, yes?" He moved out of the doorway and gestured to a small table by the door.

"Verymuchso, yes." I curtsied.

I'm not sure how much time elapsed but before I knew it, he set down a glass of water, and sat in the chair across from me. "Best drink of the night. And," he pushed a plate toward me with a couple slices of rustic looking bread on it, "to absorb the Bellini."

"Had too many o' those t'night." The water was cool and clear. "Oh, that's good. That's real good." When I bit into the bread, its crunchy exterior left crumbs all over the plate, some sprinkling onto the table. "This is dynamite, Gio. Like, a flavor explosion. Can I call you Gio? Ohmygod, I'm gonna give you all four of my apples for this bread alone. *Bravo,* Antonelli's." I began to clap, but he put his hands on mine to keep them still.

"*Grazie, bella,* but we get the fruit from a farm. Who are you with? They come here? Do you need help to get back?"

My mouth was full of bread again when I answered. "I'm here wiff my fake huvband thlash fake friend."

His face scrunched up. "You are married?"

"Nope, not even close." I swallow. "Just a so-called friend who'd rather bunk with B.O. Brenda."

A head tilt. Furrowed brows. Confusion agrees with him. "You need a taxi? Do not walk to hotel like this… uh, so late." His gray eyes showed what I hoped was concern and not pity as he leaned closer to the table. His stubble was noticeably thicker than a few hours earlier. I reached out to touch it.

A smile sprouted on my face as I looked at his. "Oh, I'm fine. I'm in Rome. I'm… I'm so fine. I found you. I found

Giovannnnni!" At the sound of my giggles his family looked over with narrowed eyes. I waved.

He turned toward his family and said something in Italian. A woman responded in an irritated tone, her words coming fast and furious, and I looked at her dumbfounded and amazed. Turning to Giovanni, I whispered, "What'd she say? Her words were so…" I snapped my fingers, "zippy."

"I take you to hotel. Okay?" He stood up and held out his hand. "A taxi will be too long."

In his baby blue Fiat, he explained that the angry woman was his sister, who was now saddled with the chore of taking their cousin, who lives much closer to Giovanni, home. I recall nothing else about the ride to the hotel, but obviously, I made it back up to the room, where I now continue reading Greg's email, my head throbbing from my late-night escapade.

I will not give Tot a hug for you. Not after the turd incident. Don't worry, I'm still feeding her, but I'm pretty sure she's going to murder me in my sleep if you don't get back soon. Look at these claw marks on my hands.

Umm, I have so many questions! Ian?! NO. And Simon asked other people to Rome before you? WHY? I will show up at the airport and kick his ass if I have to. Gladiator style. And speaking of relationship issues… Harry's totally been ignoring all my texts lately. He's still mad that I'm not bringing him home for Thanksgiving. Even though I'm totally doing him a favor!

About your mom's recipes… don't beat yourself up if you can't figure them out. Just try to enjoy yourself! You're in Italy!

Greg

❧

Attending Catholic school inevitably meant participating in weekly school prayer services and Sunday Mass. You'd think a girl with my appetite wouldn't mind attending church—there's a guaranteed snack at the end with Communion. But the Eucharist isn't exactly a gourmet appetizer. I'm not even convinced they're edible. Every Sunday, when it was time to line up for Communion, Jesus would pop up on one shoulder with his cardboard cookie glowing from the light of his halo, and on the other shoulder was Satan whispering into my ear, "Don't eat *that*; I've got a greasy pepperoni pizza with spicy red hell sauce at my place." I chose Jesus every time—my mom and teachers were all around—but I couldn't eat the Host; I literally couldn't swallow it without gagging. My body's digestion system was so shocked upon that weekly stale and flavorless wafer entering my mouth that it would not let me swallow it. I'd just chew and chew for an appropriate amount of time and then I'd hide the bland mush under my tongue until the priest said, "You may go in peace." Upon leaving the church, I'd spit out the Communion puree behind a bush when my mother wasn't looking, and then I'd ask, "Mom, can we stop at Little Caesar's on the way home?" As I got older, I was able to force it down, like hocking back a pill or taking a shot of tequila. But when I was younger, it was like eating Styrofoam.

Needless to say, I've never exactly been excited to attend church.

But today, walking toward St. Peter's Basilica, I'm adjusting to the feeling of looking forward to being in a house of worship. I'd be downright giddy if I wasn't still harboring leftover anger about learning that Simon would have preferred to be here with any number of his other stinky friends. We didn't say much to each other this morning—I apologized for my outburst and he waved it off like it was nothing—but I know he's excited to be here too. "The Sistine Chapel is nothing compared to the Basilica," he'd promised, the "Volare" lyrics still playing from his phone as he dabbed on his aftershave.

"How is that even possible?" I'd asked, reluctantly putting my ring back on after pulling on my comfy peacoat.

Simon had stopped Dean Martin mid-chorus, slipping his phone into the pocket of his jeans as we headed down for breakfast. "You'll see." Was he being short with me, or did he simply not want to give away any spoilers? I couldn't tell.

Now, hustling through St. Peter's Square—which is not actually a square at all, but a giant circle that can hold a million people—I'm overcome with a sense of grandness surrounded by white columns and statues of saints against a cloudless blue sky. It's like we're being fenced in by the strength of God's army. And leading the march is a new tour guide for the day who is hauling some serious ass.

"Can I make a pit stop?" Chuck asks.

"Bathroom breaks later," the tour guide calls out in an Italian accent, continuing to charge forward. "Most important thing now: to get in line."

Her short chestnut brown hair bobs up and down with each commanding step, her colorful flag flapping in the breeze.

"Oh, look, the Swiss Guard!" I exclaim as we speed walk

past them. Pulling out *Rome Day by Day: 31 Essential Ways to See the Eternal City*, I find the chapter on the Vatican, reading aloud as we walk toward the line. "They're the national police force of the Vatican. Wow, it says here it's comprised of one hundred Catholic Swiss men." I look up, and see them standing as still as the dozens of statues surrounding the square. Their uniforms look like they're straight from the Renaissance with blue and gold stripes, boots, and berets. "Think they'll let me take a picture of them?" I reach for my digital camera.

"Do not stop," our tour guide shouts sternly. "Plenty of time for photos later. Right now, we need to get in line." A woman on a mission, she charges forward like a bull. "If you get left behind, I cannot wait for you."

"I think she's mad you stole her thunder," Daphne says. "She didn't say squat about the Swiss Guard yet."

While there are worse places than Rome to be stranded, I don't want to be left behind like Kevin in *Home Alone*. I pick up the pace, almost jogging to keep up.

The line is already hundreds of people deep, and oddly, Rob and Vicki are nowhere in sight. My stomach drops. Is Rob angry with Simon? Or me? Is he off somewhere with this Mason fellow trying to block the promotion? Before I can think of other worst-case scenarios, Daphne asks me to take a photo of her and Chuck before a backdrop of the basilica.

"This Egyptian obelisk," the tour guide says, her eyes narrowing once they land on me, "has been standing in that very spot since 1586." After she gives us a bit more history on the monument, she gives me one more pointed look. Simon and Chuck move off to the side and start chatting, while Daphne steps over to me.

"I definitely didn't need this," I say, unbuttoning my coat.

A cool breeze brings down my body temperature a bit, the scorching sun beating down with an intensity threatening to make me pass out.

Daphne, unsurprisingly, is not interested in talking weather-related fashion problems. "What the heck happened last night?"

"One too many Bellinis."

"We were all drunker'n Cooter Brown last night, but you two were fightin' tooth and nail." She lifts her palms up in a "what gives?" gesture, expecting an explanation.

I remove my glasses for a second to rub my eyes, the darkness behind my lids a welcome relief from the blinding sun. "It was a misunderstanding. We're fine." I hope. But what if we aren't? What if, even though I wasn't his first choice, this trip is our only chance to rekindle our friendship, and my irrational outburst ruined any chance of him ever wanting to spend time with me again? Or worse, what if my behavior got him into trouble with work just as he's about to get promoted?

The sound of chiming bells, one dramatic echo at a time, rings throughout the square as we approach the doors of the massive church, adorned with an iron gate fit for a castle. At the top, a face is carved in the center with swirly leaves around it. Another bell chimes, officially knocking out the chorus of "Volare" that's been stuck in my head for two days.

Home Alone marches us forward underneath the arched entryway. From behind me I hear Simon say in an excited voice to Chuck, "Get ready."

I turn around to tease him, hoping to get back on his good side. "Are all Jewish people this thrilled when they visit a Catholic church?" He either doesn't hear my gibe, or ignores it.

That anything can top the wonder of the Sistine Chapel seems farfetched, but St. Peter's Basilica is colossal; it's two football fields long—a fact I learned in *Rome Day by Day* this morning, and confirmed by Home Alone—making it the largest church on Earth. Plus, it has all the intricate beauty of everything we saw last night, but, thanks to its gargantuan size, more of it. The golden vaulted ceiling, the color of honey and held up by massive gray columns, appears to be intricately carved as glimmers of glowing white light pass through the windows. Angels and saints are carved into every façade. The air smells of mild incense, and it feels thick and warm on my face, like a soft blanket; I can almost grab it, like it carries parts of the souls of every person who has ever sent up a prayer in here.

Home Alone slows her pace, moving reverently from one section to the next. Or maybe it's time that has slowed, rewinding toward the era of the apostles as we move farther into the church. Each area has its own gloriously painted domed ceiling. We come to one that's painted sky blue, angels flying among the clouds, shiny gold trimmings all around. Below the dome are a few windows letting the sunlight stream in, making everything the light touches gleam.

This place is like the Sistine Chapel's older, wiser big sister, and damn she's pretty.

∽

"Get ready to see a body," I overhear Simon say. Glancing at him, I can see the excitement in him as he tugs anxiously at his hoodie's drawstrings.

Chuck grunts. "What are you blabberin' about?"

"Dead Pope on display." I can hear by the tone of his voice that his eyes are twinkling with excitement. I want to turn to smile at him, acknowledge that I'm happy to be in such an amazing place with him, but I hold back, quietly observing the preserved body of Pope John XXIII as it rests inside a glass coffin.

While our tour guide explains that he died in 1963, Simon adds his own commentary. "His nickname was 'The Good Pope.'"

Persistence kicks in and I whisper to him, "As opposed to all those evil Popes?" When he doesn't answer, I attempt another joke to loosen the tension. "Should I genuflect or something? Order a round of holy water for us?"

But he turns away from me and we head for the center of the grandiose church where Bernini's Canopy captivates our gazes, glimmering with gold in the sunlight.

"The bronze canopy was erected in 1634," Home Alone says. "The columns: seventy-feet tall." They soar toward the heavens, framing the main altar. Four angel statues sit atop the canopy at each corner, with a gold cross standing gracefully in the center.

Below the canopy is St. Peter's tomb. We strain forward to get a glimpse of the burial site of one of the twelve apostles of Jesus Christ. According to tradition, our tour guide explains, St. Peter was crucified in Rome and buried right here underneath this beautiful basilica, built in his honor. I can't help but feel that my old teachers would be happy that I'm here in the presence of real popes and apostles, as if every Mass I ever fought to stay awake through, every prayer I reluctantly memorized, every Communion host I prayed would stay down, have all led me to this place.

When our tour is over, we're blessed with an opportunity to visit the bathrooms and gift shop. Before we head in, I'm determined to thaw the ice between me and Simon. I pull out my phone, ready to discreetly take photos of two statuesque Swiss Guards standing perfectly still in their striped blue and gold uniforms with red cuffs.

"Okay, on three, I'll stick my tongue out, and you moon them. Something's got to make them laugh, right?"

This is the kind of prank that would be irresistible to Simon, but when I don't hear a response from him, I look to see that he's already walking toward the gift shop. Did he hear my idea and not want to waste his time with me? Or was he already on his way walking on without me, leaving me behind? Either way, his absence makes my stomach sink—the last thing I want is to end up on separate paths again like we did after high school. But what can I do? I've pushed him away, and nothing I say is bringing him back.

Without making a face, I zoom in on a member of the Swiss Guard, tapping a few photos before closing out the camera app. And that's when I see the voicemail notification again. Maybe it's time I pay attention to the signs the universe is sending me. Ian's reaching out, and Simon's walking away. Two guys that at some point in the past few days I thought might have feelings for me. If I can have another chance with one of them, shouldn't I take it? The first thing I need to do is listen to this voicemail, and finally find out why my ex is so eager to get in touch.

CHAPTER 15

THE CITY CENTER MAZE

"Dammit!"

"Careful now, the Pope might hear ya." Daphne walks up to me, a round Christmas ornament with St. Peter's Basilica on it dangling from her fingers. "Ain't this pretty as a peach? This'll look sweeter'n cherry pie on our tree. Our first Christmas as a married couple!" She giggles.

"It's perfect. And you're making me hungry."

She hoots a laugh. "Good thing we're in Italy. So, what's with all the swearin' in God's house?"

"Technically, we're not in his actual house anymore." I shove the phone in my purse. "I was trying to listen to my messages, but my phone can't even dial into my voicemail out here. I keep getting this error tone."

"Uh huh. This wouldn't have anything to do with that call from last night, would it?" She lifts an eyebrow so that it pops above her sunglasses.

"It would. But I guess it'll have to wait."

The sight of Romans on scooters whizzing past our bulky bus with no more than a couple feet of space is a little panic-inducing. It's like being inside a real-life version of that Nintendo game where the motorcycles swerve around obstacles and jump ramps. I sneak a glance toward Simon; he's leaning so far into the aisle to talk to Rob he might as well not even be sitting next to me.

I turn my attention back outside. "How do they weave in and out of traffic like that?" My voice sounds dreamy, in awe of witnessing such scooter savvy moves.

Daphne, who's sitting in front of me, looks out the window in matched fascination. Her wavy curls, pulled into a messy bun held in place by a colorful bandana, bounce as she turns her head. "Thanks be to God they're wearin' helmets." Three scooters zip by a line of cars, swerving in between two lanes of traffic, zooming past everyone else on the road.

We're on our way to the city center of Rome where its charming cobbled streets will lead us to the Pantheon and Piazza Navona. And then the moment I've been waiting for since I finished breakfast will arrive: lunch. Our Colosseum-sized bus passes by countless fun-size cars parallel parked along the curb, leaving mere inches between bumpers. At the end of one street, a gray two-door car that's about as big as my laundry basket is wedged in sideways. Perpendicular parking, if you will. And I thought finding a spot in Chicago was tricky.

How the bus driver finds room to pull over and let us out is beyond me, but before I know it, we're walking past lovely cafés emanating the tantalizing scent of freshly baked pastries into the streets. Gelaterias display colorful mounds of fruity sweet treats. Endless parked scooters indicate it's a crowded day in these parts. The cobblestone roads curve, causing me to completely lose all sense of direction in a matter of seconds. The foldout map in my purse is nothing more than a security blanket at this point. I stay close to Home Alone, still clutching her colorful flag as she powerwalks toward the Pantheon. She stops before an eatery for a moment and turns to face us.

"This is the famous Ristorante Alfredo," she says pausing briefly in front of the restaurant's doorway. "Known for their fettucine."

"I thought that was Olive Garden," Simon quips, laughing loudly at his own joke.

I laugh too, a little harder than the joke calls for, hoping he'll notice. Home Alone, however, turns her back to us, unamused, and charges forward again. "Let's move to the sidewalk please," she soberly instructs. Simon walks forward rather quickly, in step with Rob and Vicki. I slow down a bit, staying behind with the honeymooners.

The term "sidewalk" seems ambitious; parts of the road don't even have one. This is the belly of the beast, and it's a frenzied free-for-all, a maze of cobblestone streets tunneled by buildings the color of apricot and grapefruit, lined with parked scooters and potted plants, their shiny green leaves rustling in the breeze. People stroll in the middle of the road as cars honk and sneak by whenever a gap opens up. Tables are scattered, covered with baskets of bread and bottles of olive oil. Two Italian men smoke by their scooters, propped up against orange pots sprouting lush shrubs. A tourist spins a rotating stand of postcards, magnets, and novelty calendars featuring sweaty gladiators and sexy priests.

But there's no time to peruse the trinkets; Home Alone is charging forward with the speed of a sprinter, avoiding the endless barrage of cultural obstacles with graceful precision. Bicyclists roll down the road narrowly missing the odd car coasting by. Colorful rainbows of miniature European cars parked against the muted warmth of the pastel buildings add bright pops of yellows, blues, and reds. Shopping bags dangle from arms, cameras hang from necks. All this movement carries with it an excited energy, and it's all happening in the same space. It's an endless web of cobblestone paths overlapping with cars, people, scooters, and bikes, leading us to find Roman treasures around every corner.

And speaking of treasures…

My eyes widen at the beautiful sight of *Della Palma*, a gelateria boasting more than one-hundred-fifty flavors. Chuck notices me staring into their windows.

"Gotta eat 'em all," he teases, nudging my arm with his elbow.

"If I had two stomachs I probably could."

"Just two? You'd need at least a dozen for all those flavors," Daphne adds.

What a wonderful challenge that would be, tasting all one-hundred-fifty flavors. But there's really only one that I'm interested in at the moment. "Hey, do you think they have a cheesecake flavor?"

"They better have multiple cheesecake flavors with a hundred fifty kinds!" Daphne clucks.

I peer ahead, our walking tour moving along more slowly

now that there's a crowd to contend with. "Think we have time to go in?"

She shoots me a mischievous look. "Let's do it." Turning to Chuck, she adds, "Honey bear, stay out here and holler if they get too far ahead. Or if Gerry calls!" They seal the deal with a kiss.

Della Palma is already decked out in Christmas spirit, with white lights and garland cascading in their windows. Most corners of Rome, in fact, are already sparkling with the delightful anticipation of the holidays.

"Rome at Christmas must be magical," I say, as we peruse our options.

"They must have some festive flavors at Christmastime."

"I'm picturing eggnog gelato with Nutella dripping down the cone. I'd fly back just for that."

"Well, Chuck and I ain't goin' nowhere for the holidays except home. I love it here, but I'm drivin' him crazy—I'm anxious to get back. I really want our first Christmas to be as a family." She nervously ticks her phone, hoping for good news.

"Seems to me like you're already a family." I point to the background photo on her phone, four smiling faces shining up at us.

She shakes her head. "Not an official family until the adoption goes through. I ain't losing another baby. Nothing's takin' those boys away from me."

"Official shmofficial. Chuck's probably a great dad. And you obviously love them. All three of them."

"We were so scared how they'd react to my wantin' to adopt 'em, but they're at that age where they're not cynical yet. Ten and twelve. Chuck thinks that since their *mom*," she spits out the word, "left them when they were so little, that it'd be easy for me to step in. He's always right, and he was right about that. They hugged me when we asked how they felt about it—the adoption." She laughs at the memory and looks at me, her blue eyes starting to water. "Honestly, I think I need them more than they need me."

"Nothing like a good mother." I clear my throat. "You know what, I'm betting you're going to get that family. What are we waiting for? We have some celebratory gelato to eat!"

The cheesecake gelato teases us from a silver tray, and I ask the woman behind the counter what flavors it might pair well with, hoping for a stroke of luck in my search for my mom's secret cheesecake ingredient.

"The fruit flavors will go well," she says in an accent, "We have tangerine, strawberry, pear, lemon, coconut…"

While those all sound incredible, I know none of those are in my mom's recipe. Fruit was only used as a topping, but I need to explore what could have been in the batter. "What about something non-fruity?"

"*Cioccolato* is good, almond with honey, cinnamon…"

Could cinnamon be what I'm missing? Or maybe almond? I've tried vanilla in my attempts at recreating her recipe, but of course that can't be the secret ingredient. That's too obvious. Every cheesecake recipe I've found calls for boring old vanilla. My mom must have spiced hers up in some other way.

"Girl," Daphne says, eyebrows raised, "they're all gonna be good, but we gotta go, honey."

"Honey it is then."

The woman hands each of us a dish with two scoops, cheesecake and honey almond, and we hurry back outside.

"They're not too far up," Chuck reports. "Just follow the flag."

Daphne holds out her bowl, and Chuck takes a lick. We quickly catch up to the group, which Rob and Vicki have now mysteriously rejoined, and after snaking down some more narrow cobblestone roads in the shadows of Rome, we arrive at the sunny piazza that's home to the Pantheon. With its back against the sun, this former Roman temple appears as a massive dark gray block, almost black in its own shadow. Laser beams of sunshine gleam from behind the dark corners of the Pantheon, casting a spotlight on the surrounding outdoor cafés and their hungry diners. Motivation for me to finish my gelato before it all drips onto the cobblestones.

"Built in the second century," our tour guide explains, "the Pantheon is one of the best preserved of all Ancient Roman buildings. For the past 1,500 years it has been a Catholic church." The front is a big square structure with sturdy columns holding up the peaked ceiling. Behind it is a huge concrete dome that she says is even bigger than the one at St. Peter's Basilica. The building itself underneath the dome is round; quite the architectural challenge, especially in 127 AD.

A sixteenth century marble fountain occupies the center of the square with dolphins carved into it, water sprinkling from their mouths. A cross adorns the top of the tall obelisk, shooting up into the clear, blue sky. The buildings around the piazza, with their creamy taupe paint and earthy texture of sun-faded red brick, bask in the sun's warmth, their arched windows adorned with shutters cast open welcoming in the sunshine.

"What'd ya think?" Daphne asks, spooning in the last of her gelato. "You can't stop smilin'!"

I wipe my mouth on a paper napkin while searching for the words. "Incredible. Absolutely incredible."

"So, you're tickled with that flavor combo?"

I'm not sure if it was the honey or the almond that complimented the cheesecake so perfectly—perhaps both— but I'm thrilled to make headway with another one of my mom's recipes.

"Tickled pink. That was the best flavor combo I've tasted in a long time."

"Good, 'cause we got more to try." As we continue walking, her eyes cartoonishly bulge out of their sockets at the sight of an all-cookie Christmas tree on display in a bakery's window. Layers of colorful macarons spiral up the festive little tree. She takes a closer look, her jangly jewelry clanking as she leans toward the window, and then tucks her cell phone into her cleavage so that she can point to the tree of cookies. "*Look at these.*"

"Oh, I see them, Daph. An edible Christmas tree. This is one Roman custom I'm definitely bringing back to the States."

Nibbling on a pink cookie, a bag of macarons hanging from her arm, Daphne hustles along with me and Chuck to catch up to our group again. Home Alone has one more place to show us today: Piazza Navona. We walk east to a much bigger square, but just as old. Atop the charcoal gray cobblestones, I take in the piazza's simple beauty as I stand still among a sea of people rushing in fast-forward all around me. The buildings and their familiar Italian color palettes—rustic oranges, dusty pinks, creamy whites, earthy tans, egg-yolk yellows— all drenched in bright sunlight, are a warm backdrop against the electric energy of the open piazza. Diners enjoying lunch in the fresh air. The clinks of wine glasses and silverware. The happy chatter of passersby. The ding of a bicycle bell as it rushes past me. An Italian flag waving in the wind as it flies proudly from a window above a pizzeria. Shoppers clutch their bags looking for their next memorable find. Tourists take pictures, posing near the seventeenth century Fiumi Fountain.

Before I can reach for my book, Home Alone is quick to say, "The Fiumi Fountain features the symbolic anthropomorphic sculptures of four rivers."

"I'm gonna have to read up on that one at the hotel," I whisper to Daphne, who is now enjoying another cookie.

"Over there," Home Alone points, "is the Sant'Agnese in Agone Catholic Church. Note the Baroque architecture." It's pearly white; a gorgeous sight against the baby blue sky.

While we're surrounded by treats for the eyes, our taste buds are in for a treat, too. Oodles of charming restaurants hug the perimeter of Piazza Navona. The aroma of pizza drifts to where I'm standing, and I'm thankful the sounds of water lapping in the fountain and camera shutters snapping photos cover the loud grumble in my tummy. Hey, two scoops of ice cream only go so far when you've walked as many miles as we have this morning.

"Lunch?" Simon's suggestion is met with unanimous approval. But while I nod yes, my stomach sinks just enough for me to worry if a meal with everyone will be too awkward right now. What if Rob asks questions about why we were fighting? What if our secret comes out and Simon's new job offer is revoked when his boss learns that he lied to bring a friend along? That is, if he still considers me a friend.

"*Aprile?*"

I whip around at the familiar accent, his voice as smooth as Italian leather. "Giovanni!"

In one hand, he clutches a small white box. In the other, he holds up his phone. "You see my text? Lunch today?"

I pull out my phone, surprised to see a notification for a text sent twenty minutes ago. "I'm sorry, I'm just seeing your text now. I didn't hear it. Let me introduce you."

He puts his phone back in the inside pocket of his blazer. Blue this time.

"Everyone, this is Giovanni Antonelli. I bumped into him yesterday after we went to the Colosseum." I feel him glance at me, but our second run-in is staying between the two of us. "Anyway, his family runs a pizzeria and I thought maybe I could, uh… interview him for my podcast. Is it okay if I meet up with you guys later? Simon," I hesitate, Rob looking at us with something between concern and skepticism, "cookie, is that cool with you?"

While half of this new lunch plan is an attempt at putting some space between me and Simon—after all, space is all he seems to want from me lately, not that I can blame him—the other half is, well, *Giovanni*.

"Isn't your phone busted?" Simon asks, and after a beat, "Cupcake? How will we get in touch with you?" He's either genuinely concerned, or is donning his caring husband costume for the benefit of his boss.

"Apparently, I can still get incoming calls and texts, but I can't make outgoing calls. So, if you need to reach me, you should be able to. But if nothing else, I can figure out how to get back to the hotel. I've got a map."

"That I've yet to see you open," observes Simon.

After a few more minutes of convincing, and promising

that I won't wander too far, the group reluctantly agrees to go off for lunch without me, leaving Giovanni and me behind in the piazza where we now walk toward the Fountain of Neptune. I discreetly take off my ring, shoving it in the pocket of my jeans.

"For you," he says, holding out the box. "*Sfogliatella.* Try this yet?"

I take the box from him, a sweetness filling the air as I open it. "I've not. I don't think I've ever even heard of— sfolee—sfolah—whatever you called it. How did you get my number?"

"Last night, you give me number. At hotel. Remember?" His English comes out slowly as he searches for the words to remind me that I told him I'd be in Piazza Navona today, which, as luck would have it, is close to where he works. "Then you suggest lunch."

Drunk Me really knows how to go after what I want. We reach the fountain, marvel at the sculptures, water trickling in a peaceful rhythm. Neptune is in the center fighting with an octopus as cherubs, mermaids, dolphins, and horses surround him. "I thought you worked at your dad's pizzeria. We're not close to there, are we?" The *sfogliatella* crunches lightly as I bite into it, the dough light and flaky.

"I help sometimes. In the kitchen, to wait on tables. Short on staff. But I work at a museum." He points in the direction of it, saying that he explained this to me last night. "Maybe you cannot remember…" He laughs, and jiggles his hands around his head, depicting perfectly how I felt last night and this morning. When he asks me to clarify what I'd said about interviewing him, his bushy eyebrows do an inquisitive dance, and I feel a tiny butterfly stretch its wings in the pit of my stomach.

"Oh, I review restaurants for a podcast, and am reviewing some Italian places while I'm here. The guy I was talking with—he's the friend I'm here with—we kind of had a fight last night, and things have been… off today. So, the podcast just popped into my head. I didn't know how to explain that you and I made lunch plans. Which I don't even remember making." I give Gio some time to absorb my convoluted explanation, finishing off the *sfogliatella* in a few more bites. The chocolate cream in the center makes me close my eyes and sigh. *Delizioso.*

"You not want to review Antonelli's?" He looks disappointed.

"No, actually I do, but right now, all I really want is lunch. With you. I'm sorry I didn't remember our conversation. I'm really happy you saw me. I would've been bummed if I saw that I missed your text later."

His recently shaven face stretches into a relieved smile. "*Fantastico!*"

"Did you drive to work? I hope you didn't leave your Fiat unattended."

"Vespa. Easier to park." He pauses, squinting his eyes and tilting his head as he looks at me. "Ever ride one?"

"No," I reply. "Not yet."

CHAPTER 16

MACCHERONI AND CHEESE

"THE ONLY WAY to see *Roma*," Gio says as he points to his Vespa, wedged in among several other scooters parked so tightly they look like they prop each other up. His gray eyes sparkle brightly as they catch a ray of sun, the waves of his mocha hair tousled by the breeze.

"Much as I'd love to, um, mount your bike, I really am starving," I say, gesturing to the surrounding restaurants, ignoring the rush of warmth painting my cheeks. "Should we pick one of these?"

"No. Too many tourists." He says it quietly, but with conviction.

"What do you think I am?"

"I know a place not too far. Come with me."

My stomach flips with nervous excitement. "On your Vespa?"

He shakes his head. "Close enough to walk."

While I'm slightly bummed, I'm also relieved that I'll live

to see lunch. And with a wave of his hand to follow him, we set off east of the piazza down Via delle Coppelle.

✄

I have never been more turned on. Plump, juicy tomatoes tease me with their curves as they play hide and seek among a bed of spaghetti in fresh olive oil underneath a leafy trickle of basil.

I think I'm in love.

I may have seen the site of the Gladiators, the home of the Pope, and the pinnacle of Michelangelo's career, but this is the Italian experience I've been waiting for.

"I'm so happy we're dining *al fresco*."

Gio bows his head in a hearty laugh. "We do not say that."

"You don't say what?"

"*Al fresco*. At least not like that. It is a cold place to put food and drinks. It is also slang for 'in prison.'" His smile is somehow even more charming when he's laughing at my expense.

My cheeks go even redder. "This is why I need you as my tour guide. I don't want to end up in the slammer while I'm here."

Welcome to *Maccheroni Ristorante*, a small eatery tucked away from the crowded swarm of people in Piazza Navona. In the shadows on a narrow cobblestone street, Giovanni and I sit across from each other at an outdoor table nestled next to a bunch of barrels. Across the way, leaning against a building the color of faded copper, is a line of scooters and a two-door Fiat wedged in behind them. Farther down sits another restaurant. It's a warm, rusty clay color that looks like it's been bleached by the sun over the years. A string of white lights hangs from canopies atop the tables. I've jumped straight into a charming painting. Is that "Bella Notte" I hear on accordion, or just my imagination?

Our waitress, a thin woman wearing jeans and a black apron, brings out more bread, which I promptly use to soak up the olive oil. Her black hair is cut to a chin-length bob with sweeping bangs across her forehead. She speaks English very well with an Italian accent as heavy as the black cobblestones lining the street.

"Everything okay?" she asks.

Um, yes. Everything is beyond okay.

This meal is my opportunity to check off another must-eat item: spaghetti. Between the recent luck I had with the cheesecake gelato, and a bona-fide Italian cook on my side, I might gain another insight or two about my mom's secret sauce today.

The aroma of garlic and olive oil, fresh tomatoes, and cheese is the most pleasant scent I've ever inhaled. Never have I laid eyes on a swirling nest of pasta so perfect. One potential problem, however, jumps out at me.

"Do Italians normally eat spaghetti without sauce?" That is, after all, what I'm after.

"We cook sauce, yes," Gio confirms, "but usually very light—a little bit. Some dishes have sauce, others no. Sometimes, only olive oil and tomatoes."

"We sauce it up big time in America." My mom's spaghetti sauce was thick and red, and it would cover every inch of the pasta dripping over the sides. How can I find the secret to her sauce when I've already tried incorporating the few ingredients on my plate and failed?

"Cheese?" As if reading my mind, he pushes a little tin dish of parmesan closer to me, freshly grated, waiting to melt atop my pasta. It's beautiful enough to make me weep.

"Are you encouraging me to…" I gasp for dramatic effect, "…add cheese to my pasta?"

"You stare at it." He points two fingers to his eyes. "With love in your eyes." When I offer him the dish, he holds up a hand. "Not for me."

From the cheese down, there's not a note out of harmony in this culinary composition. After a moment of losing myself in pasta perfection, I ask, "Do you always befriend tourists or just special ones?"

"Only ones who break into my *papà*'s pizzeria late at night," he teases while finishing a bite of *penne*.

Is he *trying* to make me break the *Guinness Book of World Records* for blushing? "So, which do you like more: working at the restaurant or the museum?"

"Both, but the museum—*Il Museo Nazionale Romano*—is where I want to be. I work in the *Palazzo Altemps*." When he notices my confused expression, he explains, "A palace with sculptures. More interesting than a pizzeria."

"What do you have against pizza? Pizza brings everyone joy." The question goes unanswered; he gets distracted when I twirl my pasta into a too-large beehive and cut it down to size with my fork.

"No, no, please, no!"

By the look of him, I swear he's about to faint. "Oh, my God, what's wrong?" Is he allergic to amazing food or something? Too much Italian beauty surrounding him?

He reaches over to put a hand on mine, stopping me from committing a culinary atrocity. His hand is heavy and warm, and it would feel even better on other parts of me. "You are *cutting* the pasta." He nearly chokes on the word, his face twisting into an offended expression.

"I always thought that was a joke. You really never cut spaghetti out here?"

He shakes his head. "Never, *bella*. No. You spin. Always." He emphasizes this by squeezing my hand and looking deep into my eyes.

"But what if the fork is too loaded?" Reluctantly, I pull my hands free to hold up what's left of my hive. "Do you just stuff your whole head with pasta and hope for the best?" Seriously, I don't get how it's physically possible.

"Undo that," he says, wrapping his hand over mine again to keep my fork steady, "and try again." With an expert twirl of his fingers over mine that finds me trying to push "Unchained Melody" out of my head, he bunches up the perfect amount of pasta: a dainty little nest that's both dignified in size, and satisfying. In a daze, I bring the fork to my mouth. "See? Okay, your turn, *Aprile*."

It's only when I properly spin the spaghetti on my own that his face relaxes and he finally answers my question about why working in his dad's pizzeria wasn't for him. He leans back and quietly explains that the monotony of generations of people following the exact same path didn't appeal to him. He felt blocked from exploring the world for himself. Only two options presented themselves when he was old enough to make a decision about what he wanted to do with his life: working in the family pizzeria (or another restaurant owned by his uncle), or work on the family vineyard. He chose neither.

"I wanted something different." The way he says it effuses

a wistfulness into the fresh air, and it makes me want something different, too. "Italy has good food, good wine, but it has history, too. A museum keeps the history alive."

I feel warm, and it's not from the sun or the food. "I can see the appeal."

As if his looks, charm, and inspiring desire to find deeper meaning in his life aren't enough reason to fall for him, he goes straight for my Achilles heel. "Here, try mine. More sauce." He nudges his plate toward me.

This sauce is nothing like my mother's. While this one is, well, saucier and rich in tomato, it has a little kick of heat. "What kind of sauce is this again?"

"*Arrabbiata.* Red chili pepper. Not for spaghetti." He takes a swig of red wine, and I do the same, trying to calm the zing that the chili peppers have left on my tongue.

"Definitely not, but it's very tasty." I hesitate for a moment, but only a moment. His talk about the past, keeping memories and history alive, gives me the encouragement to admit, "I'm actually trying to figure out a few old recipes while I'm here. One being my mom's spaghetti sauce. She used to make it all the time when she was alive. but I have no idea what she added to it. I've never tasted a sauce like hers since."

When my desire to find her secret ingredients was kept to myself, it was almost hypothetical. But now that I've said it out loud, I not only feel immense pressure to follow through, but also strangely fragile. The sounds of idle chatter and soft laughter from the streets seem amplified now, whisking into the air among the echo of forks on plates, the clinks of wine glasses. Does he think I've set out on some kind of crazy, impossible treasure hunt?

Gio scratches his stubble and takes another bite of *penne*, while contemplating. "*Aprile,* my *nonna,* when she was alive, made *panforte* every Christmas. A cake with fruit and nuts, spices. She always add extra cloves. *Buonissimo.* She give the recipe to my *papá.* He follow it every year. Does not taste same. It is good, but different." He pauses to top off my wine glass, and as it fills with *Sangiovese,* he drives his point home. Even if he has all the right ingredients, adds the extra cloves, bakes it for the right time at the perfect temperature, it never tastes quite right. Because, in the case of his *nonna* and my *mamma,* it's not only about tasting an ingredient; it's also about feeling the love that they put into the dish. Something which never stocks the supermarket shelves.

Still, the recipes left behind by those we've loved offer a way to reconnect with their spirit through the action of cooking. Just as I'm about to formulate this abstract notion that surely is not translated in my dictionary, Gio sums it up perfectly and succinctly. "Her recipe is her history," he says. "Proof she was here." A hint of a smile forms at the corners of his mouth. "You want to… to preserve it, yes? Like I do in the museum?"

For years, I've struggled to express to friends and even myself why it's so important to me to recreate her recipes. But, in broken English, Gio has managed to perfectly sum up this emotional and deeply personal sentiment. "Exactly! I want to keep her traditions alive. Cooking her food would sort of keep her alive in a way." I tell him about the Christmas lasagna. How I'd feel like a part of her could be with me over the holidays if only I can figure out the secrets in the layers.

"*Sí.* Italian food can be quite magical."

After an embarrassing stream-of-consciousness ramble

about sugar and onions, basil and pepper, and how I unquestionably did not inherit my mom's cooking skills, Gio offers up his own sauce strategy. Which—I mark with a mental asterisk—he learned from his father. Does the chef part of our brain become activated with child-rearing?

"Start with *soffritto*."

"Should I pull out my dictionary, or do you want to translate?"

"Onion, carrot, celery. Cook in olive oil, fifteen minutes."

A lightbulb turns on. Carrots. Mother Earth offers many natural sweeteners in her pantry (including the obvious onion which I've always used in my sauce trials), but I've coupled off carrots in a monogamous relationship with creamy ranch my whole life. Maybe Lady Carrot would enjoy an affair with Mr. Juicy Tomato.

Other lightbulbs turn on with each mention of an ingredient I'd either overlooked, or wrongly used: basil. "Must be fresh," he says wearing a look almost as serious as he did during the twirl incident, "not dried. And always add at end—when the sauce simmer."

He goes on sharing cooking tips, challenging his earlier statement that he'd rather not work in a restaurant, and I nearly erupt like Vesuvius with excitement. I might actually have something to work with here; bring on the cooking class. "*Grazie*, Gio. I must say, for someone who doesn't want to cook for a living, it sure sounds like you know your way around a kitchen."

"Maybe, one day, you see me in action." He winks and sips his wine. Does he mean at the pizzeria? Or at his place? No matter, the butterfly he keeps agitating with every Italian cadence on his words has doubled in size.

I gesture toward the bottle of wine, which is still half-full. "Hey, can we bring the rest of this with us? Be a shame to let it go to waste." His expression is a cross between confusion and horror, but I do my best to persuade him. "C'mon, we'll wrap it in a napkin, and say it's a loaf of *ciabatta* bread."

His smile is as warm as the sun. "Americans. Always in hurry. You want already to leave?" he asks.

Another Italian custom that's on the opposite end of the spectrum from America: eat-and-run is not something that's done in Italy. We stay and sip another glass of wine slowly, talking about our jobs and our lives, so separate, but colliding for one perfect meal. Which is extended as our waitress brings over a plate of *cantucci*, traditional Italian almond cookies. "They're good dipped in wine," she suggests with a wink, setting them between us.

And now cookies in wine. So that's how we'll finish this bottle. The ingenuity of Italians has me questioning my every action prior to crossing the Atlantic Ocean.

Even after dipping, the cookie remains quite dense and hard, turning the scene before me into a silent film, but instead of hearing a piano soundtrack as Gio talks, I hear *crunch crunch crunch.* Submerging my next cookie longer is a good move, as I can now hear perfectly well that he's coming on to me. "You need private cooking lesson?" He crunches into a cookie, his confident smile rhythmically noshing it into oblivion.

"How hot does your stove get?" I move my seat next to his, our thighs inches apart.

His eyes challenge mine. "You will sweat."

❧

Maccheroni: Four red, succulent apples.

Taste: The slivers of cheese curved as they softened against my warm spaghetti. Olive oil and blistered cherry tomatoes called for each bite to be savored, the stragglers slurped through my eager lips. The juicy, ripe flavors of the tomatoes tasted fresh and bright. The al dente spaghetti, cooked to perfection, were flawlessly firm yet tender. The basil's earthy sweetness and the cheese's texture and sharp burst of salty flavor rounded out the perfect plate of pasta. For dessert, simple *biscotti* did the trick. Specifically, *cantucci*: ultra-crunchy and mildly sweet, they were densely delicious, with thin, toasted almond slices throughout. Hard enough to chip a tooth, and tasty enough to risk emergency dental care. I'm giving *Maccheroni* the biggest apple in my orchard.

Service: Extra cheese and complimentary cookies: what more could one ask from her waitress? One juicy apple.

Atmosphere: My view included cute cars and an even cuter Italian. One sexy apple.

Price: Gio paid. One handsome apple.

❧

As we head back toward Piazza Navona, Gio expresses doubt that I'll learn as much as I hope to about cooking when I tell him about the upcoming class at the vineyard.

"Because it's at a winery?" I mime with my hand that I'll be drinking.

"*Esatto*! If you want to learn real Italian cooking, there is a program in Rome every year. Spring, for one month. In English," he quickly adds when he sees my expression. He explains that his cousin used to teach a course there, and now he works at the pizzeria. He can ask him for more information if I'd like.

As we pass another restaurant, I see the shutters on the windows of the apartment above sprung wide open, and wistfully, I can't help imagining hunkering down in an apartment like that next spring. Four glorious weeks soaking up Italian culture and cuisine like a bone-dry sponge. I could ride a scooter on the uneven cobblestones into town for the cooking class. Then, at night, I'd crack open the windows, letting the sounds of clinking wine glasses sparkle through the living room while sitting at a checkered-tablecloth-clad table eating the fresh pasta I myself prepared. Gio would teach me Italian slang and help me practice rolling my R's. I'd eat a different flavor of gelato every afternoon. I'd send Greg postcards every week with a new recipe. Maybe I'd even learn how to make *cantucci*. I put my hand inside my coat pocket, gripping the last cookie that I swiped as Gio paid the bill, taking it and my fantasy with me as we begin strolling along the cobbled streets before the sun sets.

And "fantasy" is definitely the right word. A cooking class back home at a community college is one thing, but here in another country? For an entire month? Donning an apron, sauces bubbling all around me as I add a pinch of pepper and a handful of basil… It almost makes me laugh. But a little information is harmless, right? "Sure, that'd be great."

CHAPTER 17

LA DOLCE VITA

THE RUMBLING ENGINE roars in my ears, the architecture blurs past my eyes in a rustic rainbow, and the wind rustles my hair—well, the tips of the strands that are sticking out from underneath the heavy helmet Gio lent me. Reluctantly lent me, I should say: only when I told him there was no way I'd face the crazy Roman traffic on a Vespa without one, he fished out a helmet that was so clean, it was either brand new, or had barely been worn—if ever. "Only short distance! Even I not wear it!" I don't care, Gio. Flatten my moussed hair; I will not die in a scooter accident.

When he first asked if I'd like a ride, I assumed he was kidding. The yelps I'm squealing into his ear as he rounds every narrow cobblestoned corner prove that he wasn't.

"Best way to get around here," he told me as I straddled the wide and surprisingly comfortable seat on his mustard yellow scooter, parked a short distance from *Maccheroni*. "I take you to *la Fontana di Trevi*. Beats walking. Trust me."

When someone says "trust me," my gut reaction is usually not to. But in Rome?

"*Andiamo!*" he shouted and hit the gas.

Now, my arms are wrapped tightly around his stomach. His Vespa seats two just fine—if you don't mind a tight squeeze.

I do not mind.

In a matter of seconds, I see that he was right about this being the best way to explore the nooks and crannies of Rome's narrow streets. Though I'm not sure which is more nerve-wracking: the people meandering mere feet from our little speed racer, or the occasional car that tries to squeeze through the maze of roads, missing us by inches. As we zip by a table of outdoor diners, I'm tempted to reach out my hand and swipe a handful of ravioli, but it remains comfortably wrapped around the tight tummy sitting in front of me. Woe is me.

Not only is riding the Vespa fun, but it's efficient. Gio swerves around tourists and Fiats with the ease of a professional slalom skier, cruising us down the bumpy cobblestones.

"We park a little away from the fountain," he shouts back to me. "Very crowded."

He's not kidding. As we get closer to the Trevi Fountain, the crowd is thick as syrup. People are everywhere, walking with Gucci shopping bags and *focaccia* slices and gelato cones. I feel like we're inside a game of Frogger, Italian style.

Only when he kills the engine do I realize how loud this little scooter can get.

He jumps off, holding the Vespa steady with one hand, smoothing his blazer with the other, his dark hair a victim of the chaotic breeze. "What you think?" His self-assured smile melts me.

Hopping off to stand, I yank off the helmet and hold it under my arm like a football. Do I admit that was the most thrilling five minutes of my life, or do I have a little fun? "It was alright, I guess."

"Come on, *Aprile*, you love it." He pinches my cheek, and the color on my face admits the truth for me.

He pushes down the lever and parks the scooter on its center kickstand at the end of a row of scooters. As he grabs the helmet from me, locking it next to the seat, he asks, "Gelato first?" I agree instantly, the flavors of the ice cream from two hours ago a distant memory.

So far, this man has patiently given me directions, driven me home when I was a drunken fool, surprised me with a tasty pastry I can't pronounce, treated me to a delicious meal, given me a Vespa tour of Rome's historic center, and now he's brought me to a *gelateria*. Would a marriage proposal from me be too much?

Behold: forty different gelato flavors.

This time, I select *amarena*—black cherry. Dark in color and rich in flavor, these cherries are so incredibly divine that if other fruits could emote, they'd be downright envious of the almighty *amarena*.

I point to the flavor I want, intimidated by how quickly the girls behind the counter are taking orders, everyone shouting in Italian all around me. One of them asks me something in Italian, and my face goes blank with dumb fear. "Um…" Flustered, I play with one of the buttons on my coat.

Gio gracefully steps in, his hand resting on my back, and translates for me. "You want cone?"

"*Sì.*"

The young woman behind the counter hands me a skinny waffle cone topped with a light pink scoop the size of a baseball threatening to melt down the sides. Little dark polka-dots of cherries are mixed in, a bite-sized golden wafer wedged atop the scoop.

As soon as my treat is in my hand, I forget about my embarrassment for not knowing the language. It's as if this cone of gelato is a magic wand, waving away all my feelings of inadequacy and replacing them with pure joy. Gio chooses hazelnut and *stracciatella:* vanilla ice cream with little shreds of chocolate in it.

We walk slowly toward the Trevi Fountain, people-watching and enjoying our ice cream without any forced conversation. My teeth crunch the wafer into oblivion, its pieces melting like soft snowflakes. It's light as air, crispy with whispers of almond and vanilla.

And inside the cone is liquid velvet. Creamy and smooth, it's already starting to melt in the sun; the white paper napkin wrapped around the bottom slowly turning a soft shade of pink. The cherries are bursting with chewy tartness; the cone crunching into sweet confetti. The scooters go silent, the rustic paint on the buildings fades to black, the bustling crowd of shoppers and diners all disappear. The only thing I am aware of is my slowly diminishing cone of cherry gelato.

The sound of men chanting explodes out of nowhere, bursting me from my trance. "What's that?"

"Game day today. *Calcio*. What you call 'soccer.' *Roma* against *Monchengladbach*, the Germans."

"That's a mouthful. Are you a fan?"

"Oh, yes. That is why I not work this afternoon."

A line of soccer enthusiasts, wearing yellow and red striped polo shirts, parade down the street, halting traffic like a line of geese. One man is wrapped in a yellow flag, chanting so loudly it echoes down the street. One look at these loud, testosterone-filled fans, and it's obvious that they take their soccer seriously.

"Giovanni!" a man shouts from the parade. He's waving a red flag displaying a wolf and the word "ROMA" in big gold letters.

Gio shouts something back in Italian which brings a smile to the man's face. He marches on, applauding and cheering.

"Wait, are you missing the game for me?"

He looks at his watch. "Uh, it not start for a few hours."

That may be so, but I suspect he was originally planning on filling his time off with activities that did not include me. *Calm down, butterfly.*

Sculpted in the eighteenth century from the same materials as the Colosseum, *la Fontana di Trevi* is the largest fountain in all of Rome.

"Eighty-six feet tall and 161 feet wide of absolute beauty! And you get to live here."

"You look at book too much. You miss real thing," Gio says, snatching *Rome Day by Day* out of my hand. He lifts my chin up so that I can take in a live view instead of the photo printed on the page.

The famous Trevi Fountain is a magnet for tourists, a cosmic aquamarine oasis sparkling with the sun's reflection. Marshmallow white sculptures of the Greek god Oceanus, winged horses, and tritons seem to jump from the water, shimmering from the lights underneath and the sunbeams above.

Gio tells me that over a million euros are tossed into this fountain every year. Each one carrying a wish dreamed up by a hopeful visitor. Superstition requires one to toss a coin with the right hand backwards over the left shoulder for the wish to come true. I'm at a magic hotspot with the power to make my dreams come to life, but only if I cast the spell correctly. Crunching on a bite of my waffle cone, I flip through the mental notes in my mind, scanning for a wish-worthy desire. One: for Simon's and my friendship to survive our week in Rome. Who knew such an enchanting city would test us like this? Two: the obvious choice as I stand in the middle of the most romantic city on Earth, Gio and I surrounded by happy couples.

"You think of wish?" he asks, as if reading my thoughts. He pops the last of his cone in his mouth and inches closer to me. Is it because the crowd is so thick?

Admitting I'd like for my suitcase to be big enough to pack him into it and bring him back to the States with me seems a tad overzealous, so I consider a food-related wish instead for option number three. "How about to be the master of my own kitchen? To find those ingredients, and make my mom proud."

Enchanted by the blue water, I chew a cherry. A sudden band of warmth heats up my waist as he places his arm around me, inching me closer. As Gio begins to hug me, I squeal. "The gelato!" A pink splotch dabs his blue blazer. "Dammit! How do I say 'sorry' in Italian?"

He wraps a hand around mine and lifts the cone to his mouth taking a heaping bite. Through a smile he says, "No worry, I change for the game." I finish the rest of the ice cream in record time. For one thing, it's really starting to melt, and for another, I want to redo that hug without the ice cream cooling off the heat between us. He draws me in and before I know it, his lips are on mine, cold and sweet from the gelato.

My heart's still racing when we finally pull away. "Are you trying to influence what I wish for?"

A self-assured grin. Bright, beautiful eyes catching a glint of sun. He squeezes me tight and rubs my back, and I think I could stay here forever with my head on his chest listening to the sound of coins making wishes come true as they plink into the fountain.

"So, this is where our favorite foodie ran off to!" The unmistakably southern accent jolts me from my own personal paradise as I turn to see Daphne and Chuck.

She peeks at Gio, raising an eyebrow. "And how did your, ahem, interview go?"

Yet another wish comes to mind. I fish a euro from my pocket, and as I toss it in, I silently plead to the powers-that-be that Daphne and Chuck forget they saw Simon's wife wrapped in the arms of a sexy Roman.

CHAPTER 18

ITALIAN SAUSAGE

"The interview! Right. We, um, well, we didn't get to the interview yet," I say, trying to loop in a casual air to my words. "Though we did talk food over lunch. We talked spices, we talked dessert..."

Daphne's eyebrow raises even higher, threatening to jump off her head.

"Gio's been showing me around a bit."

"Uh huh," her eyes flick to Gio. "I see that."

The hole I'm digging is getting so deep I can almost feel earthworms on my feet. It's time for the truth. "Daphne, Chuck, this is going to sound... ridonkulous, but Simon and I are not married. We're old high school friends, and he really wanted someone to come with him on this trip, so I agreed to play along that we're married. But you can't tell Rob, okay? Simon's worried he'll block him from that new job or something if he finds out he lied. I already caused enough trouble last night; I can't cause any more."

Her curls blow in the breeze as three scooters whiz by, while the rest of her face seems to have turned to stone in a permanent state of shock. And then, she cracks a smile. "I knew somethin' was fishy 'bout the two of y'all!" Her cackling laughter is such a relief that I exhale the breath I didn't know I was holding. "You hear that, Chuck?"

"It's all makin' sense now." He chortles.

Well, not to everyone. I fill in the gaps for Giovanni, who's a little fuzzy on the details. "You don't think I'm certifiable do you? A total loon?"

"Crazy not always bad."

"So, you *do* think I'm crazy."

"Yes, but I still like you, *bella*."

I wrap my arms around his neck and he gives me a squeeze, kissing me on both cheeks as we pull apart. How does he keep raising the bar on my charm-o-meter?

"They're havin' good luck today," Chuck says. "Maybe some'll rub off on us."

"Missin' Gerry's call isn't good luck," says Daphne, her voice huffy. "Why was your phone on silent? You knew he was supposed to call."

"And be rude while leaving the table at lunch? It's fine; he'll call again."

"Was he calling with good news?" I ask.

"The fact that he didn't leave a message doesn't seem too good to me," Daphne replies. "He's got questions about—about what happened; I can feel it. We're screwed." Her hand rubs at her temples.

"Here," Chuck says, grabbing a coin from his pocket. "No time like the present to sway fate in our favor."

She grabs the coin, turns her back to the fountain, closes her eyes, and sends it sailing over her shoulder. Plunk!

Wishes granted, we leave the Trevi Fountain and set off to find a bar. Sadly, on foot—the Vespa only seats two. Luckily, the streets of Rome don't disappoint, offering up all kinds of treasures to feed every desire. We stumble across a walk-up bar with an open window in a wall the color of ripe cantaloupe. On the ledge sit bottles of booze, towers of plastic cups, and a tin with the word "TIPS" written on it. Lemons, oranges, and cans of Red Bull sit on a shelf, while Elvis Presley's "Hound Dog" blares from inside. Daphne takes a swig of the mojito she orders, causing her brows to furrow and her lips to pucker.

"This is stee-rong!" She holds it out for me to try. "Ain't it?"

I grab the mint-infused cocktail from her hands and take a cautious sip, welcoming the flavor of rum for a change. In a word: potent. It hits my throat with the strength of a tequila shot; a far cry from the refined flavors of the fine wine that my palate has become accustomed to these past few days.

I hold back a cough. "Yes," I confirm, promptly handing it back to her. "Strong like bull."

"Ah! I know what you need." Gio says, making his way to the center of the bar. "*Quattro limoncelli per favore.*"

Daphne shoots me a wide-eyed look, her expression intrigued. I answer her with an expression of my own that says, "What can I say? He's perfect."

We sip our *limoncello* as a chill zips through the air, the sunset dimming into an orange glow.

"So, why aren't you two with the others?" I ask.

"We split up after lunch," Daphne answers. "We needed

some time alone at the fountain. God, I sound so desperate. Resorting to a wish to keep this family together."

"Which we're not even gonna need," Chuck interrupts reassuringly before turning to me and Gio. "We're plannin' on meetin' up with everyone at the hotel later to figure out dinner."

"I hope Simon doesn't feel like a third wheel if it's just him with his boss and his wife," I say feeling a little guilty about my afternoon joyride.

Chuck waves away my concerns with his burly hands. "I reckon that's not so. He and Rob were talkin' shop all through lunch. Don't tell him this," he leans in and lowers his voice, "but I was happy to get away from them for a bit. We're in Rome right now, not rentin' trucks. Those two don't know when to punch out sometimes, I tell ya."

The sound of a car honking causes us to stop and squeeze behind a parked Fiat to let the driver pass. "Poor Vicki," I say. "Listening to her husband jabber on about work all day has got to get old."

"Oh, honey," says Daphne, finishing the last of her *limoncello* as we resume our stroll, "she's been samplin' all the fine wine this country has to offer since her plane landed. She's peachy."

We come to a store that sells nothing but Pinocchio. Nutcrackers, necklaces, mobiles, clocks: all Pinocchio-themed and carved out of wood painted firetruck-red, shining brilliantly in the window against the setting sun. Outside the store sits a human-sized Pinocchio on a bench.

Chuck sets his beer down on Pinocchio's lap and sits next to him. "Hon, have a seat," he says, indicating the empty space on the other side of the famous long-nosed fable-dweller. Daphne sits and playfully grabs his oversized sniffer and smiles for a selfie.

Not sure how comfortable Gio is with taking a photo with me, I grab his attention and nod toward the puppet in a wordless inquiry. He nods back and sits where Chuck was. I take the other seat and we both put our arms around the over-sized wooden marionette while cheesing for the camera—at least my phone is capable of capturing some memories while I'm out here.

Not far down, we come to another store with unexpected inventory catching our eyes. I've seen a lot of naked men—that is, *statues* of naked men—during my stay in Italy so far. I've adjusted quite well to Europe's ability to embrace nudity, yet no amount of sculpted manly nakedness could prepare us for what we now see inside a souvenir shop.

"Oh my God, we gotta buy that!" Daphne shouts with childish glee upon seeing a unique kitchen apron hanging from a rack.

"That would look good on me," Chuck jokes, his eyes disappearing as his laughing smile takes over his face.

This tacky apron doesn't have Sicilian lemons or luscious grapes embroidered on the front. Instead, it's taken one of the most revered images in art history and turned it into a drunken tourist's dream souvenir: the naked body of David, Michelangelo's masterpiece statue, with variably sized, shall we say, "Italian sausages."

I look to my new Italian friend. "Gio, have you ever braved the tourist shops around here?"

The look he flashes me gives me my answer, but to be sure his message gets across he says in crystal clear English, "Never."

"That's about to change." I playfully grab his blazer's collar, pulling him into the store, and then we become the opening line of a bad joke: Three Americans and a Roman walk into a souvenir shop to peruse a rack of risqué kitchen aprons.

Daphne and I rummage through them like two shoppers at a Black Friday doorbuster sale. We pull apron after apron off the rack looking for the right size—pun intended. It's only a matter of seconds before Chuck and Giovanni abandon us and head back in the fresh air.

"I'm gettin' one o' these for Chuck," Daphne whispers with a playful smile on her face.

We giggle uncontrollably like pre-teens in sex ed, the *limoncello* getting to our brains.

"This has my cat sitter's name all over it," I declare, heading to the register with an apron featuring a well-endowed David. Daphne nods her approval before doubling over.

We continue walking through the narrow cobblestone streets, walls the color of faded oranges and mustard yellows tunneling our vision to the sliver of another road ahead, like a rainbow maze made of acrylic chalk. Space is still scarce, as people continue to dine outside and stroll with overflowing shopping bags. Are there fewer Romans riding their scooters, or am I so used to the sound of them zipping by that I no longer notice them?

"*Aprile*, I must leave." Gio taps the gelato stain on his jacket. "I change before the game. You will find hotel okay?"

"Well, I was looking forward to another Vespa ride, but I've got my trusty maps. And, unlike mine, I think their phones actually work," I reply, pointing to Chuck and Daphne.

He kisses both cheeks again. "*Ciao, bella.*" And with a wave of his hand and an unforgettable smile, he walks off toward the little yellow Vespa that gave me the most memorable tour of Rome I'll have all week.

"*Ciao, bella?*" Daphne's eyebrows are wiggling so much they look like they're doing jumping jacks. "Girl."

"Everyone's back at the hotel," Chuck announces while reading the text on his phone. And thanks to his GPS, we smoothly navigate our way back on foot, but not before stopping at another bar first. It's small but posh, the purple lighting too enticing to ignore. Another round of *limoncello* is all Daphne and I need to paint American tourists in a not-so-flattering light.

"Let's put the aprons on," she slurs giddily.

And that's how, on the colorful, quaint streets of Rome, two grown women end up walking to a five-star hotel wearing Statue of David nudie aprons—once we finally get our heads through the neck loops. Our motor skills are sub-par at the moment.

The two of us, arm in arm in our tacky aprons, turn heads, every Roman who crosses our path taking notice. A couple walking a dog does a double take, polite laughter not quite concealing their confusion—revulsion? Stopped at a red light are two men inside a work van who honk their horn as they watch us stumble along. Two people even ask to take a photo with the Apron Twins, landing this proud moment into a stranger's scrapbook.

Bumbling along *Via Ludovisi* in our tacky aprons is working up quite the appetite. Remembering the cookie that I stashed away in my pocket earlier is just the thing to class up this scene.

I pinch my treasured *cantuccio* between my fingers, flick off the lint, and bring it to my mouth. The crunch is so loud that I can't hear the line of Vespas zooming past us. I wave in case one is Gio. Crumbs spray miraculously from my mouth to the cobblestones like I'm *la Fontana di Aprile*.

"Oh, hon," Daphne says, "it's a good thing Gio hit the bricks when he did." I cover my mouth so as not to spray her with crumbs while giggling.

When we reach the lobby of our hotel, I brush off the crumbs from my coat, reach into my pocket, and replace the ring on my finger. "Okay, guys, I think it's time I talked with my 'husband,'" I say, my fingers making air quotes on the last word. "We have a lot to talk about."

CHAPTER 19

THE PASTA HATERS CLUB

OVER BY THE hotel bar, the light dim and the music quiet, Rob and Simon have their heads together in a booth while looking at the former's cell phone. Vicki is Krazy-gluing a bottle of red wine to her hand.

"The coastal markets are going to be an adjustment," Rob is saying as we walk over. "You have to factor in wildfires in the west, hurricanes in the east. It messes with all the transport schedules." He looks at Simon now, his face beaming at his favorite employee. "But you'll be fine. Though you'll still dabble with the larger Midwest clients from time to time, and that, of course, will be no adjustment at all. The contracts, however, have more clauses you'll need to familiarize yourself with."

Simon forces a smile.

"You weren't kiddin' about the shop talk, Chuck," I say under my breath. "Their conversation sounds as exciting as a pizza with no toppings."

When we reach the table, the life returns to Simon's face. "Hey! You're back! We were just about to figure out dinner." His smile vanishes when he looks at me.

I shuffle into the booth next to him, and despite his cold greeting, give him an unrequited sheepish grin. Instead of worrying about how difficult it might be to clear the air with him later, I let a happy anticipation stir up my appetite as a distraction. Will we have pasta smothered in pesto? Stuffed manicotti? Meaty lasagna? It's Rob and his perfectly gelled hair who bursts my bubble:

"Whatever we eat, I don't want any more pasta."

He may as well be speaking in dialect because I didn't understand a single word he just said. "No more pasta?!" What kind of sick joke is that?

He shakes his head confirming my worst nightmare. When it comes to pasta, tonight we'll be having *niente*.

"My gym won't recognize me if I eat another plate of pasta," Simon agrees with a laugh.

Blasphemy.

I feel compelled to defend Rome's pasta, stand up for starchy carbs everywhere. But before I find the words, Chuck—sweet southern Chuck who makes everything sound charming—says the most uncharming thing:

"I need a break from pasta, too."

Traitor.

Friends don't deprive friends of pasta. Who are these… *strangers?* My foodie's guidebook lists twenty-five different types of must-eat pasta. We've tried only an embarrassingly small fraction of that list. We've yet to try the elf hats, the little ears, the wagon wheels, the cork screws. With no tour guide holding us to a strict schedule shlepping us around town, we can cover an immense amount of Italian culinary ground tonight.

"A-ha!" I say, fishing for the perfect guidebook in my purse. "This sounds like a job for *Eating Italy: The Foodie's Guide to Rome*!" After all, it doesn't have to be pasta to be world-class Italian cuisine. We could have pizza or a fragrant garlic lemon chicken dish. I'd even settle for seafood, which is saying something. I hand the book to Chuck. "You might find something in there."

"Whoa, what do we have here?" He casually fans through the pages, his cell phone resting on his jean-covered muscular thigh. "You came prepared."

In a tone coated in sarcasm, Simon explains, "April carries everything in her purse. Even maps she can't open."

"I open them! It's *closing* them—" I mime folding a map in mid-air "—that I struggle with."

He sips an old-fashioned, one ankle propped up on his knee looking as care-free as ever. "Care-free" does not describe how I feel as my book now finds its way into Rob's hands. The man who already reached his pasta quota after only two days. The man who waived dessert from our lunch yesterday. The fate of our dinner is now in his hands. Skeptically, I side-eye him while he flips through the guidebook, never staying on any one page long enough to make a culinary commitment. The room feels warmer now; I sip my water. And then, in one swift move, he pulls his phone from his pocket with one hand, and with the other, passes the book to Chuck who passes it back to me.

My heart beats a touch faster. What does this mean?

"How about this place?" Rob holds up the glowing screen. "It's in Chinatown."

If this were a movie trailer, this is the part where an ear-piercing record scratch sound effect would play, followed by a pregnant pause of tense silence.

Chinatown?

I muffle a scoff. Crab rangoon and wonton soup are nowhere to be found on my Must-Eat-in-Italy list. I did not endure ten hours of flying over the Atlantic, lose an entire night of sleep, and learn Italian—okay, *try* to learn Italian—to eat some kung-pao chicken.

Rome giveth, and Rob taketh away. I'm speechless, in shock at this unexpected turn of events. A pasta-free Italian dinner is disappointing, but I was still willing. But China-town? In Italy? Inside, I'm steaming hotter than a container of pork fried rice.

"And it looks pretty quiet, too," Rob continues, all but making the decision for the entire group. "I can give you the four-one-one on some of those national reps you'll be working with, Simon. Not to mention some of the pain-in-the-ass clients. There's one in D.C. you'll have to stay on. You thought the Sandersons were bad. That's nothing compared to these guys."

One look at Simon's glazed-over face and it's clear that he's had enough shop talk for one day. "Actually, Rob," I interject, "would it be okay if I borrowed Simon tonight? I haven't seen him for hours, and I'd love a dinner just the two of us." No protesting from Simon. I'll take that as a win under the circumstances.

"Oh," Rob says, disappointment coating his words. "Well, sure. Of course. But let's go over some of this stuff on the train tomorrow, okay, Simon? Your workload is about to get crazy, and I don't want my main guy to get swallowed up in National's red tape bull—"

Vicki grabs hold of his shoulder. "Leave work at home. Haven't I been saying that? I *beg* you." She releases her grip, rolls her eyes, and applies more Krazy glue.

"We'll see you guys tomorrow," I say, scootching out of the booth. "Have an egg roll for us." On the way to the elevators, eagerly anticipating a room with no co-workers and no chop suey, I say to him, "Hope it's okay I stole you away from them."

"If I hear one more rundown on one more client, I will quit and move to Italy," Simon says in an exasperated voice as the elevator doors close. "We're gonna need to avoid them on the train to Florence tomorrow."

"We'll sit on the luggage racks if we have to. Or stow away in the bathrooms!"

His reflection looks at mine in the mirror-covered elevator, and his shoulders bob with the smallest hint of a laugh. I'll take it. The doors open, and we walk to our room. "I've been wanting to talk to you," I say. "But let's figure out dinner first. I'm starting to get hangry."

"Uh oh, we don't want that." He grabs a protein bar and plops down on the bed. "It *would* be nice to have something other than pasta though. We had *carbonara* earlier. So good, but my gym might kick me out if I keep eating this way." He pats his stomach.

"I think your six-pack has a long way to go before it turns into a keg."

"It will though if I keep eating pasta."

I plop down on the opposite bed. "Okay, you don't want pasta, and I don't want non-Italian. How about we find ourselves a nice caprese salad? I haven't had buffalo mozzarella all day and I think I'm experiencing withdrawal." I tell him

I know a good place that's not too far. But first: an *antipasto*. Remembering the airline rolls stashed away in my bag, I dig them out, shamelessly biting into them.

He laughs. "I'll share my protein bars with you, you know."

"Becks, I'd rather lick my shoe." The bread is beyond stale. I gnaw at it with my teeth until they feel like they're going to fall out of my mouth. It's hard as a rock. "You were wrong; Bob Seger wrote that song about leftover airplane bread."

♨

The roads are lit by streetlamps and headlights, the air is clear, but my head is murky with undiscussed what-ifs as we walk to dinner. The kisses I've shared with Simon: enjoyable but confusing. And the fight that exploded between us has me worried that I've ruined our reunion and possibly friendship. At least I can take solace in the fact that, based on Rob's nonstop Nationals advice, he's clearly not fired. And then there are my recurring memories of Ian, prompted by his incessant calls: irritating yet comforting. Plus, on top of all that, this new thing with Gio: absolutely delightful despite the fact that it can never be anything lasting. I desperately need to get some things off my chest.

"I'm really sorry about blowing up last night. I'm not used to drinking so much wine. And those Bellini drinks— they should come with a warning label on the glass."

"April, it's fine, in fact—"

"No, it's *not* fine. I mean, here I am in Rome for a week for free. That should be enough—more than enough! Who cares if you asked a few other people before me? High school is ancient history. Of course I wouldn't have been the one to pop into your head right away; you've got other friends—newer friends, and—"

"But, you did," he interrupts. "I thought of you right away. A week of eating Italian food? Who'd love that more than April Appleby?"

We stop at a red light, finally facing each other, and his face cracks a smile as he continues. "All those spaghetti dinners at your house in high school… I knew you'd want to come; I just didn't know if it would be weird after all this time. Kind of a big ask. And the whole spouse thing…"

"Are you kidding?! We were always goofing off when we hung out. Pretending to be married? Pfft."

He laughs. The light turns green, but we remain standing, looking at each other as if we're really seeing each other for the first time on this reunion. The excitement I felt after he kissed me that first night has been replaced with a comforting nostalgia. Here I am, in the most fascinating city in the world, with a friend I'd seriously started to wonder if I'd ever see again. Which is all the clarity I need to make sure those stolen kisses were nothing more than a product of getting swept up in the romance of Rome.

"There was something else I wanted to bring up," I say. "Last night, when I said that my friend thought you might have, you know, feelings for me or whatever—"

"We should cross. It's green." He ushers me across the street with his hand on my back, and I mentally kick myself for bringing it up. Maybe I shouldn't have flirted with him, kissed him back, ogled his shirtless physique. How will he ever be comfortable around me again?

But to my surprise, he answers my unasked question. "About your friend's theory. I never meant to give you the wrong idea when I—I didn't mean to make you uncomfortable." He glances at me. "Literally, everyone on this trip brought either their husband or wife, or their kid. And, I dunno, you get some alcohol in me—"

"And Red Bull."

"And espresso."

"And flower petals…"

"I *might* have gotten a little carried away."

"You *might* have kissed me. Three times."

Through an embarrassed laugh, he says, "I'm sorry. I've never brought a friend with to one of these things—usually I bring my mom or someone. I didn't want to get caught breaking the family-only rule, you know?" We stop walking, and he awkwardly taps my shoulder with a friendly fist. "Wanted to look convincing. Sorry if I made things weird, Appleby. Friends?"

Relief floods through me. No more wondering if he wants more than friendship. Which, most importantly, is safe: I won't have to say goodbye to another person I care about, relying on only memories to visit him. "What's a reunion without a little weirdness?" I punch him back. "Gotta say, I'm relieved. I didn't want things to change between us. Not that you're not a good kisser." I abruptly turn to keep walking. Out of the corner of my eye, I see that he's smirking.

"The restaurant's not far," I say, changing the subject. "Keep going this way." As we round a corner, I exclaim, "Hey, let's go up to Summerfest next year. Maybe we can stay for the whole week this time! Rumor has it Styx will be one of the headliners." Penciling in another concert feels good, even if it is barely legible on-the-go chicken scratch.

"Oh man, that would be killer," he says, pausing as his

words are drowned out by an accelerating scooter. When it passes, he continues, placing a hand over mine to stop me from scribbling in my notebook. "But now I'm not sure if—"

"Oh! Speaking of our 'marriage,'" I interrupt, not wanting to forget perhaps the most important thing I have to tell him. "I really hope I didn't blow it, but I had to tell Daphne and Chuck about us. When I ran into them earlier, I had to… well, I had to explain when they saw me and Giovanni at the Trevi Fountain. He sort of had his hands all over me. But I told them not to say anything."

"Oh, the jig's up. But not because of you. I told Rob the whole thing. He started asking me all kinds of questions about how you and I have to—about all kinds of stuff. But I'll tell you about that later. What does 'hands all over you' mean? Are you okay? I thought you were just going to talk about this guy's restaurant."

Antonelli's Pizzeria jumps out in front of us, the outdoor tables underneath the awnings already claimed by hungry diners. "His *dad's* restaurant. And here it is." My hands make a *voila* gesture, but confusion still lines Simon's face. "And it was just a friendly hug. And maybe a kiss." I give him a reassuring smile, and my cheeks turn into cherries.

"Oh, I bet it was friendly alright." He wiggles his eyebrows as he holds the door for me. "Sounds to me like you're having a little Roman rendezvous. How could you cheat on me like that?"

I lightly punch him in the stomach as we head for an open table. Soon, a plate of tomato-topped bruschetta and two caprese salads arrive. I go for the buffalo mozzarella first. Its soft texture and mild flavor are complete bliss, and a satisfied moan escapes me that causes Simon to shift uncomfortably in his seat across from me.

"So, about this—this Giovanni guy… He gonna be here tonight?"

"No, actually. He said he'd be at a soccer game."

Despite limiting his carbs, Simon can't resist the bruschetta and takes a bite, crunching loudly. "And you're wishing he was here instead."

I snicker at his suggestion, stabbing a hunk of tomato. "Maybe. Think Rob took the liberty to order egg rolls for everyone?"

"Probably chose the sauce for 'em all, too."

❧

Antonelli's Pizzeria: Four apples so shiny you can see yourself.

Taste: The caprese salad was generous with its basil, its tomatoes plump and divinely red, and the mozzarella ball was the freshest yet. The bruschetta was sublime, perfectly crunchy yet tender with each bite. The olive oil drizzled over each slice, enticing in flavor and aroma. The metaphorical cherry on top? The complimentary *Vin Santo*, fruity with a hint of caramel and hazelnut, a gift from Gio's sister. One juicy apple.

Service: Fast, friendly, and a gratuitous digestive. One perfect apple.

Atmosphere: Rustic, authentic, and family-owned. An attractive and generous family, I might add. A big-ass charming apple.

Price: Simon paid. Another entire apple.

To: gregorystorms@wrck.fm

Subject: Rode a Vespa, Met Pinocchio, Ate Mozzarella

I see your request for a pic of Gio, and I raise you a pic of me, Gio, and Pinocchio. He gave me a ride on his Vespa today. No, that's not code for the horizontal tarantella.

I finally cleared the air with Simon. We're all good. Even have a whole summer of concerts lined up next year. No need to go gladiator on him.

Why are you so scared to bring Harry to your parents' house? They're going to love him. It's been two years. Time for him to meet the 'rents!

Had the best spaghetti of my life today. Nothing like my mother's though, and I feel weird saying that. Gio told me his sauce strategy today, and I think the missing ingredient could be in there. He also told me there's some cooking abroad program in Rome next year. (Insert hysterical laughter here.) Poor guy's delusional. Sexy as hell, but delusional.

Attaching pics of all the food I ate today.

Buona notte, Greg!

April

CHAPTER 20

A TRAIN TO TUSCANY

HE DOESN'T EVEN have to ask anymore; I've become accustomed to automatically holding out my hand so Simon can pass me the carbs that will threaten to dismantle his six-pack that day. At the moment, it's a complimentary granola bar. And this time, I won't wait two days to eat it.

We've just left *Roma Termini,* leaving the gray rainy skies of Rome behind for the capital of Tuscany. The train ride to Florence is an hour-and-a-half, which is all the time Simon needs to make himself at home—a rather easy task considering we made sure to sit in a car with no sight of his boss. He kicks off his shoes and peels off his socks, soaked from this morning's downpour. After all the grief I've caused him, I don't have the heart to tell him how grotesque his pruny, wet feet are.

The granola bar is sweet and chewy, with more chocolate than should be allowed this time of the morning. "*This* is what I pictured Italy to look like," I say, rolling green hills blurring past the windows as tiny rays of sunshine peek through the clouds. "Though I've gotten used to seeing graffiti everywhere."

"It's very political here," Simon explains, pulling a protein bar from his rainproof black jacket. "The graffiti will come back in Florence."

At 250 kilometers per hour, we track toward hilly terrain in no time, flashing past Tuscan vineyards and barreling through winding, pitch-black tunnels. My ears pop incessantly as Simon naps through most of our journey, head back and arms crossed over his chest. Connecting to the train's wi-fi, I open up my email.

> *To: aprilappleby@wrck.fm*
>
> *Subject: Re: Rode a Vespa, Met Pinocchio, Ate Mozzarella*
>
> *OMG that is some massive mozzarella.*
>
> *You call him GIO?? Does he know that you can probably find a way to ruin cereal?*
>
> *But seriously, don't even try to convince me you wouldn't want to take that class in Rome. I found that flyer for Cooking 101 in your kitchen drawer! How are you still hedging on that?? How long is the program in Rome for? You could shack up with Gio, and he could give you private lessons, if you know what I mean.*
>
> *What do you think the missing ingredient is??*
>
> *Glad things are good with Simon, though I'm still 1,000% jealous that I'm not the one traipsing all over Italy with you.*
>
> *And I'm not scared to introduce Harry to my parents, but he's been a city boy all his life, and dragging him to*

Nowheresville, Nebraska is going to be some serious culture shock. I don't want to put him through that. It's bad enough that you and I have to explain every year to all my aunts and uncles that we're not dating. Can you imagine their faces if I walk in with Harry?

I'm attaching pics of the SKID MARKS on your bathroom floor. Tot's going in a time out.

Greg

Leave it to Greg to see right through my hesitation about enrolling in this month-long cooking class. Would I like to leave responsibility behind to chop garlic and smell simmering sauces for four weeks? Obviously. But, for starters, what's the admission process like? How much is tuition? And I can't take such a large chunk of time off work, can I? I only get three weeks' vacation. Oh, and the minor detail of living in a foreign country for an entire month. The Beatles said it best: it's all too much.

Before slipping my phone back into my bag, I wipe out another voicemail notification. Ian called in the middle of the night again, leaving another message. With Simon still breathing heavily as his head lolls to the side, I attempt to listen, but my phone still won't let me check my messages. In vain I attempt to text him, but that's no good either. The pit in my stomach grows heavier. What could possibly be so urgent? It's unlike Ian to leave a voicemail, not to mention multiple. I could email him and explain why I haven't been answering or calling back, but I'd really like to know what he's got to say first—especially if he's going to bring up getting back together. Whatever this conversation is, it's probably going to be serious. Which means it'll have to wait, preferably until we're both on the same continent. Enjoying my time in Rome should not include inviting my ex into the experience.

Switching my focus to snacking while window gazing takes my mind off Ian. I'm not sure if it's the second granola bar I open with its foil wrapper crinkling loudly, or my humming "Volare" that wakes Simon up. (Hey, if he's going to insist on playing that every morning in the shower, he can't expect it not to get stuck in my head.)

He yawns, reaching for his socks. "Ugh, they're still wet."

"I didn't even bother taking mine off," I say, pointing to my soaked shoes. "My toes probably look like raisins by now."

Soon, the streets begin to fill with scooters and tiny cars, buildings painted in hues of tangerine and pear.

"And there's your graffiti," he says, pointing just beyond the train platform as we coast to a stop. "Welcome to Florence."

⋙

Squish squish squish. My socks are cold wet rags, my skinny jeans damp from the knees down sticking to my calves like glue. We slug our way off the crowded platform, eventually finding Rob and Chuck, all of us prepared for more precipitation in dark rain coats.

"Where's the rest of the tour group?" Simon asks.

"Not entirely certain," comes Rob's reply. "Let's head this way."

Thank God for Teal Thing One and Teal Thing Two: Vicki and Daphne are wearing matching seafoam blue waterproof jackets, arms draped around each other's shoulders as they bob their way through the sea of humanity like two neon buoys floating toward the tour guide. We keep our eyes on the flash of color, eventually making our way to the group.

Our tour guide evidently expects us to keep an eye on her basic black umbrella instead of a colorful flag. "Looks like we've got Mary Poppins today."

"Maybe for a little bit," Simon says through a chuckle. The sparkle in his eye is almost a gleam when he looks at me. "But I've got some things tucked up my sleeve."

᠊ᢀ

The Renaissance art capital of the world, home of fine leather, and what I'm tickled pink about: motherland of gelato.

We step out into Florence, a chill biting through my thin raincoat. Our tour begins down a street lined with scooters leaning against graffiti-covered buildings, splashes of baby blue, neon green, magenta, and red popping against the brown walls. Simon laughs as I snap a few pictures—my obsession with Italian street art and tiny European vehicles has only intensified since our arrival. The marmalade-colored buildings lining the streets tunnel our vision as we pass endless Florentine treasures.

The fifteenth century Basilica di San Lorenzo wears a brown, unfinished plainness on the outside in complete contrast to its beauty on the inside: another Michelangelo achievement. But it's the Medici family who left their legacy imprinted on all the nooks and crannies of the capital of Tuscany. From the *Monumento a Giovanni della Bande Nere*, the statue that commemorates the military leader of the Medici, to the Riccardi Medici Palace, built in the 1400s, Renaissance remnants shine on every corner. The latter features remarkable architecture, rustic stone walls, and a garden of green grass and trees sprouting citrus, white marble statues poised all around.

But it's a certain material that's popping up on every street. In one boutique, bags in hues of every shade paint this gray day with vibrant color.

"There's enough leather here to outfit every member of Judas Priest for a year," Simon says. He looks in, as if considering making a purchase.

"I can even *smell* it out here," I reply, breathing in the scent slowly, cherishing its richness. It's as strong as the scent of freshly brewed espresso or stewed tomatoes that I've begun to take for granted in Italy. "Actually, that gives me an idea," I say, remembering the concert promos we're airing on WRCK. "They're going on tour next year. Bet I can score free tickets from the station." He walks ahead without replying, while I scribble down our fifth concert in my *Order Up* notebook. Our concert calendar is growing so effortlessly, I give Simon a bear hug from behind.

Towering above us is a fourteen-foot sculpture that's been standing triumphantly since the early 1500s. Inside the *Galleria dell'Accademia* stands Michelangelo's famous statue of David. I've seen pictures of it—and have worn aprons of it—but I've never realized how large of a sculpture it really is.

While basking in the hushed chatter that is so characteristic of museums, I think of the text I received from Gio while on the train this morning. *"My sister tell me you see David today. Why you not come to my museum?"* He attached a selfie of himself next to a sculpture. "*You make Dionysus sad.*" My high school mythology course earned me that lone F on my transcript—meanwhile, Simon passed with flying colors—so I cracked open *Passport to History* while Simon was still snoozing. "Dionysus, the Olympian god of wine, ecstasy, festivity, madness, and insanity, represents all the side effects of overindulgence." God of ecstasy? Gio has to know this, the history buff that he is. Out of all the statues in his museum, he chose the god of pleasure? I feel warm all over again recalling the photo, his face.

But here at the *Accademia*, my focus turns to David. "Wow, did you know Michelangelo began sculpting this when he was only twenty-six? And he wasn't even the first to attempt to sculpt David. It says here that other artists attempted the sculpture but never finished the project." All my tour books were about Rome, so while the rest of our group was going through the security check, I swung into the museum's gift shop to pick up *una guida ufficiale.*

"We have a tour guide, you know."

We do indeed. She's eyeing me and my official guidebook right now with resentment. "Sometimes I can't hear them or I forget what they say," I whisper into his ear, while admiring one of humankind's greatest artistic accomplishments. A tall, naked David, standing in chiseled muscular glory, wavy curls atop his head as he looks on toward infinity.

"Why are David's hands so big?" someone from our group shouts, almost as if to be searching for flaws in this masterpiece.

"Oh, it's because Michelangelo wanted viewers to spot more detail from afar." I interject, holding my booklet into the air, all eyes on me and a general chuckle spreading through the group like they're doing the wave at a baseball game. "It says that 'The veins, fingernails, and lines in David's hands were carved with painstaking detail—details that would have been lost had he sculpted the hands to scale.'"

Mary Poppins smiles politely at me. "*Grazie, signora,*" she manages to say through her teeth. Her eyes roll into their sockets as she turns away.

"I never knew you to be a teacher's pet, Appleby."

Stuffing the guidebook into my purse, I let Mary Poppins point out the real flaws on the statue of David, though their existence is not through any fault of Michelangelo. She tells us that in 1991, a man attacked David with a hammer, damaging the toes on the left foot of the statue. Since then, a protective glass wall encircles the base of the statue, keeping crowds at a safe distance. Luckily, unlike the veins in David's hands and the curls in his hair, these smashed toes are details that *can't* be seen from afar. Still though, a disturbing reminder not to take anything or anyone for granted—they may not be here tomorrow.

I nearly fall flat on my face leaving the museum. Side-stepping what appears to be an original work of art lying in the street causes me to lose my balance, clumsily bumping into the artist.

"Sorry," I say, smoothing out my hair.

This painter has chosen the worst possible place to display his talents. Nonetheless, a dozen or so unframed paintings are scattered on the cobblestones beneath a cloud-covered sky that could drench them at any moment.

The rest of us file out, each person's feet coming danger-ously close to stomping all over the artwork. Simon, lagging behind me after making a pit stop, comes out and in a move that's as graceful as a drunk hippopotamus on roller skates, plants his dirty footprint right on a painting.

"Oooh," the crowd winces painfully, like fans at a game whose team just missed the final shot.

"Major party foul," I add.

Simon looks down, immediately seeing his contribution to this man's painting. A nasal chuckle flitters out of his mouth as he instantly reaches for his wallet. "Just my luck." Smiling, he holds out a few notes to the Florentine. "Can I take this off your hands?" After a moment, he asks again in muddled Italian, "Uh, *compro*? Can I buy this?" He holds up the wad of euros higher.

"*Grazie, signore, grazie, grazie mille, troppo gentile, troppo gentile.*" The man hands over the painting, and Simon and I take in the rich golden colors drenching a sunset scene of *Ponte Vecchio*, the remnants of what could have been Bigfoot stomped across it.

Simon rolls it up and hands it to me. "Something to remember our time in Italy by." He smiles, and somehow, under the clouds, his brown eyes catch a twinkle that fills my heart with gratitude, not only for a beautiful painting (stamped with a funny blunder), but of a week with a friend who came back to me from the past. And, after clearing the air, I finally let myself believe that he's no longer a friend I used to know—a friend I'd lost touch with. He's here to stay.

I grab the roll of paper gently, cracking a joke to keep my tearful gratitude at bay. "And your shoes, too. Looked like good tread. You wear those to the gym?"

☙

"That car!" My eyes widen as I give Simon a look like a kid who just saw a puppy. "It's so cute!"

Simon laughs as I tap a photo of a schoolbus-yellow Pasquali, a three-wheeled electric European car so tiny its thin tires look like they belong on a Schwinn bicycle. It pulls over letting an ambulance pass, idling behind the outdoor tables at a restaurant taking up no more space than a big potted plant.

"April, look up," he says. "You're gonna want a photo of what's next."

Straight ahead at the end of the road, a sliver of the most magnificent church I've seen all week peeks through. Lavishly decorated with a pearly white and charcoal gray exterior topped with a massive copper dome, the word "church" seems much too modest to describe the Cathedral of *Santa Maria del Fiore*, more simply known around these parts as the Duomo. Once we get to the end of the street the full enormity of the church comes into view.

"'The architecture of this Gothic church, one of the biggest in the world, inspired the dome on St. Peter's Basilica. Construction began in 1296, but it wasn't until almost 200 years later that it was completed with the breathtaking dome.'" As I look up from *101 Must-See Churches of Italy*, Simon is in mid-eyeroll, his annoyance on full display. "What? I got it when we were at the Vatican."

Mary Poppins holds up her black umbrella and leads us to the front of the cathedral. Its magnificent black doors look heavy enough to be made from iron, while intricate carvings of saints and religious figures soften its heavy appearance, adding a delicate texture. Arches, sculpted saints, and images of Jesus Christ adorn its exterior. Pops of gold and shades of pink add a delicateness to this massive Gothic structure.

Giotto's Bell Tower stands tall next to the church entrance, like a skinny *ante-litteram* skyscraper reaching for the heavens.

But if I'm going to have a religious experience in Florence, it won't be at a medieval cathedral. It'll be at a place like *Venchi Cioccolato*. On either side of the gelateria's entryway stand two giant decorative cones of gelato, each nearly as tall as I, luring in hungry tourists ailed with a sweet tooth.

"Should I ask Mary Poppins if we can stop in here? I mean, we're in the city where gelato was invented."

Simon points to our tour guide as she charges up *Via dei Calzaiuoli.* "Her umbrella already carried her too far." He sees the disappointment on my face and peeks inside the gelateria. "But it doesn't look too busy. Be fast."

While he waits at the door for me, the woman behind the counter prepares my two scoops of *cioccolato*—no need to peruse flavors at this chocolate haven.

Back outside, we're headed for *Piazza della Repubblica,* an open square surrounded by cafés, shops, and vendors. A grand twinkling carousel, the *Antica Giostra Toscana,* sits in the middle of the square, a quirky carnivalesque sight among the piazza's quaint cafés and Renaissance-inspired archway. A clown wearing a red and white fuzzy shirt and hat makes balloon animals.

"Hey, over here." Simon tugs at my sleeves and nods his head toward the carousel. "Wanna show you something." We begin walking at a quick clip toward a food vendor not far from the square.

"We're gonna fall even farther behind the group. What are you doing?" I skip a little to keep up.

"Finish your ice cream. It's time for a real treat." He gestures to a sandwich stand.

"What's *lampredotto*?" I ask, reading the sign and inhaling an enticing beefy aroma.

"Cow's stomach. But that's not why we're here." A mischievous grin forms on his face as he points to the bottles of wine behind the display of sandwiches. "Wanna play hooky?"

Mary Poppins' umbrella is already leading the crowd out of the piazza. Turning back to Simon, I beam ear to ear. "Let's do it."

Simon orders two drinks and the man hands him two plastic cups of red wine. "Now we can explore this city the Italian way."

As we begin strolling back through the piazza, I ask, "Are you sure we can drink this out in the open?"

"They were selling it on the street. Why not?" He chuckles and takes a sip. "Up for a carousel ride?"

"That's what the walking tour was missing. Well, that and wine." I take a sip.

We go up to the ticket booth, holding our cups low at our sides. Simon hands a man four euros in exchange for two tickets.

"Let's ride!"

We each mount two horses side-by-side, one hand on the pole, the other on our adult beverages. As the ride begins to spin, the gold lights shining on our multi-colored horses galloping up and down, I throw my head back and laugh without inhibition. Our high school trips to Great America and the Wisconsin Dells rotate around my mind as we rotate around this Florentine gem, and a happiness that I'm reunited with my friend swells up inside me. "Alcoholic carousel ride… Becks, this might be your most brilliant idea ever!"

He laughs, too, sneaking a sip of wine and saying, "*Salute!*"

When the carousel comes to a stop, we reluctantly dismount. "That was far too short," I say. "You're a much better tour guide than Mary Poppins." My smile is now starting to make my cheeks sore.

"Tour's not over. Got somethin' else to show you." He nods his head toward the south of the square, and I follow willingly. Soon, we stroll into the heart of Florence: *Piazza della Signoria*. I do a double take at the sight of Michelangelo's most famous statue—again. "This is where David used to be," he says, pausing to take a sip of wine, "before they moved him."

"You really paid attention in history class."

"I just remember from when I was here with my mom. It's a replica, see? They put it up after they moved the original to the *Accademia*. I've got one more stop for you."

"Donatello, Leonardo da Vinci, Michelangelo... Where's Raphael?" I ask, as we walk through *Piazzale degli Uffizi*. "We need the last Ninja Turtle."

He laughs as we breeze past a line of statues. "I don't know, but wait till you get a load of this view coming up."

When we reach the Arno River, the famous *Ponte Vecchio* steals the show.

"It's Italian for 'old bridge,'" he explains. "It's from medieval times. Known for its jewelry and souvenir shops now."

It has three arched sections, above which are painted warm hues of cherry, nectarine, and pineapple. Through the windows of the shops, I see people strolling along, looking at all the jewels, selecting which trinkets to take home. The buildings are lined up on either side of the river, painted in shades of sunny yellows, tan, and creamy oranges, all lined up in different colors like a box of crayons. The bright hues reflect off the Arno, rippling along the gentle waves like sherbet melting in the sun.

Which, at some point since we got off the train, has actually peeked out now that the skies have cleared. Simon takes a selfie of us with the bridge in the background. "Florence looks so much warmer and brighter when the sun's out, doesn't it?" he says.

"It's beautiful. It's practically gold." I shift my gaze from the bridge to my friend. "You've gone above and beyond here. Do you still feel guilty about not asking me to Italy first or something? 'Cause I forgive you for that. We're totally cool."

He takes a deep breath, and his smile fades. "I know. But, the new job… I don't know how many of those concerts I'll be able to go to with you. I have to relocate. Company headquarters are in Houston."

I almost choke on my wine. "Houston? I don't understand. I thought you were remote."

"For this job I'm remote, but I'm only regional now. For the national gig, it's big time. I've got to be in all these meetings with all the top execs, regional reps, clients. Weekly status reports and client rundowns. Something called a 'logistics transportational accessibility schedule.' Rob's been trying to fill me in, but bottom line: they need me on Ground Zero for this one."

A gentle breeze rustles my hair, and I suddenly realize that despite the sunshine, it's still a chilly fall day. I shake with a quick shiver, the warmth from running around piazzas and sipping wine suddenly gone. "Do you *want* to move to

Houston?" I hate that there's a quake in my voice. I pretend to adjust my glasses.

His face softens with sympathy. It's not really about the move, he explains, but the job. He needs it. "I can't stay in rentals another year. I can't. My salary's capped; I'm basically trying to out-commission myself every year." He guides me out of the way as a couple approaches the river, cell phone in hand for their own selfie. "Plus, I used to live in the south for a couple years, so it won't be a huge adjustment. I travel so much as it is that I'm hardly ever home anyway, so what's the difference?"

The difference is that we'll be three states away from each other instead of three towns. We *just* reconnected. A familiar feeling comes over me: the feeling of our lives splitting when we went to two different colleges.

The paper tears out of the notebook unevenly, leaving a ruffled scrap behind. I crumple the sheet with my fist, my loopy script written down in excited haste now balled up in defeat. "It was only five shows anyway."

CHAPTER 21

A BIG PIZZA PIE

IN A MATTER of days, I've morphed from a gluttonous American who gladly eats Spaghettios by the can alone in her living room, to a student of Italy who's learned to savor and appreciate the flavors, smells, and textures of a freshly prepared meal at some of the most exquisite eateries on the globe.

We're at an outdoor table at *La Borsa,* and I'm about to check off another must-eat item: my first authentic Italian pizza. An experience that's practically sacred.

Simon and I, the last to arrive for lunch due to our impromptu personalized tour of Florence, join the rest of our group who have already begun eating.

"Ah, Mr. and Mrs. Becker, so nice of you to join us," Rob says with a friendly smirk.

"Yeah, yeah, yeah," replies Simon.

"And where did your little adventure take you?" Rob asks. "We missed you from the group."

"Oh, around." I exchange a knowing glance with Simon.

We sit at one end of the table next to Rob and Chuck, and at the opposite end are Vicki and Daphne, keeping cozy beneath a heating lamp. My thin raincoat remains on, doing little to provide warmth. But hey, lunch is about to be served: that'll warm me up in no time.

"You guys want a slice?" Rob asks, holding up a plate of pizza topped with würstel. "It's *pizza Americana*. Little taste of home."

Home. Noisy trains rumbling along the L. Sirens going off every five minutes. Sub-zero winters. Tater Tot. "Well, I am a little homesick."

"I'm not homesick, but I am curious." Simon reaches over and takes a slice, too. "*And* I want to make a contribution to your restaurant reviews, April." After his first bite, he dramatically clears his throat, his voice coming out unnaturally quiet and slow as if he were on public radio. "We have here a crispy crust, and, what's that I'm tasting? Oregano, perhaps? The sauce," he pauses to click his tongue a few times, "is very... saucy. Topped with a generous layer of fresh, melty—" Oh my God, those hand gestures mean he's going to attempt an Italian accent "—*mozzarella*! And let's not forget the final flavor rounding out this pizza that represents America in the best possible light: hot dogs. Gives it a nice frankfurter finish. I award this fine establishment my highest rating: One-million stars." He cackles, taking an awkward bow while still seated as we humor him with applause.

"Don't American tourists have a bad enough reputation? Now we're synonymous with hot dogs on pizza?"

"You don't like it, Appleby?"

"I didn't say that." The slice disappears. When my own pizza arrives a few moments later—prosciutto pizza—I'm immensely pleased with my choice. Dare I say, it's the most flavorful pizza I've ever consumed. And I take pizza very seriously; I'm a Chicagoan. It's with this pie that I now understand what Elizabeth Gilbert meant when she wrote that she was having a relationship with her pizza in *Eat Pray Love*.

Girl, me too.

"Hey, April," Chuck says, "want me to take a picture o' you two?"

"Yeah, that'd be great." I hand him my phone and get up to crouch next to Simon.

"No, no, you and the pizza." Chuck says, pointing to my plate.

Simon cracks up while a big toothy grin takes over my face and I proudly hold up the cheesy pie, my arm cradling the circle like Pizza and I have just gotten engaged.

Chuck taps the screen, handing it back to me. I couldn't look happier if I my arm were wrapped around Gio's torso—okay, maybe I *could* look happier. I wonder if I'll have time to go back to Antonelli's and see how their pizza fares against this one. Something tells me if Gio served it, it would blow this one out of the water.

"Anyone want a slice?" I regret the question the second the words leave my mouth; I want every single slice for myself. But I hold up my tray of pizza anyway as a polite gesture, now missing a quarter of it, hoping that everyone is already too full to take me up on my hollow offer.

It's Vicki who bursts my bubble. "I'll try one."

I force a smile on my face as she reaches over and grabs a slice of my pizza. My perfect, mouthwatering, Italian pizza. Luckily, my generosity is immediately rewarded with someone else's unselfish gesture:

"Who wants a taste of this soup?" Daphne asks.

My hand shoots up in the air like the teacher's pet. *Me! Pick me!* The soup is like minestrone on steroids. I'm not sure what's in it, but it's delicious and hearty enough to be a meal in itself.

I savor every last bite of the remaining two slices, wishing I could sit here in my pizza coma for hours until time stops. Instead of feeling guilty about the likelihood of gaining a couple pounds this week, I feel happy about the friendships I've gained. Friendships that have blossomed over divine cuisine.

I think back to something Giovanni said over lunch yesterday about the human connection we feel when enjoying a meal together. Food this delicious is meant be shared. Food so tasty that we want our friends to experience the pleasure with us. A good meal has the power to bring people together, even strangers which is what most of these people were to me just days ago. Now, we're offering each other pizza, sharing spoonfuls of soup, slicing off bites of each other's lasagnas, scooping each other's salads onto our plates. Eating is a reason to celebrate; to be social. Not only am I filling up on zesty sauces and fresh cheeses, but also of human connection. Food pulls people together around a table, whether they're family or strangers, lovers or enemies, encouraging the heart to reach out to new wonderful people, and bridge the gap between two estranged friends. Food is love.

Of course it is. My mom was the first person to teach me that.

❧

La Borsa: Four of the reddest apples in the orchard.

Taste: Meals begin with the eyes, and, boy, did mine feast on the sight of this one. The red and orange hues were full of promise. Then, another sense was treated as the fresh aroma of tomatoes, cheese, and cured meat teased me. Finally, the flavor. Its crust: a flaky yet sturdy base. The sauce: a perfect consistency with just the right amount of oregano. And that mozzarella: *delizioso!* Topped with thin slices of salty prosciutto curling up at the edges: the finishing touch. And, nothing hot dog-esque about it. One meaty apple.

Service: Food was waiting for us before we sat down. I will now be late for all future group lunches. One hearty-sized apple.

Atmosphere: Is there anything more charming than dining on a tasty pizza outdoors while watching the shoppers of Florence stroll by? One dreamy apple.

Price: Worldswift sales team foots the bill once again. One big ol' free apple.

❧

Leather-banded watches, gold butterfly pins with blue painted wings, vintage ivory cameos strung on gold chains, pearl earrings, diamond necklaces. I can only imagine how much more *Ponte Vecchio* would glimmer if the sun's rays were still casting down on these jewels.

"This damn rain had to come back, huh? It's gonna make my curls frizz," Daphne says.

Our umbrellas shield us from the drizzle as the wet cobblestones glow with the reflection of the bright lights from the jewelry shops. A gold Pinocchio necklace dangles from a window, countless more necklaces shimmering behind. But as the seconds slip away, our only day in the gelato capital of the world is almost over. Which makes our next stop a unanimous decision.

"We need some gelato." Vicki says.

The surrounding churches reach that part of my spirit that hasn't prayed since my days of choking down Eucharist wafers. "Amen!"

We stop at the first *gelateria* we see, where I order one scoop of lemon with one scoop of melon. Chunks of fruit are mixed in; it's refreshing as an ice-cold lemonade on the Fourth of July.

"You like the fruity ones, huh?" Simon observes, while scooping up a big, green spoonful of pistachio.

"I like the creamy ones too, but I wanted something refreshing," I explain. As if to make a liar out of me, a mountain of tiramisu flavored gelato catches my eye and a craving for decadent sweetness hits. "How did I miss *that* flavor?!"

Simon laughs at my having been cheated out of what's probably the most heavenly ice cream on the planet, bringing another green scoop to his mouth.

The window is a huge leather dreamcatcher made of bags in every color: a sky blue with gold stitching, a cranberry red, a mocha with dark brown straps, candy pinks, mustard yellows, creamy ivory. The rich smell of the leather wafts out the door and into the street. We step inside, and I'm immediately grateful for the warm air caressing my cold hands, my fingers now icicles after clutching ice cream in the rain.

Chuck grabs a large mahogany-colored bag that looks like something Mr. Banks from *Mary Poppins* would carry with him to the bank every morning. It's hefty with thick brown straps, yet gorgeously chic.

"I'd look good with one o' these." He brings the bag close to his face to inspect the stitching, his dimples appearing as he smiles at the bag.

Everyone plunges farther into the store, but with only six remaining euros in my purse, I don't anticipate finding anything in my price range in the city where Gucci got his start. I make my way for the door, content to soak up a solitary moment on the quiet, cobbled street, glistening in the drizzle.

Okay, fine, I need to take a closer look at the god of pleasure again. I grab my phone and pull up the text thread from Gio.

Vicki sees me heading back outside and hands me her dish of gelato. "Would you mind tossing this for me? I've got to narrow down these purses." Before I reach her cup, she's already turned back to the wall lined in leather handbags of all sizes.

"No problem."

Most people probably wouldn't list taking somebody else's trash out as a highlight of their tour of Italy, but this moment is an opportunity for me to complete my destiny.

Vicki barely made a dent.

Isn't it a punishable crime not to finish one's gelato in the city it was invented? This is my time to shine. For I am April, finisher of all unfinished meals. Proud licker of all pre-licked gelato. Standing here alone in the rain in my white shirt and black coat, I might as well be a raccoon, pre-emptively dumpster diving as I devour half-eaten ice cream by the mini-spoonful. The creamy gelato is now a candied soup—a delicious one.

Simon was right: I should have gone with sweet over fruity.

My phone dings: a text from Gio.

"Aprile—" oh my God, he even texts my name in Italian *"—here is the information on the cooking school. They have a month-long pasta program."*

The link dares me to click it, its blue underlined text teasing me with potential answers at the tap of a finger. Could it really be that easy? Sign up for a class, learn authentic Italian cooking, and bring my mom's recipes back to life? The temptation to do it—to sign up for the class, to master the art of cooking that Mom did so effortlessly—burns hotter within me. But logistically, I still don't think it's possible to come back to Rome so soon and stay for an entire month.

Gio, oblivious to my time-off-work and tuition concerns, sends a second text, and the bright screen makes the alley seem even darker. *"The school name is CII. The Culinary Institute of Italy. In Eur, southern Rome. They have a pastry program too."*

Then, he sends a third text which includes his email address and what appears to be an enticing offer, but the shock of it leaves me at a loss for words. Could something have been lost in translation? I reread the message three times, but it only puzzles me more. My phone's inability to reply is a blessing in disguise right now because I have no idea what I'd say. At least not until I can get some clarity on what I think he's suggesting.

❧

Heading back to the train station, we fill the streets, our umbrellas bouncing in unison. The carousel in *Piazza della Repubblica* now glows a bright orange, its lights swirling vividly in the shadows of dusk. Our path is illuminated by the lights from inside the stores painting everything with a citrusy glow, Christmas lights twinkling in the night. String hangs above our heads across an open walkway like thick tinsel, shiny round ornaments dangling from it, wet raindrops splattering against them, glistening. Cold, gray rain has never felt so warm.

Simon and I once again sit in a different car from the others. Other than the patter of rain drops on the windows and the chatter of two Italian women sitting across the aisle, it's quiet, the gentle vibration of the locomotive slowly lulling me to sleep.

A bright flash wakes me. "You need a pick-me-up." Simon's holding up his phone, chuckling at my startled reaction to the flash of its camera app.

"Then you better have some tiramisu for me." I feel groggy, every muscle in my body relaxing as the cushioned seat props me up.

"I was actually thinking that we could walk back to Rob and Chuck's car." He runs his hand through his hair while his leg bounces up and down. "We still have an hour."

"When did you become nocturnal?"

His nasal laugh breaks the silence of the car. "I'm a vampire. And I think I'm immune to jet lag."

"You really do travel too much." I sit up straighter, grabbing my phone. "I just need a minute to wake up. And maybe get your opinion on something." I tell him all about the cooking school, how next spring for the entire month of May, Rome's finest culinary masterminds could instill within me a skill I'm severely lacking. A skill that would bring a small part of my mom back to me.

"Have you signed up yet? You should do it!"

"I don't know if it's possible. For one thing, I only get three weeks' vacation. I haven't even looked into the cost yet. And then there's my cat—"

"Excuses, Appleby," he interrupts. "W-W-J-D?" As he stands up, his eyes twinkle as he nods toward the car behind us. "Let's see what everyone else thinks."

"Okay," I say grabbing my bag, "but I can't exactly picture John Fogerty rustling up eggplant *parmigiana*."

He laughs, grabbing on to each seat to steady himself as we walk to the next car. "You know what I mean."

Unbeknownst to us, a raging party has taken on a life of its own in the next car. Music is playing from somewhere— someone's phone?—while plastic cups seem to be affixed to everyone's hands.

"Howdy!" Daphne's eyes light up at the sight of us. "Café car is two cars back."

Simon nods and charges back, retrieving us each a cup of red wine. Just as "Pour Some Sugar on Me" ends, he takes the opportunity to be dee-jay, filling the car with the smooth vocals of Dean Martin. "Time to class this party up." He snaps his fingers to the beat of "Volare."

"To Florence!" He holds up his cup, and we toast merrily. Simon maxes out the volume, but with the surrounding chatter and *chug chug chug* of the train, it's not exactly surround-sound audio. But that doesn't stop us. "Everybody!"

The six of us sing along while Simon holds up his phone. We sway and snap like uncoordinated backup singers. A foursome across the aisle—also from Worldswift—joins in. Simon finishes his wine in record time, abandons the empty cup under the seat, and stands in the aisle. "Volare!" he sings, waving his hands like he's directing an orchestra until more and more people join the chorus. Then another couple adds their harmonies, and another, until nearly the entire car is crooning in unison.

"*Basta*! *Basta*!" Two men storm into the car.

"Wait, I know that word."

Before I can reach for my pocket dictionary, Vicki stops me. "It's security. They want us to stop singing and keep it down." She waves Simon over to come back to his seat.

When the crowd settles a bit, Vicki says something in Italian with an apologetic tone until they're satisfied and leave the car in a much quieter state.

"Well, now that we've landed in hot water with security, I'd say we checked everything off the list." Chuck says, meeting Simon's high five over the accomplishment.

"Not everything." Simon's voice is laced with a playful air.

I cock my head.

"Pull up that text, click that link, and sign up."

At everyone's confused expressions, I explain about Gio's text, the culinary school, and its month-long programs.

Daphne inhales sharply. "You gave Gio your digits? Are y'all a thing?" She stomps her cowgirl boots in excitement.

"What's a Gio?" Chuck asks.

"*Who's* Gio," Daphne clarifies, playfully punching his shoulder. "As in Giovanni. The Trevi Fountain Italian charmer that was attached to April's hip, remember?"

"Okay," I say, holding up a hand, addressing everyone before they can hurl any more questions at me, "I gave him my number only so he could text me the cooking school info."

"That all? The two of you took a little scooter joy ride from what I recall," Daphne says, volunteering some colorful details. "What'd ya call that thingy again?"

"A Vespa." I take a sip of wine, glancing out the window to avoid everyone's staring faces, but the florescent lights from the train reflect back making it impossible to see the landscape blanketed in nightfall.

"Someone's getting a lot more out of this trip than history and Renaissance art," Vicki observes.

"Just information on an Italian cooking course." Right now would be a great time to revive the singalong.

"Something's cookin' alright." Simon's dazzling white teeth sparkle as he laughs. "Okay, enough stalling, April. Pull up that text and sign up." Everyone else unanimously agrees, chanting over and over, "Sign up! Sign up! Sign up!"

"Chill, guys," I plead. "You want security to come back?" After haggling with Simon like he's a used car dealer, I offer a compromise. "I'll sign up—" I stress the following phrase strongly "—only to get more info. How's that?" I connect to the train's wi-fi and tap in my email address once I pull up the school's website. "There. They're going to send me more information. But I'm not registering yet."

"Yet?" Simon raises his brows, "So, you're going."

"She's *so* going. Pooh bear, go back and get us another round." Daphne places her hand on Chuck's chest. "Let's give our little April a proper toast."

✑

To: gregorystorms@wrck.fm

Subject: Hypothetical Question…

In the event that I should one day need you to Tot-sit for, say, an extended period of time… would you be willing to scrub skid marks off my bathroom tile for a month? You can say no. I ask because remember that month-long cooking abroad program in Rome next May? Insanely, I'm considering it. That is, if I can get the time off work and can figure out a way to cover the tuition.

Honestly, it's probably a moot point, so don't feel obligated.

And, yes, it took your family a while to accept who you are, but your parents have come a long way, and they love you. They'd be happy to see that you're actually in a committed relationship this time around—not with some jerk who was using you.

We went to Florence today! As you can see, it's a mecca for art and ice cream!

Here's Gio with the god of wine and pleasure. I think he's trying to tell me something.

In gelato we trust,

April

CHAPTER 22
OIL, FLOUR, AND EGGS, OH MY

To: aprilappleby@wrck.fm

Re: Hypothetical Question…

Whoa, is that the Statue of David or are you just happy to see me?

I'm gaining weight just by looking at all those hilly gelato lumps!

Moot point my ass. You're going! Let's see… hanging with The Queen of Cats for a month, gee, what torture. Of course, I'll Tot-sit! But you better do some potty training with her before then. She's literally pooped outside the box since you left. I think she just laughed at me as I typed that.

Don't you get, like, a month of vacation days? I swear, you take every Friday off to eat your weight in donuts at Lutz's.

As for the cost… what about financial aid? They've got to have some sort of financing option.

I'll consider bringing Harry home to meet my parents, but I need a little more time to get comfortable with the idea.

Okay, now I have a question for you: have you seen Gio naked yet? I'm pretty sure HE'S the god of wine and pleasure.

In litter boxes we trust,

Greg

❧

Maybe it's because I woke up to such a positive response from Greg, or maybe it's the scenic views worthy of a romance film that surround me—grapevines and olive groves set against a tranquil backdrop of rolling green hills—or maybe it's because I've had two glasses of white wine before noon, but I'm feeling downright flirtatious. I have my eye on a handsome guy—a cute ginger, hair as orange as fruit—and I'm armed with liquid courage. Why is Italy filled with so many gorgeous creatures?

I walk toward the olive tree where he's standing, careful not to let the wine knock me off balance. "*Buongiorno!*" I roll my *R* as best I can, trying to impress him. Which is ridiculous. He's surrounded by a crowd of adoring females. He's probably a heartbreaker who feeds on women's attention.

Which I'm more than willing to supply at this rustic winery.

I push my way through the women, ready to make my move. He sashays my way, and I see how young he is. To get his attention I stroke his hair, soft as silk, and our eyes meet. His are two green gemstones, charming their way directly into my soul. Before I can properly introduce myself, the owner of the winery, Alberto, begins talking from farther down the gravel path nestled among the olive trees, greeting us and telling us about where we are. My international flirting will have to wait.

"Welcome to Cantine Santa Benedetta," Alberto shouts with pride, "the oldest winery among the *Castelli Romani* region." It's here atop these gently rolling hills made of volcanic ash that the Benedetti family and their guests have overlooked Rome for the past three hundred years. From the olive groves they produce olive oil. From the vines, grapes, which are then transformed into the delicious wine my friends and I have been sipping since we arrived this morning.

Alberto looks to be in his sixties, with short gray hair thinning on the top of his head. He wears a V-neck sweater the color of fertile soil with brown elbow patches. His rimless glasses are almost unnoticeable underneath his bushy dark eyebrows. It's difficult to understand what he's saying—not so much because of his strong accent, but because my attention keeps drifting to the young, ravishing redhead next to me.

We make eye contact, and I smile at him, glad the other women have switched their focus to Alberto. I stroke his red hair again, and he wags his long tail in appreciation, pouncing atop a short stone fence along the perimeter of the vineyards. That's when I notice two more cats: an elusive gray tabby wandering the grounds, and a fluffy black cat with a luxurious coat of velvet.

My inhibitions might be low enough for me to flirt with an actual human if it weren't for these divine slices of garlicky bruschetta soaking up the booze. The crispy edges crunch loudly as I take another bite. Toasted, crusty bread, olive oil, and a touch of garlic rubbed on top—how simple can it get? And yet, how tasty! Over by the gate, tall and made of old heavy stone weathering away after standing for centuries, stands a man holding a tray of these garlicky treats; it seems to keep replenishing itself no matter how many slices I grab.

So, to recap: I'm at an Italian vineyard drinking all-you-can-drink wine, eating all-you-can-eat bruschetta (with much more food to come), and petting all-you-can-pet cats. Is this Heaven?

It's here among the hills of Italy where we'll be preparing our very own pasta, a task that intimidates me even more than flying over an ocean or spending a week in a country with neither cell service nor adequate knowledge of its native tongue. The estate, the color of marshmallow fluff underneath a roof of curved red shingles, stands behind the patio. Potted plants add pops of green on the rustic gray stones, where we gather for a lesson in Italian cooking. But we American students can't learn without full glasses of wine in hand. A man with dark hair tops off everyone's wine, while Alberto introduces us to our teacher.

Having gone from tipsy to buzzed, I don't catch our teacher's name. Let's call her Mama Pasta. An older woman, Mama Pasta has worked at the winery for forty-five years.

"She is like my sister," Alberto says, melting the hearts of each one of us in the crowd, before quipping, "Make that, my grandmother."

She wears a white apron and a huge white chef's hat obscuring her graying hair. A proud smile beams across her face at the sight of her eager students ready to witness her culinary talents.

On the table before her are a wooden cutting board, two brown eggs nestled on a bed of flour, a bottle of olive oil, and another of wine.

"Only four ingredients?" I look at Simon, skepticism in my eyes. "This shouldn't be so hard."

"Maybe we could get jobs at Olive Garden when we go back home."

It's when the lesson begins that I realize how wrong I was. After nearly a week in a foreign country, I see now how spoiled we've been. Because when Mama Pasta speaks, not a single word of English pops out. This cooking lesson just got a whole lot more challenging. I mean, she's teaching us how to cook: an activity I always manage to fail in English.

Before I can say "*grazie*" to the man who keeps pouring wine into my glass, eggs are cracking, olive oil is glugging, and clouds of flour puff from Mama Pasta's hands.

I send a concerned look to Simon. "We better pay attention."

He shrugs and takes a big swig of wine.

She starts working the dough with a rolling pin, overcome with a love of cooking so deep that she conveys it through song. Mama Pasta is now the star in her very own culinary opera, Italian lyrics spilling from her lungs. Moving as her performance is, the Italian words aren't any easier to comprehend when they're sung—though I don't think we're even trying to understand the pasta-making process anymore. We've begun cheering her on like the crowd at a one-woman show, holding up our wine glasses in a toast to Mama Pasta and her culinary creations.

"*Lasagne!*"

Finally, a word my American brain comprehends. The

newly crafted pasta dangles from her flour-covered fingers. We'd applaud, but we're all holding glasses of wine—which are once again topped off. By the time we've taken a celebratory sip to show her our utmost appreciation, Mama Pasta kneads the dough again, cutting and molding it with fervor like a magician transforming shapeless dough into delicious pasta behind a mysterious cloud of flour.

"Tortellino!" she shouts, her left cheek covered in flour. She folds and twists the dough around her finger, sealing the edges to give an idea what the finished product would look like as Alberto explains they'd normally stuff it with beef or pork. It's almost unhuman how quicky her hands are crafting these delicate creations, some of which look rather intricately constructed, the dough twisting and curving in sinuous patterns.

"I'll just take hers," Simon whispers into my ear.

"We'll be lucky if our pasta is even edible."

She sings again, showing off more fresh pasta that, only moments ago, was a messy pile of flour and egg yolk. We can't keep up with her. *"Fettucini! Tagliatelle! Maltagliati!"* One after another after another.

"Every kind of pasta," Alberto explains, "will have a different sauce. *Maltagliati all'amatriciana* is the pasta you'll be eating today. Tomato, bacon, cheek of the pork, pecorino cheese…"

My mouth waters. It seems we'll be eating like royalty once again on our last full day in Italy. How can we be going home tomorrow? I'm not ready to leave all this behind me. And yet, after almost a week in a foreign country, I can't help missing my cat. Any my best friend. (Don't judge me for listing my cat first. I'm drunk.) It's strange feeling so homesick, yet simultaneously wanting to stay here forever. I may not depart Rome with a sexy Italian love slave chained to me—Gio would never leave his museum behind, would he?—but I'll be damned if I don't bring home some much-needed cooking skills. Especially since there's a fat chance my name will be on the roster of students at CII next spring.

The cellar is cold and dim with rows and rows of bottles of wine and olive oil against a long wall. On the floor are boxes of rolling pins. Two quaint chandeliers hang from the ceiling, and a couple long florescent lights brighten the corners of the room. Large wooden tables fill the space, topped with tiny hills of flour and eggs waiting to be transformed into lunch.

"Over here?" Simon points to a large table in the corner wedged behind two shiny silver fermenters. The six of us claim a station. After I drop my bulging purse down to the floor below the table, I pull my hair back into a messy bun, ready to get my hands dirty. It's chilly in the cellar; everyone leaves our coats on except Daphne.

"I ain't hidin' all this," she says, moving her hands up and down the side of her body like Vanna White showing off a brand-new car. "I bought this outfit special for Italy." Few people can pull off a cougar print blouse; Daphne is one of them.

"I hope you don't get flour all over it. Actually, I hope I don't get flour all over me." My black coat somehow seems even blacker now that there's a pile of white, powdery flour mere inches from it. "Where's a naked David apron when you need one?"

As for Vicki, it's her diamond ring that I'm most concerned about; it's sure to lose its sparkle in a matter of seconds.

I crack my egg on the side of the wooden table, silently sending up an Our Father in hopes it doesn't drip into my purse. I mix the egg with the flour, add a dash of olive oil, and after a couple minutes Alberto comes by to add a glug of wine to my mixture. Ironically, I'd forgotten that step in my inebriated state. Why on earth am I fantasizing about doing this for an entire month? I'd likely suffocate in flour. Already feeling flustered, I glance over at Simon to see if he's faring any better. His eggs are spilling out all over the table in goopy globs, like an erupting, edible Mount Vesuvius.

When Mama Pasta manifests in the entryway of the cellar, our spirits are lifted. Her apron is covered in flour, and her face is all smiles. She belts out an Italian song at a volume loud enough for the Pope to hear, hands gesticulating wildly in the air, like she's performing a pasta aria. It's anyone's guess what she's saying, but I'd like to think she's encouraging us to dive into our flour mounds wholeheartedly, that she's proud of how far we've come since witnessing her demonstration mere moments ago. The warmth and love emanating from this woman are as strong as the fresh *vino* boiling inside the fermenters next to us. Her spirit is grandmotherly, and I feel a sense of connection with everyone gathered in the cellar cooking together. I turn back to my dough, kneading it with a renewed vigor, delighting in its cold softness squeezing between my fingers. Who knew getting one's hands dirty with flour and eggs could be so liberating?

Mama Pasta starts for our table with an excited look on her face.

"Oh my God, she's coming our way," Simon says, his eyes

sparkling with anticipation. He stops mixing immediately as if star struck, hands held out in front of him dripping egg yolk on the table.

Before you can say "*ciao bella*" she grabs some dry flour from our table and playfully slaps Vicki's cheek while exclaiming something in Italian. Flour flies everywhere, leaving a layer of white dust on anything within a few feet. Note to self: black attire does not mix with pasta-making. Rob brushes away the dusty remnants from his coat, squeezing himself in between the two fermenters until he's out of reach of Mama Pasta's floured hands. Vicki's smile stretches out on her face, the entire left side of which is now covered in flour. She grabs her phone, leaving white finger prints all over it, and snaps a selfie with Mama Pasta. I want her to flour me next, hoping in her powdered smack she'd infuse all her culinary knowledge into me, but just as soon as she arrived at Vicki's side, she scampers off to another table to make her mark on her next unsuspecting victim, like an Italian flour fairy.

Which means it's all up to me. My mom's gone, and so is Mama Pasta. I need to prove to myself that I can do this.

Rolling pins are handed out: it's time to flatten the dough. This should be easy.

Right?

Chuck, struggling to smooth his dough, makes a perceptive observation. "Mine looks like a butt," he says, perplexed. He scrunches up his face, lines crinkling on his forehead.

We peer over, and sure enough, it does, in fact, look like somebody's pasty rear end. Two round cheeks of dough smile up at us with a thin crack down the middle. Not exactly the perfect circle Mama Pasta rolled out twenty minutes ago.

"Don't feel bad," Simon observes, "April's looks like when

all the countries were together before they broke apart." His laugh echoes off the fermenters.

"You're not wrong," I concede, leaving floured finger prints on my lenses as I push my glasses up my nose. "Mine is barely staying together." In my confidence wielding a rolling pin, I've flattened the dough too much, rendering it thin, brittle, and ragged on the edges. I'm unable to navigate with any of the maps in my purse, yet somehow, I've managed to blend cartography with the culinary arts. Maybe I'm not cut out for this. It would be crazy for someone like me to try to master the art of pasta-making for four straight weeks. It was crazy to even dream about it. Enrolling as a culinary student in a place known for its food? Who do I think I am?

As if sensing my self-doubt, Simon puts a positive spin on it. "It's abstract art!"

When we finish slicing off strings of pasta, they're all collected in one giant tray.

"That wasn't so bad," Daphne says, clapping her floury hands together. "I'm fixin' to make some pasta when we get back to Myrtle Beach."

"You'll be scrubbin' those counters 'til the cows come home." Chuck holds out two fists full of dried flour clumps as visual aids to the guaranteed mess that their kitchen will endure.

Daphne places each of her palms around his messy fists and kisses him on the lips. "I reckon you and the kiddos will help me."

⁂

Turning four simple ingredients into pasta wasn't as easy as it ought to be, but I got through it. But it's when a tray of additional ingredients is presented to us that my intimidation for cooking escalates into emotional warfare. Basil, garlic, olive oil, parmesan cheese, and pine nuts.

Pesto sauce.

My mom and I noshing on a plate of pesto cavatappi at Noodles and Company before I went off to college. Before my life completely flipped upside down. The memory is so vivid it could have happened yesterday.

"What do we get if we win?" Simon asks with one brow raised, his hands now clump-free after rubbing them with a handful of dry flour.

I pat him on the back leaving a handprint. "Tough to say, Becks. Probably more free wine. Maybe one of the cats."

Before you know it, Vicki and Rob are slicing and dicing garlic and pine nuts. Simon starts mashing in some basil while I mix in a bit of parmesan cheese and olive oil. The aroma is intoxicating. Chuck dollops the thick green sauce on top of some pasta, delicately stacked by Daphne like Jenga blocks.

"It's all about presentation, y'all."

More sauce is smeared on the plate in the fashion of a Michelin-starred restaurant.

Simon admires our finished product for a moment, rotating the plate slowly as if ensuring it looks perfect. "This would totally be good enough for Olive Garden."

"That's it." I reach for the bottle of wine we used in our pasta. "This is now a drinking game. Every time you make an Olive Garden joke, everyone takes a drink."

"Good Lord," Chuck says, "we'll need rehab before dinner!"

But we all abide by the rules. "*Salute!*"

The panel of judges is impressed with our table's creation. After tasting all the dishes, Alberto declares two winners: our table wins for presentation, and the table next to ours wins for flavor. While we might not have won the higher honor, I still feel the warmth from a flicker of hope inside me. Runner-up isn't anything to sneeze at.

The winners begin to sing Queen's "We Are the Champions," waving their flour-covered hands in the air in celebration.

"Is anybody gonna eat that?" I point to our second-prize dish. "Seems like a waste not to." Will it taste as sweet as that bright spark of a memory?

Rob slides the Frisbee of flavor across the wooden table to me. It's a bit thick and heavy on the garlic, but it's delicious nonetheless. Needs more oil to thin it out. Before I can play a verse on air guitar, it hits me that I didn't hesitate to think of how to improve the recipe. On a whim. Just like that. Intuition. The flicker of hope burns brighter.

I drizzle some oil over the pasta. "No one else wants to try our winning dish? We got the silver medal, after all." I push the plate toward the center of the table. "It's actually not bad."

Everyone else digs in, exchanging their own pleasantly surprised reactions.

"So, this is pesto, huh? This right here is a first for me," Chuck says, stabbing a second forkful. "Ain't too shabby."

"Like you have somethin' to compare it to," Daphne teases.

"Pesto is absolutely divine," Vicki gushes. "And that *basil*. Oh my *God*."

Simon holds out his hands palms up. "No one's gonna pat me on the back for my excellent smashing technique? Rob, do I smash basil as well as I rent trucks?"

"Best smasher this side of the Atlantic."

I stab some more pasta, eating slower than perhaps, well, ever. To enjoy a meal together, as one group sharing in the sensory pleasures of food—that's the key ingredient. I see that so clearly now. Would these flavors blend as perfectly without Simon's Olive Garden jokes? Would the aroma smell as appealing without Daphne and Chuck dabbing sauce off each other's faces? Would we appreciate the creamy texture had we not been the ones to prepare it? It's people—and the care and time they put into their preparations—who supply the essence of a good meal.

For a moment, I flash back to that Noodles and Company, sitting at a table across from my mother, the both of us delighting in a plate of pesto cavatappi, our forks tap dancing on the plate. The memory is as vivid as the flavors on my tongue, coming alive amidst a freshly prepared meal. Garlic, pine nuts, basil, olive oil, and parmesan on their own: simply a list of ingredients. But when strategically combined, they form an elixir powerful enough to revive a cherished time in my past. Gio was right: Italian food can be quite magical indeed.

CHAPTER 23

BUON APPETITO

"R‍AISE YOUR GLASS."

Alberto, the winery's owner, is standing in the center of the dining hall holding a glass of the white wine we've been enjoying all morning. His dark sweater now has a white hand print on the front—not even he is safe from Mama Pasta's flour attacks. He begins to make an impassioned toast; between his accent and my current blood alcohol level, most of it is going over my head.

Simon is sitting next to me. I look over at him, each of us holding up a brimming glass, and say, "We've gotten pretty good at this." He nods proudly in agreement. After nearly a week in a country known for, among other things, its wine, we have indeed gotten pretty good at this.

The dining room is adorned with framed pictures of lush landscapes, animals, and people—perhaps ancestors of the Benedetti family. Orange flames dance in the fireplace, crackling. The walls boast tapestries, olive-green drapes, copper pots and pans, and mirrors hugged by gold frames. The ceiling is painted with flowers and birds, and quaint chandeliers dangle over the tables, giving the room an enchanting luminescence.

Alberto's toast lasts several minutes. On more than one occasion I lift my glass to my lips after a pregnant pause in his toast.

"Is he done?" I whisper out of the corner of my mouth.

"Not sure…" Simon says, looking around to see if anyone else is drinking yet.

"I can't wait any longer," Daphne chimes in.

"I'm parched." Vicki grabs her glass.

We tip back our glasses, and the flavors of blackberries and pineapple with gentle floral undertones hit our taste buds. But we're premature; Alberto continues. And let's just say, there really is no elegant or inconspicuous way of depositing our wine back into our glasses. Believe me, we try, and turn more than a few heads while doing so.

"He's killin' me," Chuck huffs, wiping his mouth with a napkin.

Finally, the moment is upon us. "*Salute!*" everyone rejoices, our glasses clinking like windchimes in an autumn breeze.

Wine has been a constant during this trip, but only now, here among the green, rolling Italian vineyards, do I feel like I can officially—properly—check off wine from my list. I've gone from guzzling to sipping, sipping to tasting, and finally understanding. Promise to self: I will never drink wine from a mug again.

❧

On my plate sits buffalo mozzarella the size of a softball. Next to it, a tiny halved cherry tomato on a dollop of pesto. Leafy greens and a few artichokes fill out the rest of the plate.

Chuck wastes no time slicing into his cheese. It squirts him as his knife spears it, landing on his brown and tan plaid shirt. He looks up to see if anyone noticed.

"That's how you know it's fresh," I tease him.

Daphne giggles, reaching for her wine glass. "I'll drink to that."

Next to our table is the door, wafting in cool air from the outside as the staff rushes in and out carrying bottles of wine and trays of cheese and bread. Across from me, Vicki wraps a scarf the color of espresso around her neck, while Simon zips up his puffy black coat. But to me, the breeze feels refreshing after hours of wine consumption, my face warm and flushed.

"*This* is Italy," Simon declares, picking up his wine glass. Every inch of our table is covered in enough wine and food to be a royal feast. To start our meal: roasted potatoes, broccoli, and a dozen types of cheeses. We start with the familiar first: fresh chunks of pale, crumbly parmesan. Rounding out the spread are oranges fresh off the tree, adorning our table like little golden suns orbiting our plates. Edible, yes. But so pretty that Simon jokes they're only for decoration.

"Ohmigod, *amici, Order Up* is about to break new ground with this place." The buffalo mozzarella is divine as I sample another taste. "I mean, I know this place isn't technically a restaurant—" I pause to let the flavors of the wine compliment the mozzarella "—but based on the cheese alone I'd award this place the entire apple orchard."

⊷

"How did you end up with two?!" Simon peers across the table at Rob, who has somehow been lucky enough to have been served not one, but two bowls of eggplant *parmigiana*.

"Chuck stole half my caprese salad the other day," he retorts, "and you are leaving me for Nationals. I'd say I earned it."

With this course of the meal, we've now moved into red wine territory. The staff brings a bottle of *Tre Vecchie* to our table, a cabernet sauvignon. It's not long before a few of us give the universal sign that our tummies are nearing full capacity: the satisfied sigh. I take a couple more bites, but storage space is running dangerously low. And to top it all off—literally—the wine keeps flowing.

"More red, *signore*," Simon says.

"Someone's accent is getting stronger," I say, "but you still can't roll your R's if your life depended on it."

Our glasses are already brimming, thanks to Vicki, who is clearly not ready to go back to mom life. But the staff brings us several more bottles anyway. I mean, it's a winery—plenty to go around.

Next up is the pasta that we ourselves prepared. One of the first things I notice is that the pasta itself is inconsistent in size, shape, and thickness. Normally, I'd peg that for a sign that we can still learn a thing or two from Mama Pasta. But Alberto explained earlier that *maltagliati* means "poorly cut;" it's supposed to be inconsistent in size. We succeeded at being imperfect. Perhaps that's the key to conquering cooking. Not being afraid of the imperfections. To improvise the recipe and delight in its surprises.

I take my fork for another spin. "You know, we're not half bad at this. *I'm* not half bad."

The head table is adorned with a huge pork roast that looks ceremonial in its arrangement. The men in our group walk over to take a photo of the spread, complete with a tray of cured meats, rustic bread, and a whole pig. Am I, a carnivore, hypocritical for not sharing in their awe of the pork? I'll admit, it's a sight to behold paired with an enticing aroma, but it feels barbaric no matter how delicious it promises to be. Maybe Americans, with our love of convenient pre-packaged meals, are too far removed from the food chain. In any event, I'm beginning to feel extremely full, and, as Simon comes back to the table, I say something that nearly causes my old pal to question our friendship altogether.

"I might skip the pork."

"Skip the pork?!" he says, appalled, wasting no time to guilt me that I'll not only disappoint him, but also the pig. "At least take some prosciutto." Ensuring he's persuaded me, he adds, "It's like royal bacon."

As soon as we stand up to get in line, my head feels woozy enough to nearly knock me off my feet. I steady myself by holding the back of my chair, take a deep breath, and follow the others toward Wilbur; it's probably a good idea to get as much food in me as possible to absorb the endless stream of wine pouring down my throat. Even if it is a cute farm animal.

Under normal circumstances, dessert wine makes me deliriously happy. After all, it's alcohol that tastes like cake. But instead of wiggling with glee after being poured a glass of sweet wine the color of champagne, my stomach sinks. The end of this glorious meal is near. Do we really have to leave?

"I need a breather," I announce to the table, my words slurring. I'm unsteady on my feet, my head dizzy.

"Do you really need *both* those glasses?" Simon gestures first to the dessert wine in my right hand, then the red wine in my left.

I take sip of the cabernet. "It's for research."

The cool air hits my cheeks, and I stop by a stack of barrels beneath the trees whose leaves have been dyed red and orange by the autumn sun. I let my hair down, my locks warm against my neck. I try not to stumble down the gravel path amongst the olive trees, taking in the view of the expansive and peaceful vineyards. Is this what Gio's family vineyard looks like? Why wonder about it when I could ask him?

I set down my wine glasses, tilting precariously on an uneven rustic stone, and sit down on the ground. Once I have my bedroom eyes and come-hither smirk on my face, I tilt my head to just the right angle and lift my phone up. Right as I snap the photo, The Gray One walks into the shot, perched atop moss-covered stone in the garden, emerald green stems dotted with tiny pink flowers surrounding the frame. That's Instagram-worthy. Soon, The Black One approaches, sitting off to the side doing what cats do best: passing judgment.

I draft a text which I will later send as an email. *"These vineyards are almost as charming as you. ALMOST. You know so much about the god of pleasure, but can you make my kitty purrrr? Inquiring felines want to know."* As first drafts go, it's not terr—okay, it's terrible. But it's only a first draft. I'm sure the final email I send to Gio once we return to the hotel will be irresistibly flirtatious, not at all embarrassing, and might actually include a thoughtful inquiry about his family's vineyard.

My phone rings. Does he know I'm thinking about him? Butterflies immediately start doing laps. But then they turn into moths when I read the caller ID. Unfortunately, in my inebriated state, I'm all too willing to answer even though the wrong guy is calling.

"Ian! What a coinkydink that you'd call when I can finally answer. You're not gonna believe where I am. The Bedinitta—the Bondinighty—I'm at a winery! With cats!"

"Pardon? April? You're cutting in and out. Are you all right? My attempts to reach you for weeks have failed. I have extraordinary news to share!"

"Oh? Should I turn on CNN?" I laugh at my clever hilarity. "You shoulda gone into broadcasting with me if you're reporting the news. Hang on a sec." I prop up my knee like Captain Morgan, managing to push myself back up to my feet, causing the blood to rush straight to the place of my brain that encourages me to say things that make people uncomfortable. "Ian. What happened to us? We were such a great team. I miss your face."

"Beg your pardon? You're breaking up. Are you alright? You sound—"

I wait to find out what I sound like. "Well?"

My screen tells me that the call died. In vain, I call back. Texting him is just as fruitless. Waiting to connect to the hotel wi-fi seems like the best solution; tracking down the winery's wi-fi password would be mission impossible in my current state.

The Gray One distracts me by jumping up on a stone

fence, rows of vineyards stretching out behind her, pine trees in the distance.

"I'm gonna call you Mambo," I declare proudly. "Mambo Italiano." While singing and dancing, I pet the cat, her warm fur comforting in the cool air, which blows the clipped conversation with Ian over the hills and far away.

⬦

Before we board the bus, Simon and I stand before the vineyards, a sea of green stretching out for acres, the grass on the hilly waves rippling in the wind. I clumsily clasp my fingers around the stems of my two wine glasses, wrapping my free arm around Simon. He responds in kind.

As we take in another eyeful of the vines and olive groves, I adjust my purse on my shoulder, now even heavier after I embraced my inner kleptomaniac—I wasn't quite ready to say "*arrivederci*." So, I palmed the biggest oranges from the table, frantically tossing them in my bag as a parting gift. Then, fistfuls of wine corks, lobbing them in like balls of confetti. Tragic that my bag isn't a skosh bigger to accommodate a cat or two.

While we take in the view, Simon extends his free arm gesturing to the green hills, holding up his red wine as if in a toast.

Here's to friendships: the old ones that feel comfortable and nostalgic, and the new ones that are exciting in their limitless possibilities. Here's to good food and its power to corral people together around a table. Here's to the meals and memories borne of family recipes. Here's to seeing the world; visiting places so different from our own that they alter our perceptions of life. Here's to being connected to humanity through layers of history that run centuries deep. Here's to drinking wine before noon, wet mozzarella, olive oil as thick as maple syrup, sugar dissolving in dark espresso, and fresh citrus. Here's to grabbing life by the flour, getting your hands dirty, and letting raw egg run down your fingers. Here's to parmesan so flavorful it doesn't need to be sprinkled on something to be enjoyed. Here's to tiny cars and fast scooters. Here's to meeting a part of yourself that you didn't know existed. Here's to Rome.

❧

> ***Cantine Santa Benedetta:*** Four apples so shiny you can see yourself in them, plus an orange for absolutely ruining all future meals for me.

> **Taste:** From the moment the meal began, we were treated to an array of cheeses and veggies that took their job of warming up our taste buds quite seriously. Then, the eggplant *parmigiana*, coupled with a cabernet sauvignon. From the wine's fruity flavors, cherry was the most vivid, and it paired beautifully with the eggplant, mine covered under some extra sprinkles of parmesan that dissolved into the warm red sauce. Next, our own *maltagliati*, its red sauce surprisingly salty, was served with the valuable lesson that achieving goals really is possible, no matter how out of reach they may seem. Our cooking was not only up to snuff, but the savory taste was a

delightful change in flavors. When we arrived at the main course, the meal was off the charts. The pork roast was tender enough to melt in my mouth, savory without being salty, with a hint of subtle sweetness. It was the best pork I've ever had the pleasure of eating—including crispy bacon. The prosciutto was next, dark maroon in color, almost purple, and as soft as flesh. The flavor was savory, yet mild. Slightly chewy, but also delicately tender. And for dessert: three divine cream puffs, soft and airy like the cloud of an angel, with melted chocolate cascading down the sides and eggnog-colored cream dolloped in the centers. *Delizioso.* One oversized apple that keeps giving and giving.

Service: Bottomless wine, too many courses to count, and the passion of Mama Pasta infusing each course on which we dined. One *bellissima* apple.

Atmosphere: I don't know if I'll ever be lucky enough to experience an afternoon at an Italian family winery again, but if not, the image of Italy's grassy countryside spreading out all around me as my feet were anchored on rustic stones, the vines and trees standing with me, will be one forever etched in my memory. One pinch-me-am-I-dreaming? apple.

Price: No amount of euros can buy the feeling this place gave me. One apple, the one with the sweet aftertaste that leaves you licking your lips long after the last slice is gone.

CHAPTER 24

OLD FLAMES (REPRISE)

"How many girlfriends ya got?" The words fly out of my mouth unfiltered as we walk into our hotel room. I feel that I have a right to know about my fake husband's love life.

If Simon is taken off guard, he doesn't show it. Instantly, he quips, "I've got one in every state." He kicks off his shoes and plops down on the bed. "Why? You want a piece of this?" He thumbs his nipples in circles through his shirt.

"We already had this talk. But, if I may be so superficial," I say, tripping over my own shoelace on the way to my bed, "you're loaded and a dog dad. That's the total package."

Simon cues up "Volare" from his phone. "Why thank you, but the amount of travel I do… It makes relationships kind of hard. And shouldn't you save your flirty comments for Gio?"

"That reminds me…" I connect to the wi-fi and copy the email address Gio texted me, pasting it into the recipient field of a new email. I attach my vineyard selfie and boldly go with the first draft saved in a text, adding on a whim: "*Want to come by the hotel tonight? Dinner and dancing. You can crash the party.*" Let's hope that lands in the correct inbox.

Turning back to Simon, I shrug. "Gio lives in Italy. I mean, I'm having a blast with him right now, but what happens when there's an ocean between us again?"

"What about Ian? Seems like you've been doing an awful lot of talking about him lately."

Ian! I open the call history on my phone and am quickly reminded of our unsuccessful conversation. A fuzzy echo of what he said rings in my mind. Something about news. It's the text notification that clears things up a bit. After our truncated phone call, he sent a text.

"April, you seem very unlike yourself. I'm quite worried about you. Call me back. I have something to tell you."

Not even my wine fog can shake the bad feeling in the pit of my stomach. I fill Simon in.

"Sounds important." His eyes go big like they did when our English teacher gave us pop quizzes.

"Yes, but I'm not getting back-together vibes. He's kinda freaking me out."

"Do you wish he was giving you back-together vibes?"

Unable to untangle the many strings of emotions swaying inside me, I don't respond. Simon stops the music and burrows under the covers, breaking his "no nap" rule one more time.

If I'm going to face my ex and his news, I'll need fuel. I dump out the contents of my purse onto the bed, and three huge oranges tumble out. I start peeling the biggest one, leaving the scraps on the bedspread. The only sounds in the room are Simon's heavy breathing and the tearing of the fruit's flesh. The citrus fragrance fills the stale hotel air. I push apart the slices with my fingers, letting the juice drip down my hands, and start devouring them one by one. It's fair to assume that, in addition to Mama Pasta's flour attacks, she's also responsible for sprinkling flavor dust on the citrus groves of the Benedetti family winery because these suckers are as sweet as Mother Teresa. And juicy enough to fill a whole glass.

I lie back against the pillows, brushing away bits of pulp. As I open my social media app, I tell myself that I'm being courteous. Can't have Ian worrying about me on the other side of the globe.

"In Rome. Phone doesn't work here. Can't even check voice-mail. Will call you next week when I'm back."

There. Whenever he sees my message, he'll know that I'm fine, and that we'll talk in a few days. But before I can even close the app, I see three blue bubbles pop up indicating that Ian is already responding.

"In Rome? How unexpected."

I instantly regret opening the lines of communication. I'm sitting here on plush gold-stitched five-star comfort devouring oranges, and I'm choosing to let my ex crash my European bubble of bliss? Why am I not G-chatting with the attractive Italian guy whose lips felt perfect against mine?

"Pray tell, what brought you to the eternal city?"

That one's easy. I send a gif of a plate of sparkling spaghetti.

Wait, what am I doing? Engaging in this conversation will only extend the time it takes to reach its finish line. I steer my messages back on track, asking him if everything's okay—four days in a row of calling an ex raises a few red flags.

"Things couldn't be better actually," he types. *"I have some news."*

Why does learning of his good news make me feel like I'm about to receive bad news? I desperately want to put this conversation off until I return home, but now that we're in the middle of it, I don't see how I can delay this any longer.

"Oh?"

I pop another orange wedge into my mouth, bracing myself for his news, but no amount of pilfered citrus could prepare me for:

"I was hoping to tell you over the phone, but I suppose there's no time like the present! I'm getting married."

A pile of half-chewed orange flesh sits on my tongue, as I forget how to swallow, and my world drops out from below me. I re-read the last word. Married?

Time passes. Seconds? Minutes? The quiet in the room is suddenly deafening, and I feel trapped with nowhere to go. More blue bubbles pop up. Is he going to tell me the name of the person who replaced me as the woman he'll take a vow for?

"Apologies if this comes as a shock, but I didn't want you to be blindsided when you received the invitation. I'd love it if you could be in attendance. With a guest of course."

The jet lag, wine, and surprise of his news all take what should be a simple "congratulations" and turn it into the message of someone who is trying way too hard to play it cool: I send a gif of a cat dressed up as a pirate.

Okay, that might not fully convey my congratulatory wishes. I offer an explanation for my odd response, which I hope will double as a hint that I really can't talk right now:

"Sorry… I'm so wasted! Spent the day at a vineyard. Gotta sober up for dinner, dude."

I hope he takes the hint that I need to get ready. Can

we end this unexpected, geographically distant, emotionally unbalanced, half drunken conversation? Not yet.

"Who's accompanying you?"

I look over at Simon, lightly snoring in the bed next to mine, oblivious to my current state of poor judgment. I could keep our fib alive and say that I'm in Rome with my new husband who has zero percent body fat, and make him all kinds of jealous.

Who am I kidding? Ian has found the woman he wants to spend the rest of his life with; he wouldn't be jealous. The fact that I'm even pondering ways to make him envious doesn't make me proud.

But I'm human. A single human who's had nothing but disastrous relationships ever since Ian and I broke off our engagement. I know it shouldn't matter, but I'll feel pathetic admitting I'm here with just a friend, especially now that he's found The One.

"Simon. You might remember that name… I think I mentioned him to you in college."

"Yes, of course! I was unaware that you two rekindled your friendship. Or perhaps it's grown into something more?"

I am now freefalling headfirst into the rabbit hole. My ex-fiancé is asking if I'm dating my fake husband. My head hurts. Tell him the truth, and I admit I'm a lonely spinster; insinuate that there's more to my relationship with Simon than there actually is, and I lose respect for myself for being so insecure and dishonest. Disgusted with both options, I shut off the screen and toss my phone on the bed while thinking up a response that won't make me seem as pitiful as I feel.

I could blame the wine, the shock, or even my exhaustion from being single, but the truth is that my ego is bruised and ready to fight back. Its intentions are honorable though: trying to shield me from humiliation. What better way to do that than by spinning a deceitful web of a romantic Roman rendezvous, a tale of international lustful passion?

"We got married. We're on our honeymoon."

The second I hit "send," I'm swallowed up by a murky pool of regret. Shame. What am I doing? Why did I open this can of worms? He's going to have more questions. Why is the Internet in this hotel so goddamn reliable? Quick! I need an enticing distraction:

"Stole oranges from the vineyard. So fresh."

My attempt to divert my ex with tales of my vitamin C thievery fall flat. The bubbles start blinking on my screen again. In a panic I close the app, bailing out of this conversation that I've lost all control over. I know what's coming next, and I don't want to be here for it. The notification bar at the top of my phone lets me know that Ian has sent his response. I should ignore it—I'm on vacation. But three dings get the better of my morbid curiosity, and I open the app again.

"You got married?? Wow… I had no idea you and Simon were even courting. My heartfelt congratulations!

"I know you're probably well-occupied right now, and I'd never want to impose on your honeymoon, but I found some of your things, and put them in a box for you.

"Let me know when you return, and I'll happily drop them off. Have a lovely time in Rome, April."

Well, I *was.*

Now he wants to give me my stuff back. A gesture filled with so much finality that I might as well kiss goodbye any remnants of friendship we might have still had. I click off the screen, and a face lined with disappointment stares back at me. It's the face of a fool who feels the sudden severing of another relationship. It's the face of someone who should've just taken a damn nap.

CHAPTER 25

A NIGHT AT THE OPERA

HAVE YOU EVER walked past a mirror and thought, for a second, that your reflection was someone else? An attractive couple looks back at me through the glass, she in blue heels and a dress of dusty-rose flowers; he in a navy-blue jacket, white button-up, and khakis. It's almost like looking at a home movie of me and Simon from fifteen years ago, all dressed up and heading off to our senior prom, where we swapped dates, the two of us tearing up the dance floor in all of our awkward youthful glory. Is this some sort of funhouse mirror showing what used to be? Or perhaps it shows what other people perceive: a married couple headed for a fancy dinner. What the mirror can't show is how good my non-husband smells after spritzing himself with cologne after his second shower of the day, which was, of course, once again to the tune of Dean Martin's greatest hits.

The ballroom's transformation from breakfast-buffet warmth to glitzy five-star dining hall is stunning. The tables are covered in apple-red cloths, the chandeliers seem to twinkle brighter as they dangle from the gilded ceiling, and fiery red lights are cast against the walls, highlighting the room's marble columns. At the door, a man greets us with a tray of bubbly. "Champagne?"

Well, I *almost* reached sobriety today.

"*Sí, grazie.*" The drink fizzles on my tongue, a sensation I've become quite accustomed to this week. Simon passes on the champagne, and instead, heads over to the bar to order something a little harder: an old-fashioned. While Chuck keeps him occupied at the bar, I snatch my phone and open the reply Gio just emailed me.

"*There is only one way to find out, cara. I can come to hotel after work at the pizzeria tonight. I give you the dance of your life. Yes?*"

Okay, these butterflies are now doing an Olympic-style gymnastics floor routine in there. I type out a hurried "*yes*" and hit send while my heart is pounding out of my chest. Is he really going to show up?

Daphne is sitting at a table in the corner, her only companion a cell phone with which she appears quite miffed. She's wearing a stylish and uncharacteristically simple black dress with a ribbon of white flowers across one shoulder.

"Hey, Daph, mind if I join you?" I'm in the seat next to her before she answers, my hors d'oeuvres wafting a tantalizing aroma.

Her face transforms into a smile at the sight of me. "Hey, darlin'. Chuck isn't lookin' for me, is he? Our lawyer's supposed to call back any second, and I ain't missin' the call again. Told him to call *my* phone this time. Chuck'll never answer if he calls in the middle of dinner—thinks it's too rude."

"I think he's at the bar. Can I ask what 'trust' is all about?" I point to the word in ink on her wrist.

She takes a sip of wine. "Got this a year after I started seein' Chuck. He's everything, that one. One of the few men in my life who haven't broken it."

"Your life?"

"My trust." She sets down her phone and sighs. "My relationships haven't always been this rosy. Was with a guy for a long time—eight years—controlled my every move, my thoughts, everything. Just when I thought I'd get a family of my own, he made sure that wouldn't happen." She taps her phone, checking to make sure she didn't miss a call in the last ten seconds. "Tell ya, if this decree is denied because of a procedure I didn't even want to happen, I don't know what I'll do."

A moment passes, and the lighting changes color to an electric blue. "Oh, Daph. I'm so sorry. You must be going crazy waiting. But if I may quote the wise and enlightened Bob Marley: every little thing is gonna be alright."

She throws her head back in a cackle. "Hon, you sound like Chuck!" She takes a deep breath, her pearly smile stretching across her face.

"I thought my ears were burnin'," Chuck pulls up a chair next to Daphne, setting down a glass of wine. "You ladies gabbin' about me?"

"All good things," I reassure him.

The rest of the group finds us and sits down. Rob, looking dashing in a black suit and red tie, approves of our table's unobtrusive location. "It's like we're in a time-out over here. Perfect for Rentals—we get rowdy." He holds up the drink in his hand as proof. So far, our rowdy rap sheet consists of

Simon swallowing a lily, Rob shattering a wine glass, and Vicki smuggling a bottle of wine back to the hotel. And let's not forget my own contribution to the list of shame: my drunken Bellini-fueled outburst. The opportunities to add to that highlight reel are endless here in the shadowy corner of the ballroom.

The menu promises another never-ending parade of delights, most of which I can't pronounce. The wait staff, looking dapper in their suits and bowties, makes their rounds to the tables with the first dish: crab salads. We're presented with bowls of leafy greens, olives, and yellow and red cherry tomatoes topped with crab meat. But it's the U-shaped corn waffle resting atop each dish that puzzles us.

Simon studies the shell in his hands. "I think they confused crab salad with taco salad." Amused, he sets it back down on the bed of greens. "They're *Americans*," he continues, playfully mocking how the chefs must have dreamed up the first course, "Americans *love* taco salads!"

"Damn right, we do," I say. "I make mine with Doritos. And they're nothing short of amazing."

"Are we supposed to fill it?" Rob asks.

"Of course, you fill the shell," says Vicki as she adjusts the big pink statement necklace dangling around her neck.

"But then it's a taco. Not a salad."

I don't possess the ability to eat tacos neatly, so I have alternate plans. I crunch the shell into bits, mixing them up among the greens. "The last thing I need is a lap full of crab meat. Major party foul. And the color would totally clash with my dress." That wouldn't be a good look when Gio gets here. *If* he gets here. He's probably messing with me. I'm just some clumsy American tourist.

"I like that idea," says Chuck, nodding approvingly. "Break it up into chips. All we need now is some *queso*."

"Wrong country, hon'."

Further courses prove to be less confusing, or maybe the wine that Vicki keeps pouring for us is kicking in. Beef and prawns with rosemary potatoes: so soft they crumble at the touch of my fork. Pumpkin ricotta almond timbale: an enchanting flavor combination I've never before experienced. With each bite, my stomach expands like a sped-up pregnancy—I hope those timbales don't start kicking. The meal is capped off with espresso, pie, and petit fours.

I lean back in my chair, discreetly glancing at the door as if that will make it open. What, is that thing bolted shut or something? I shake my head, trying not to let my frustration get to me. "Those five-mile runs along the lake will be a challenge when I get home."

"What my gym doesn't know won't hurt it." Simon gestures to the many plates on the table, the odd crumb here and there the only bits that survived such a scrumptious dinner.

"I'll be rolling my way along the lake like a chubby tumbleweed."

"I'll take naps on the bench press."

Napping is the last thing on our minds as four women now stride into the ballroom, each holding a wireless microphone. Their hair is dark as espresso; their lips painted to match their sparkling, strawberry-red, backless gowns with dangerously low plunging necklines. The vibe in the room goes theatrical when the lights melt into a burnt orange.

Pizzicato strings pluck out the bass line of "Habanera" from the French opera *Carmen*, each singer taking a turn with a vocal solo, sauntering to different tables to mesmerize the audience with their impeccable voices. When they sing the famous refrain, Simon looks to me, mimes the French lyrics, and exaggerates his face to make it look like he's belting out his own opera. The next number is just as incredible, singing in four-part harmonies. Their voices, like echoes of angels, hypnotize us, their grand performance being captured on tiny phone screens throughout the ballroom.

"I was hoping for a Journey cover band," Simon quips over the cheering of the crowd as another song ends. Seconds later he shouts, *"Bravissimo! Bravissimo!"*

It's when the women launch into a tune straight from Simon's shower playlist that enjoying the show while seated is no longer an option.

"That's what I'm talkin' about!" Simon exclaims at the first note of "Mambo Italiano," his eyes alive with sparkles. "Let's stand." He pushes back his chair, and I follow him to the back wall, glad to burn a few calories. Our feet tap to the beat of a song finally getting proper acoustics after hearing it from his cell phone speakers all week. The catchy lyrics fill the air, invigorating the ballroom with the energy of live music.

The women circle the room as if they're on the prowl. With each hip swivel, their dresses shimmer under the ballroom's vivid lights, reflecting the flashes from photos being taken. Just when I think our dance party for two will double at the sight of Chuck and Daphne jumping out of their seats, the newlyweds run out of the ballroom, a phone pressed to Daphne's cheek.

The lights flash from blue to purple and back again, and Simon and I dance like we're at our own personal nightclub. My bones vibrate with the notes blaring out of the speakers, my body channeling the melody as the women's gorgeous

voices send a wave of goosebumps down my arms. The slug-
gish buzz from all the wine, the dry eyes from inadequate
sleep, the heavy gut filled with fine cuisine—all forgotten.
We just… dance.

I cheer as loudly as if I were at a rock show, shouting at
the top of my lungs the battle cry of an enthusiastic con-
cert-goer: "Woo!"

Who *am* I? This is opera, not Aerosmith.

But I'm not alone here in operamania. When the quartet
sings ABBA's "Dancing Queen," the crowd's energy explodes
to near ear-splitting levels. Every foot taps in unison, every
pair of hands claps in synchronicity, and every set of vocal
chords vibrates. We are one big choir.

Not even bench-pressing, protein-eating Simon is
immune to getting swept up in the moment. He grins goofily
at me, dancing and singing in his nasal voice. We're all under
the spell of this performance, uniting us through music. A
song made popular by a Swedish band, performed by Italian
opera singers to a crowd of Americans. Like food, music also
has the power to bring people together. And here by the back
wall of the ballroom, our dance party of two has taken on a
life of its own.

Simon points toward the singers and asks me, "Want to
go dance with them?"

"Have you lost your marbles?"

He sets his drink down on the table. "No! Let's get
out there!"

The person I really want to dance with is a no-show. Why
sulk about it? Tipping back my glass, I drain the rest of my
wine and kick off my heels. "Let's do this!"

Sauntering to the middle of the ballroom barefoot wasn't

part of the plan for the evening, but what's life without a little improvising? I shake my hips as the sexy quartet sings about having the time of our lives.

Simon grabs my wrist twirling me toward him. "Let's show 'em how it's done."

My eyes widen with fear and impulsivity. "You're crazy! I don't even know what dance this is!"

"Just move your body, Appleby!" He flings me away and my dress fans out as I nearly ram into one of the singers. Excitement sparkles in her eyes as she motions me to follow her. We slink over to Simon, and the three of us move in a mismatched choreographed dance that would look a lot less appealing if the bustiest singer of the quartet weren't in the middle of us. Soon, the other three singers join us, and the quartet forms a circle around me and Simon who has now lost all composure as tears spill from his eyes.

"What are we doing?" he shouts through an uncontrollable laugh, extending one arm on an angle in a move straight out of *Saturday Night Fever.*

"This was your idea!" Before I know it, I'm doing my best disco dance, too, ignoring the pain in my side from too much laughing paired with too much food.

When the song ends, everyone in the crowd rises to their feet, cheering for more. The singers motion for everyone to join us on the dance floor, and the lights freeze into an ice blue, setting the mood for their final song, made popular by Andrea Bocelli: "*Con Te Partiró.*"

Simon holds out his hand, palm up. "Care to have this dance?" His chest rises as he catches his breath.

I respond with a smile, putting my hand in his, and the music takes over.

A wide beam of light flashes on the dance floor as Daphne and Chuck walk back in through the doors. Daphne's face is red, and tears are streaming down her cheeks.

"She looks hysterical," I say, my heart breaking for her. "We should go over there."

"I dunno," Simon responds, his voice sounding hopeful. "Look at Chuck."

And there are the deepest dimples I've ever seen anchoring an ear-to-ear smile on his face. Holding hands, they find a spot next to us on the dance floor where they embrace in an all-encompassing hug, swaying to the song. When they finally pull apart, they're both smiling.

"So, congratulations are in order?" I ask tentatively, and she nods, her eyes glistening. "You're one hot mama, Daph,"

She laughs, more happy tears falling down her face. Simon and Chuck fist-bump. The latter has a smile almost as big as Daphne's, but he's enjoying a different performance. His eyes, glued to the bouncing blond curls before him, don't so much as glance at the four sultry singers for the entire song. She's lost in the happy moment, and when she finds her way out, Chuck and his boys—*their* boys—will be at her side.

But it's at my side where a familiar blazer and dark stubble catch my eye. "*Aprile*?" Giovanni makes a gesture asking to cut in. Simon goes wide-eyed and happily obliges, patting Gio on the back as he steps aside.

"So, you dress up while making pizzas now?"

"I change back. I wear this to the museum this morning." He raises an eyebrow at me. "You like my moves?" He pulls me in close and takes my hand in his, leading so confidently that I don't even have to think about what my feet are doing.

"You can cook *and* dance? Dangerous combination."

We move around the perimeter of the floor, his hands firmly yet gently guiding me in the right direction. When he asks about the culinary school, everything inside me is telling me to go for it. Quit worrying about the details! But my wine daze is fading and a logical response comes out. "I don't know if it's possible."

"*Tutto é possibile.*" Everything is possible, he tells me. I can have whatever I want if I try. If I believe. "You think about it. And my offer."

We pivot and turn in unison for another verse before he lets go of me. "Your friend—" he waves Simon over, watching us from the side lines "—I think he want to be in my place."

Simon walks over, embracing Gio in a bro hug as if they were old fraternity brothers. He then pulls me in, and I watch Gio take a seat at our table. Even from the shadowy corner, his smile sends me aflutter, the exciting possibilities of the night sending a wave of chills over my body.

"I'm going to miss you and your stupid protein bars when you move to Houston, Becks."

He squeezes his arm a little tighter around my waist. "I'll visit." Then, with a wink he adds, "I've got to bring Esther to visit my parents every now and then. They spoil her with the good treats."

The four songbirds glide through the ballroom, gracefully floating between the couples, serenading everyone, reaching straight into our souls. They hit the high notes with absolute perfection; I feel warm, like a candle inside my heart has been lit, the flame flickering with intensifying heat. Goosebumps make my skin come alive.

In English, Gio told me, the song title literally means "I'll leave with you," but it's often loosely translated into "time to say goodbye," a perfectly bittersweet sentiment on our last night in Rome, and perhaps another last hurrah between me and my friend before our lives split into two paths again.

The key changes, the strings swell, and another round of chills crawls over my skin and finds its way directly into my beating heart. The only sound in this glowing room: four angelic voices. Getting swept up in the music, Simon belts out operatic gibberish during the famous soprano melodies, and a shaky laugh escapes me as I try to hold back tears. He attempts to dip me, but I clumsily bump into someone.

"Forget the cooking class," I say as I stand back up, "we should have taken dance classes."

He tilts his head to the side a bit, the way he always did in high school when he got contemplative. "I think we're doing alright."

The song ends, and for one magical moment, brought to life through the music, Simon and I are no longer in Rome being flawlessly serenaded by an opera quartet. We're in Joliet, Illinois, at the Rialto Square Theater. It's my eighteenth birthday all over again, and my old buddy and I are watching CCR on stage, on our feet, cheering as if this is the only moment we have.

⌒

To: gregorystorms@wrck.fm

Subject: Almost time to say arrivederci :(

I just did some ballroom dancing with Simon and Gio while an opera quartet serenaded us. Who am I?

The cooking class was amazing today, and I didn't even learn anything new about what my mom's secret ingredients could have been, but I'm strangely okay with that at the moment, because we made pesto sauce which was one of her favorites. It sort of felt like she was with me. Gio was telling me tonight—while we took a moonlit walk in the Borghese Gardens… swoon—that I should invent recipes of my own inspired by hers. He says that's what he does with his nonna's panforte. Maybe I'll learn how to do that if I get up the nerve to enroll in that cooking abroad program. I just don't know if I can swing it.

I might need to request your presence for a wee bit longer at my place after I get back. I finally found out why Ian's been calling: he needs to drop off a box of my stuff. Because he's getting married. And I'm apparently invited. If you could be there with me when he comes by AND be my date to the most awkward wedding of the century, that'd be fantastico!

Ciao,

April

CHAPTER 26

ARRIVEDERCI

WHAT I WOULDN'T give for Simon to crank up his phone right now and play Dean Martin.

The only sounds in the shuttle bus are the occasional clicks of a turn signal and the whoosh of the road rushing by underneath: the sounds of leaving Rome behind.

Simon made the best of our last hours in the eternal city. I woke up to the sounds of a certain Rat Pack singer crooning in the background, as Simon was already up and at 'em. The first thing he said to me as I sat up in bed rubbing my eyes was, "I switched our flight to a later one."

Translation: Let's stay in Italy a few more hours. That quickly became my new favorite phrase in the English language.

As his nasal voice filled our hotel room with song while we packed, a bittersweet feeling came over me. For one thing, everyone else had already departed for the airport. Daphne, Chuck, Rob, and Vicki were gone, and who knows if I'll ever see them again? But the news of stealing a couple more hours in delicious, gorgeous, historical Italy softened the blow. Plus, what I was really happy about was that my old friend and I would share our last moments in Rome with no one else crowding us. And after the news of his moving to Houston, I really needed that.

The hum of a window being rolled down breaks the silence, and a cool breeze fills the warm shuttle. The irony hits me that the only day we've experienced light traffic is the day we're leaving this wonderful city behind. I'd give anything for a line of scooters to cut us off, causing the driver to slam the brakes and extend our stay, even if only for an extra minute.

Pedestrian traffic was light today, too. Earlier, at the concierge booth, Simon, perhaps remembering how bummed I was for missing them on our first day in Rome, asked for directions to the famous Spanish Steps. The man handed him a map and explained, in an accent as heavy as travertine stone, that it was a short walk with what sounded like hundreds of turns. Thankfully, Simon was paying attention because, despite my incessant nodding, I didn't comprehend a single word. *Non capisco.*

It was a perfect morning in Rome. The streets breathed with space. Perhaps everyone was sleeping off Saturday night's escapades, or maybe they were praying for forgiveness for them in one of Rome's many churches. The sky was an ocean of blue, the Italian sunshine unobstructed, the air cool and refreshing. We walked in a comfortable silence toward the famous steps, past palm trees and "pesto" pine trees, past statues guarding grand estates, past Italian flags waving in the wind. We walked close together on narrow sidewalks past slews of scooters and Fiats. The buildings of buttery yellows, oranges, and reds shone under the brilliant sun.

The top of the Spanish Steps treated us to a wonderful

elevated view of Rome. The domes of churches glistened under the sun's rays, palm trees blowing in the breeze.

It wasn't until we descended the steps that I realized how many, in fact, there are: one-hundred seventy-four according to *Passport to History*. Going down them is one thing, but the reverse trip…

"I'll buy you lunch if you give me a piggyback ride back up," I said, squinting from the sun as the breeze rustled my hair.

Simon slapped his thigh and said, "Oh, c'mon! Don't you want buns of steel?"

Walking up over one-hundred steps was exactly what we needed though; for the better part of a week, we'd replaced daily five-mile runs and CrossFit workouts with nightly pasta parties. Our hotel did have a gym, but it wasn't half as appealing as pork, pasta, and parmesan.

Upon reaching the bottom of the steps, we spent a quiet moment by the *Fontana della Barcaccia*, or "fountain of the boat," a Baroque fountain in the shape of a half-sunken ship with water overflowing over the sides.

It was a serene, peaceful goodbye to a timeless place, capped off with a simple breakfast of eggs *con formaggio*, juice, coffee, and croissants, the latter of which he promptly handed to me one last time sticking to our well-established routine. Happily, I buttered it while it was still warm.

"Hell of a high school reunion, right?" Simon says, bringing me back to the highway.

"Huh?"

"Our fifteen-year reunion in Rome. Way better than a school gymnasium."

"Way. I feel like I won the *Price is Right* showcase showdown. But the good one. Not the one with a lame dinette set."

He laughs and pulls his phone out of his pocket. "One more time for the road?"

I affirmatively nod, not needing any clarification.

His fingers tap the screen, and his phone starts crooning. For the rest of the shuttle ride, we hum along quietly as we watch the eternal city blur past us.

❧

I feel grossly underdressed, once again donning my gray travel lounge pants and Rolling Stones T-shirt, now with a week's worth of wrinkles. But on the plus side, our seats are actually next to each other for our quick flight to London.

Having had no time this morning to check my email, I connect to the airline's wi-fi.

To: aprilappleby@wrck.fm

Subject: Re: Almost time to say arrivederci :(

I can't for the life of me picture you dancing to an opera quartet. I almost want to see that more than Gio naked. Almost.

About this cooking class in Rome… What do you need me to do to help you make it happen? You obviously want to go.

As for Ian… I'm not going to type what I'm thinking because I don't want there to be a paper trail leading back to me of how I think you should handle him. Much to discuss when you get back.

Fly safe! See you soooooon!

Greg

"Just about another hour," Simon says, readjusting his ear buds, "and we'll be in London."

"At least we'll be able to speak the language this time."

❧

Shit. Brits are impossible to understand. Lingually, I'm less confident here than in Italy.

"*What* did they just say?" I ask, straining to hear the announcements as we get off the plane and hoping the airport sells English-to-English dictionaries. Because, based on what I'm hearing, British English and American English are two totally different languages.

He charges through the terminal. "Just follow me."

Not much later, we're aboard another plane, this time Chicago-bound, which means we're in for another long haul. Nine hours in the clouds, countless failed attempts to nap, and enough airline food to feed a small Italian village.

A melancholy fills my soul, knowing I'm leaving such a wonderful place behind me. I close my eyes for a moment, resting my head on the back of the seat, envisioning the warm colors on the buildings, the fountains spraying water in the Roman sunlight, the gelato rainbows in every window. *Sigh*.

The map on the big screen ahead distracts me from my thoughts, the little red dot tracking our progress over the Atlantic. Simultaneously, I'm feeling both relieved to see us inching closer to Chicago, and saddened to see the space between our plane and Rome expand. It's quite the distracting conflict of emotions. Not even the four movies I watch during the flight can hold my attention.

"You've never seen *Bill and Ted?*" Simon asks sounding shocked, as he unbuckles his seatbelt to make a bathroom run.

"I was always more of *Wayne's World* gal," I say, though truth be told I'm not paying it any attention. This movie was supposed to be *excellent*. But, perhaps everything, even entertaining cult classic films, will now seem duller in the aftermath of being in the center of the most spirited place I've ever visited. Did the past week divide my life into two sections? Life Before Italy, when I accepted reality as it was without question and never lifted my head high enough to see beyond my own basic existence; and Life After Italy, when my pre-existing reality will no longer satiate my new hunger for the wonderful place that literally allowed me see the world from a new perspective. In Rome, the colors are brighter, the food is tastier, the language is sexier, the trains are faster, the art is richer, the churches are grander, the history is older, and their fun-size Fiats get more miles to the gallon than any American car ever will.

No wonder an eighties movie about teenage time travel isn't holding my attention.

From my carry-on, I pull out my *Order Up* notebook, making sure my restaurant reviews are legible. It's the scribbles from my secret ingredient hunt, however, that aren't as fleshed out.

> 1. <u>*Spaghetti sauce*</u>
>   *Melt in some cheese?*
>   *Cook with wine? Doubtful.*
>   **Soffritto** – *Carrots, onion, and celery*
>   *Fresh basil*
>   *Add love, quantity unknown.*

2. _Lasagna cheese_
   Mozzarella and a mystery cheese.
3. _Cheesecake batter_
   Exclude lemon?
   Add honey?
   Maybe almond extract???

Instead of finding answers this week about my favorite dishes of my mom's, I've somehow ended up with more questions. If only I had the money and time to enroll at CII. A heavy sigh escapes me, and Simon looks over.

"What's that? Meal prepping for when we land? Do you ever think about anything other than food?"

"No." I look up from the notebook. "Remember when we had lunch before we left for Rome and you asked me about my mom's red velvet cupcakes?"

He beams with pleasure. "Well, I remember the cupcakes, that's for sure."

"And I said that I wish I knew how to make them? Well, this whole week, I've been trying to figure out the secret to some of her recipes." I hand him the notebook, listing my favorite dishes she used to make, about which I'm still clueless. "I thought for sure I'd figure something out in Italy. But now I'm even more confused."

He looks over my chicken scratch, and after a moment, hands me back the notebook. He opens his mouth for a moment as if about to say something, then closes it.

I go on, trying to explain. "I've just visited a corner of the world where the food is superior—"

"Hey, America invented bacon donuts."

"—and now I'm heading back home with…" I slap the scribbles on my notebook in frustration, "*this*."

Simon listens intently. His eyes feel like they're burning a hole through my face, or maybe that's just my anger for coming up so royally short after the opportunity of a lifetime.

"I dunno, maybe I should give this up. Stop obsessing over it. You saw what my dough looked like." I fold the notebook closed and tuck it back into my carry-on. "It's time I accept that I'll never be able to cook. At least not the way my mom could."

"That's not how I see it. Looks to me like you've got some ideas to explore… even some new ingredients to try for a couple of those dishes. What'd you expect, to reach Master Chef level after only a week in Italy? Most of which was filled with sightseeing, by the way. What were you gonna do? Bust into the hotel's kitchen every night for private lessons? C'mon," he nudges my shoulder. "Talk about putting pressure on yourself."

My eyes lock with his, which are sparkling with compassion. "I guess I set the bar a little high."

"Yeah. And just because you didn't figure it all out this week doesn't mean you won't. I mean, you could go home and experiment with what you've written. It's not like you had time to actually cook anything this week—other than making some clumpy dough. Maybe after you make a few attempts at home, you'll get closer to figuring it out, or maybe you'll come up with your own spin on it."

"That's what Gio said I should do." Gio. His text message with the cooking abroad info is still in my phone. I click the link again. "Registration closes New Year's Eve for this pasta program."

Simon says through a laugh, "You totally want to do it."

"Wanting something and being able to actually do it are two different things. But, you're right," I admit, "I do want to do it."

"Now we're finally on the same page." He grins and puts his arm around my shoulder giving me a reassuring squeeze.

"Maybe in a few years I can make it work."

He throws me a disappointed look.

"There's a lot of prep! I have no idea how I'd afford airfare, tuition, and lodging, plus, get an entire month off from work. There's no way."

"Don't sweat the details. Details work themselves out."

"Says the man who bought a truck without measuring his garage first."

"What's the hold up? Shouldn't we have landed by now?" After multiple flights in the past week, I finally feel brave enough to peer out the window. Not that I see much—between nightfall and snowfall, visibility is practically nonexistent.

"We're circling. Happens sometimes at O'Hare. Probably just in line waiting for our turn."

After another half hour, the plane descends. "Finally," I mutter.

"The joys of air travel in bad weather."

Landing: it's normally my favorite part of the flying experience. But as soon as the plane touches down, something feels off. Way off.

"Shouldn't we be slowing down?" My heartbeat picks up, and I grip the arm rest as we start to swerve wildly on the runway.

"Passengers," the pilot says through the P.A., "please remain seated with seatbelts fastened."

A woman behind me gasps and the plane fills with worried murmurs. We continue sliding jerkily, still barreling forward with enough momentum to feel like we're taking off again. "It's ice!" Someone shouts. The runway is whited out by it, slick and frozen, and there's only so much room on it before we'll crash into the airport.

CHAPTER 27

HOME FROM ROME

I SUCK IN my breath, holding it, my knuckles as white as the fat, uncaring snowflakes falling outside. "Oh my God! Oh my God!" My hands shake.

The plane skids, and we swerve to the right.

"Don't panic," Simon says wrapping an arm around me. "We're on the ground."

My hands grip his back. "Going a million miles an hour headed straight for the terminal!"

We begin to tip sideways, the right wing scraping the ice-covered runway loudly, but it's not enough friction to slow our speed. I squeeze tighter, feeling like we're on an amusement park ride gone terribly wrong.

"Jesus! We better not die! You and your stupid later flight! I'll kill you if we die!"

"We're not gonna die." Those words would be a lot more reassuring if Simon's eyes weren't two saucers wide with fear.

"God, I never even tried Giovanni's pizza!"

A few women shriek as we regain balance and the plane rights itself, but we're still sliding fast on the runway like a giant ice skate. "That's it. No more excuses. I'm gonna do it. I'm gonna enroll in that Goddamn cooking class if it's the last thing I do, just, God, let me off this fucking plane."

We start to tip again, and the plane skids off the runway. Someone screams. We rumble onto snow-covered grass, the wing dipping down until it digs into the earth, halting the plane with an abrupt thump.

I finally breathe. "How did I not toss my cookies during that?"

Simon laughs as though we've just been on a thrilling carnival ride. "Congrats! I think that means you're officially a pro flier."

⚬

After surviving the world's largest slip 'n' slide, being bussed back to the terminal, having to take a pop quiz to get through customs, and being called "ma'am" by a customs official, we're finally in a rideshare heading back to Simon's place, the sleet splattering into wet globs on the windshield. With shaky hands, I text Greg an update.

His response is almost instantaneous. *"Tot is waiting."* The accompanying photo shows my cat sitting in a loaf position on the radiator in the living room wearing her signature grumpy expression.

In a matter of minutes, we're pulling into Simon's complex.

"Now, remember what you said as we landed. About the cooking class?"

"Nothing like the fear of God to make me come to my senses." I prop up my luggage in his kitchen. "Can I leave these here while I use your bathroom? Surprised I didn't wet myself…"

"Now I know to bring adult diapers on these trips." He laughs. "Down at the end of the hall on the left."

After spending half a day in the air, little luxuries like a bathroom that's bigger than a broom closet are blissfully sweet. The view from the mirror, however, leaves something to be desired; the blues of my eyes look dull, tired. My reflection could do with some sprucing up, but delirium-inducing travel fatigue and pangs of homesickness convince me to abandon any attempt at freshening up.

I stay just long enough to grab my keys from his kitchen counter, hiding behind the oversized jug of protein powder where I left them. Remembering the leather boutique in Florence, I quickly dig in my luggage for the little keychain I bought. Simon thought my selection was hilarious. "We're all getting nice expensive bags and stuff, and you're getting a little doggy keychain?" he asked, playfully teasing me.

I attach the leather pooch to my keyring, and my fingers rub over the words that are stitched on the dog's belly made of pure leather:

MADE IN ITALY
VERA PELLE

A sigh escapes me as I face my friend for the final time this week. "Remember when we went to Rome? That was cool."

"Maybe we'll do it again some time." He laughs.

"Just not in fifteen years, okay? I know you can't make

the concerts, but if you have any time off before your new gig starts, let's at least try to do lunch."

"Or we could have a *Labyrinth* screening."

I nod. "There wasn't nearly enough David Bowie on this trip."

He laughs again, but the twinkle in his eye loses its luster as he tells me that his new boss wants him to start much earlier than either of us anticipated: next month. "December second to be exact."

"Before Christmas?!"

"I'm Jewish."

I emphatically gesture toward the oversized Christmas tree twinkling in his living room. "And that Christmas party you told me you were throwing for your gym?"

"They'll have to find another party. And, actually, Hanukkah is the week of Christmas this year, so I'll be coming back that week to stay with my parents. Vacation time's already approved."

The worry lines on my face soften. "All eight crazy nights?"

He smiles. "Yep. And if you're around, yes, we should do lunch again. All the bread you want, on me."

We hug for a moment, and as I let go, I look into those brown eyes of his and say, "I'm going to hold you to that."

"You better." He drags my luggage to the car, loading my bags in the trunk. Wet snowflakes fall on us as I back out of his garage, my window rolled down, Simon walking beside my door. We wave goodbye one last time as I shift my car into drive, leaving him standing on the wet blacktop. At the gate, I look in the rearview mirror, but nightfall obscures everything, swallowing up my friend from view like he's not there anymore.

The radio serenades me quietly as I drive home on roads slick from falling sleet. Still a bit shaky from the landing, I channel my inner Sunday driver, cruising well under the speed limit. The radio calms me, sounds of guitar and drums replacing a week's worth of smooth crooning and opera. The traffic lights and headlights reflect off the wet asphalt, painting the black roads with streaks of red, green, and white, like an abstract water color interpretation of the Italian flag. The flag I'll once again see waving in the wind in six months. If I can manage to figure out how to tie up all those loose ends.

At home, Greg smothers me in a hug, practically shouting in my ear, "*Ciao, bella!*"

I squeeze back. "Somebody's been practicing!"

After rolling around on her scratch mat, belly flopping this way and that, my plump cat inspects my luggage, giving it a thorough sniffing. "Obviously, I'll need to hide the *biscotti* from her." Retrieving the bags of cookies, I fill Greg in on the past week as we crunch into our cookies and pore over photos of Rome.

Twenty minutes later, he says through a yawn, "I hate to be a party pooper, but I've got to get up for work tomorrow and I need to sleep in my own bed. Your couch is lumpy."

I rise from said couch. "Well, I guess I can let you go. Tot looks as chubby as ever and the bathroom tile is positively gleaming. A-plus!" I pat him on the back, and hand him a plastic bag containing his souvenir. "Thank you for Tot-sitting."

He pulls the apron out of the bag and immediately fits his head through the neck loop. "Oh… my… God." He walks to the hallway mirror, modeling the apron from different stances.

I do my best cat call. "Is that sausage you're cooking or are you just happy to see me?"

"You couldn't have brought me back a leather wallet or something? Maybe some olive oil? Something without genitalia on it?"

"Don't pretend you don't love it. And I'll expect you to wear that the next time you cook me dinner." I hold the door open for him.

"Me cook *you* dinner? Nuh-uh. You could be the expert here—if you stop dragging your feet and sign up for that damn class."

∾

Not only did Greg brave tiny cat claws and diligently scrub away skid marks on the bathroom floor, but he stocked my entire kitchen. Tomatoes of every shape and color greet me from the crisper—no doubt homegrown from his own kitchen windowsill—while a jumbo pack of string cheese sits on the top shelf. In the cupboard: olive oil and balsamic vinegar. And it's the new fresh basil plant on my windowsill that will complete the recipe. A shiny green giftwrap bow is stuck on the terra-cotta planter next to a Post-It note with Greg's handwriting:

"Ta-da! A plant you can eat! Now you can have caprese salads here, too. (You'll have to settle for string cheese though. I have no idea where one buys freakishly big balls of mozzarella.)"

"He's going to turn me into a green thumb if it kills him," I say to myself, shaking my head despite the smile on my face.

I grab a handful of fresh leaves, popping one in my mouth, tasting the freshness of it. It's a world away from the dried basil in my cupboard, and it's sure to improve my attempts at spaghetti, a box of which I now notice stocked in my pantry.

Even though the moon has already clocked in for the night shift, I cast the blinds open all the way up, ready for the morning sunshine to not only wash over the basil, but over me. And with that warmth, I'll welcome a new day and the prospect of a new, less lonely, beginning.

It's another interpretation of the Italian flag: red slices of tomatoes, white chunks of mozzarella, and a handful of green basil are arranged on my plate underneath a drizzle of balsamic vinegar and olive oil. In between bites of appreciation for the salad's fresh flavors, I peek outside. Chicago is totally whitewashed as the snow erases the green grass, the cars, and the blacktop. My body is here, in the snow-covered Midwest, but my thoughts are an ocean away, in the middle of a sun-drenched piazza. Somewhere in the distance I can almost hear an accordion.

Should I implement Simon's strategy? Enroll and let the details fall into place? That seems reckless. I could lose a lot of money if the trip falls through. The devil is on my shoulder shouting, "Just enroll, you idiot! Open a second credit card if you have to. Sell a kidney!" And the angel on my other shoulder is saying, "Go to bed."

Go to bed? Huh. Well, who am I to question how God works?

I change into an oversized tie-dye Jim Morrison T-shirt and dig deep in my sock drawer looking for the fuzzy slipper socks I only wear on the coldest of nights, when I find it: a folder with the bank account information from when my mom bequeathed her money to me. The funds were first deposited into the account on December first, 2009; almost a full year after her passing. And with the exception of a withdrawal for a used car and another for the down payment on my apartment, I haven't touched it in nearly five years. To spend it always felt like I would somehow be giving away not her money, but her memory—her spirit. Like I'd be using up what was left of her. I've used it so rarely that I'd actually forgotten about it. For one thing, I do my banking at another institution. But it was easier to set up the account as her beneficiary at her bank, and I've never bothered to transfer the money over.

But now I can spend this money to learn how to do what she always did for me. That would be the perfect way to honor her. And who knows? Maybe I will be able to invent my own take on pasta sauce or lasagna after taking this course. She'd be proud of me for that—and happy to know I'm over-the-moon happy. Plus, the chance to see Gio again wouldn't be the worst thing either.

The moon shines from behind wispy clouds, a bright spot in the velvety blackness. I feel my mother's presence while looking at that smiling moon, and I thank her for always coming through for me. The thought that she's still paying for my education makes me laugh a little hysterically. Here I am jumping over the first hurdle on my way back to Rome.

After my computer boots up, I type in the web address for The Culinary Institute of Italy, ready to let in what I've been so scared to ever since I lost my mom, my own personal master chef who loved me more than life itself. I click on "programs," and find the four-week pasta course. The first week is spent learning the history of Italy's pasta-making tradition while observing demonstrations and enjoying guided tastings from renowned Italian chefs—I know I'll ace the tasting portion. Weeks two and three include hands-on cooking sessions that cover everything from dough preparation, pasta-shaping, cooking strategies, sauce theory, and wine pairings. And the course culminates in the final week with a student-prepared dinner for the ultimate final exam feast. I find the tuition information. As I suspected, I'll have to dip into the money from my mom; paying in full is much higher than my credit limit on my charge card.

It's been years since I last logged into her bank's website, and I'm faced with answering more security questions than I can fathom. Eventually, I manage to reset my password, but an unsettling welcome message in red type taunts me while I trip over this hurdle that was much higher than I realized:

Dormant account. Please contact your financial institution to unfreeze assets.

CHAPTER 28

A BOX OF MEMORIES

THE FAINT SOUND of the L rumbles along the tracks outside
my apartment. From my eyes, I rub away the sleep that never
came. Under normal circumstances, waking up at three
o'clock in the morning would be soul-sucking, but I use this
time to research what I need to do to unfreeze the account,
which, according to the bank's website, needs to happen, like,
yesterday, otherwise my mom's money will be handed over
to the state once a period of five years of inactivity has been
reached. That date is coming up in January, but I need access
much sooner if I'm going to enroll at CII. The fire that this
lights under my ass could not be hotter. I leave half a dozen
messages and emails for several personal bankers, hoping at
least one of them will respond today. And as if that's not
stressful enough, I have to face Ian tonight.

My suitcases, still sitting in the living room where I left
them last night, offer a distraction. In the front pouch of
my carry-on I find a framed photo of me and Simon at the

Colosseum. He must have slipped this in when we stopped at his house. A crumpled sheet of notebook paper is flattened out and taped to the back. In addition to the five concerts I'd written, he added:

South by Southwest, March 8th – 17th, Austin. Short drive from my new digs... Pick a date you can come to Texas for our concert tour. I'll fly back for the others.

-S

I stand the photo on the mantel, our two smiling faces looking back at me as the Colosseum stretches wide behind us. Looks like next year will be filled with concerts after all. At least one thing in my life is on track.

And I thought flying over the Atlantic was nerve wracking. Turns out, waiting for my ex to ring my apartment's intercom is another activity that fuels my anxiety.

"Are you sure he's coming tonight?" Greg peeks at his watch. It was his grandpa's.

"Yes. He texted me and said he'd swing by after work today." I get up from the couch to peer out the window, my curtains cinched with two ribbons to let more light in during the day, the sunset now dwindling to a whisper pink along the horizon. "Maybe he's trying to find a space to park. My block fills up pretty fast."

Back on the couch, Tater Tot squeezes herself in between the two of us, purring while being petted from all angles.

"I promise we'll dive into these donuts after Ian leaves.

Thank you for bringing them, by the way. My stomach is just one giant knot right now."

"Speaking of stomachs, are you going to wear a bikini to the beach with Gio? You need to show some skin. None of this wear-a-tee-shirt-over-my-swimsuit nonsense."

"I don't even know if there will be a beach to visit now." I take this opportunity to fill Greg in on my latest predicament, reassuring myself more than him that someone from the bank is bound to get back to me sooner or later. "And when they do, I'll be packing up my oven mitts and heading back to Rome. And, no, I won't be packing a bikini. I'll have a spaghetti belly by the time they're through with me. One-piece with shorts is more my style."

"Sounds like a swimsuit for a nun."

"Well, it's a holy city."

And maybe that's a good thing—I explain to Greg that the boss didn't sound too happy when I told him I was planning on being out of the country for the entire month of May. (I figured I might as well try to clear at least one hurdle today.) After a little selfish praying to the big guy upstairs, we were able to make it work. My three weeks' vacation plus my personal day only left four days to account for. Eventually, my boss agreed to advance me those days from the following year. Our weekend jocks were apparently over the moon to fill in for me. Still, I feel a bit guilty for such an extended absence. Nothing a top-notch bottle of prosecco can't smooth over.

Buzz! Greg and I exchange a nervous glance, and Tot bolts into the bedroom.

"I wish I could hide in there with her."

"It'll be fine," he reassures me. "He'll hand you the box,

you'll say 'thanks,' and he'll ride off into the sunset and you'll never see him again."

"Except for his wedding."

"We'll talk."

Seeing one's ex is always a bit awkward, but I don't think never seeing him again would make me feel better. Handing me a box of my stuff because he's settling down with someone else feels like a final goodbye before he goes to the ex-afterlife. A melancholic air seeps into the room.

I buzz Ian in and unlock my door. Turning to Greg, I point my finger at him. "Be nice."

Three polite knocks. "April?"

"We're in here," I call from the living room. "It's open."

He lets himself in and in an instant, I'm flooded with every emotion I'm capable of feeling. I'm an everything-but-the-kitchen-sink recipe: a heaping spoonful of anxiety mixed with a dash of regret, half a teaspoon of embarrassment, and a pinch of sadness garnished with a twist of nostalgia. Served with a side of guilt for which I'd rather substitute fries.

He holds a modest-sized cardboard box in his hands—the remnants of my place in his life which he no longer has a need for—and looks at me for a moment with a friendly yet forced smile. "Greetings!" Too much enthusiasm.

"Hi." I take the box from him with a sheepish smile. "Thanks for bringing this by."

"Not a problem at all. Apologies for the delay."

"Traffic's a bear in the city."

"Indeed it is, but I was referring to all the years this went ignored while sitting in my parents' basement." When he notices Greg, confusion lines Ian's face, which looks much more rugged than I remember. He's clearly in between haircuts, the shaggy brown waves framing his jawline, which is now completely hidden underneath a well-manicured beard. "Greg! Didn't think I'd find your smiling face here."

Greg, overprotective skepticism all over his face, now gives the faintest hint of a grin.

Tater Tot's curiosity at the sound of a new voice brings her back into the living room with us. She sits in front of the fireplace, looking up at the motley crew of humans who don't know quite how to interact.

Greg looks to me as if seeking permission to address the ghost of my past. I nod subtly. "Well, I am her best friend." Thankfully he keeps the bite out of his tone.

"Of course," Ian agrees, still standing a foot from the door, "Though, I must admit, I was expecting to be faced with Simon." He turns to me now, curiosity in his gaze. "Is the man of the house home? I thought I'd congratulate the pair of you," he says while reaching into his jacket pocket, retrieving an envelope, "whilst personally inviting the both of you to my upcoming nuptials." Upon handing it to me I see it's addressed to a nonexistent couple: "Mr. & Mrs. Becker."

And that's when the memory rushes back to me faster than a pack of Vespas fleeing the *carabinieri*.

"Oh…" My mouth opens to explain, but I don't know where to begin, held back by the sheer mortification that I lied about my marital status to my ex-fiancé. How could I have done something so mortifying? Oh right. Gallons of wine.

"Simon is… he's not here. Come on in! Have a seat." I gesture to the couch, quickly picking up Tot's blanket covered in a layer of fur. "I should probably explain. Um…" I trail off. Greg, seated between us, looks just as confused as Ian. "You know, it's kind of funny. I may have crossed some wires during that conversation. Simon and I—me and Simon—we're, you know, we're friends. We're not married. *You're* getting married. We're—I'm single. There was a lot of wine. Would you care for a donut?"

Tot jumps up on Ian's lap and purrs at full volume. Traitor. He absentmindedly pets the cat without bothering to look at the dozen donuts I'm holding a foot from his face. "Pardon my confusion, but what are you talking about? I thought you were on your honeymoon." He glances feverishly between me and Greg, awaiting an explanation that doesn't come. "You're... *not* married?"

I ignore the look they're both giving me, and instead take a deep, calming breath inhaling the scent of frosted dough. I grab a Boston Crème and take a bite, mostly so that I don't have to talk any more. "Uh-uh," I say, shaking my head, savoring the custard.

My answer doesn't seem to satisfy either gentleman, and the room fills with the sound of me chewing and Tot purring even louder now as she starts to shed on Ian's black shirt. I set the donut down on a napkin, and face Ian. "I was—it was a joke. I thought it would be funny to tell you that I was married and honeymooning in Rome since you—you're tying the knot!" I try to act excited for him, but a crazed smile threatens to strangle my face and my eyebrows feel like they've lifted off my head. "So, who's the lucky lady? Don't keep us in suspense, you!"

His eyes dart back and forth again for a second. "Alrighty! Um, okay, well, her name is Ingrid, and I met her while doing some freelance work for her. A co-worker introduced us—she needed a complete website rebuild."

Greg discreetly turns to me mouthing "Ingrid" with a look of disgust on his face. I shove a piece of my donut in his mouth.

"Wow, that's—that's great! When did you meet? All this time, I thought you were still dating what's-her-face from that restaurant."

"Heavens no, that was over before it started. I met Ingrid shortly after that. I purposely took my time rebuilding her website; that was incredibly simple. It was building up the courage to ask her out that was proving challenging." Shyness softens the angled features of his face, and it reminds me why I felt so safe with him in college. Tot makes several hundred biscuits on his thighs before settling into a croissant position on his lap. "We're going to Germany on our honeymoon. She has family out there." He waits for us to match his enthusiasm, which, if he were a puppy, would manifest in the form of a happily wagging tail. "*Prost!*"

"Germany! Wow! That's—that's so far." What an observation, April. My face turns pink. "Eat some chocolate for me while you're there." My hair feels flat and greasy as I anxiously scratch my head, turning my gaze back to my donut. "Sure you don't want to stay for dessert?" My voice sounds cold and distant, despite the fake smile etched on my face.

"I must politely decline. Bit of a drive to the 'burbs for my return trip according to this barrage of Swerge notifications." He keeps stroking Tot, her fluffy belly rising and falling slowly, oblivious to the awkward tension in the room. "Curious that your cat isn't scared off by the canine scent I'm doused in. Ingrid and I have a dog. She's a maniac. Jumps all over me when I come home from work. Time escaped me, and I couldn't change."

Picturing Ian and Ingrid with their precious pup should make me jealous, but surprisingly, a little flame of warmth lights up inside me. It's comforting knowing that someone who was so important to me is happy. He's moved on, and I finally feel like I am, too. Or at least I'm trying.

He sits up a little straighter, shifting his weight. Tot takes the hint and jumps down. Ian holds out his hand toward Greg who politely accepts the handshake while remaining seated. Then he turns to me. "April. Very good to see you. I sincerely hope you can be in attendance." He gestures to the envelope, sitting on the coffee table.

While I walk him to the door, he adds with an exaggerated amount of nonchalance, "Just mail it back whenever. Yes or no, either way." He stops at the door and looks me in the eyes, his smile still just as innocent as it was in college. "Though I hope it's a yes."

"A 'yes.' Did you hear him?" Crumbs of donuts spit out of my mouth as I ask the question, while aggressively eating my feelings. "Doesn't he know how excruciatingly awkward attending my ex-fiancé's wedding will be?"

"Almost as awkward as making up a Roman honeymoon." Greg can't help chuckling.

My head rests on my palms. "Oh my God, he must think I'm a nutbar. He's probably thrilled to be rid of the last of me." I take the top off the box and see my belongings that I didn't even know were missing neatly stacked inside.

"He obviously still cares about you."

"Why would you say that?"

"He held onto all your crap! Any normal person would have chucked it in a landfill or set fire to it, but he held onto it because he was holding on to the hope that he would see you again."

"And he saw me alright. To personally deliver an invitation to his wedding to someone else."

"In any case, he still cares. I mean, what do we even have in here? Old books and—and a boombox. Wow." He releases a hearty laugh. "And, oh my God, an iPod Touch. What year is it?"

"*That's* where that thing ended up!" I reach over and take it from Greg's hands, marveling at it like it's a rare fossil.

"Someone who didn't still care would have pitched all this junk."

"Hey, be careful what you call 'junk.' I still listen to CDs." I pop open the boombox's CD tray, delighted to see a blue disc with the image of roller skates. "*Seventies Roller Disco!* We each brought a guilty pleasure CD when we drove to San Francisco. This was mine; he hated this album. It must have been in here for years." I close the lid, plug it in, and hit play, and the sound of clapping as the Bay City Rollers spell out "Saturday" blares out of the tiny speakers.

"Yeah. This CD definitely should have been hurled into a dumpster." He starts pulling out the other contents of the box. "What about these books? You don't even have any shelf space left. Looks like you live in a library, you big nerd."

I scan the spines. "These aren't books—well, yes, they're books, but they're *cookbooks*."

"You owned cookbooks? Little Miss How-Do-I-Make-Scrambled-Eggs?"

I roll my eyes, though I did call him once to ask him that

very question, albeit a long time ago. I'd just rented a cheap apartment for a few years, on my own for the first time after my engagement went up in flames, and all thoughts were consumed by the suffocating aloneness I'd been suddenly subjected to. Adding milk to my eggs to make them fluffy—an old trick my mom had shown me long ago—had temporarily slipped my mind.

"No," I say, scanning the title more closely, pulling out *Betty Crocker's Italian Cooking*. Flipping through the pages, a hopeful spark ignites at the sight of handwritten notes in the margins; the unmistakable loopy script of my mom as clear as if she'd scribbled in these pages yesterday. A frazzled energy makes my hands shake. "My mom did."

CHAPTER 29

THE APPLEBY CHRISTMAS LASAGNA

THE GROUND BEEF sizzles in a sauce pan bubbling with olive oil, chopped onions, and garlic, the aroma mixing with the crooning vocals of Dean Martin's Christmas album as they blast out of my old boom box sitting on my kitchen counter.

"What can I bring?" Greg had asked over the phone. "I don't want you to be the only one slaving away in the kitchen on Christmas. Plus, I want to use my nudie apron again. It looks fabulous on me."

"I certainly don't want to stand in the way of you and your apron," I'd replied, laughing. "But I think I can handle our feast for two. Are you sure your parents don't mind that we're not coming over? I'm just so excited to try cooking my first Christmas dinner."

"They're totally fine with it. Besides, Thanksgiving was enough family time for me. I think my uncle is back to thinking you're my girlfriend." I could hear his eyes rolling through his tone of voice.

I wedged the phone between my head and shoulder to pour a mug of Italian hot chocolate—a family recipe Gio had shared with me over a recent video chat. "Not to jump to conclusions but he might need a dementia screening."

"No, he's just a Nebraskan." He's the one family member his parents couldn't get through to so they stopped trying.

"Well, it's better this way anyway. I've had enough pretend romance for a while. And Easter isn't that far off—we'll be seeing them again for the ol' egg hunt." I took a sip of chocolate, content in anticipating the tradition.

"Not only that, but I might be bringing *two* guests home for Easter next year."

"Tater Tot does not travel. You know this."

"No. Harry. I'm finally going to ask him to come with us. If he's up for it. My family can be a lot."

"Oh my God! He'll totally be up for it. Look at you, being all brave and stuff. And speaking of brave, lasagna's one thing, but I don't know if I can tackle dessert, too, so I'm putting you on dessert duty." I'd secretly been pining for an opportunity to flex my newfound cooking muscles ever since meeting Mama Pasta, but it wasn't until I finally found the secret ingredients to my mom's recipes that I felt the final push I needed to summon my confidence behind a hot stove, which I've been doing almost every night for several weeks. Following her handwritten tweaks to Ms. Crocker's recipe feels like she's standing here in my kitchen talking me through the process of preparing the traditional Appleby Christmas lasagna.

When the meat is browned, the sauce cascades into the

skillet. Sprinkles of parsley and freshly chopped basil fall into it like little snow flurries of sweetness. I fist-bump a bushy part of the plant. "Thanks for your help, stud." The basil has thrived so much on my kitchen windowsill over the past few weeks that I've already looked into transplanting it into a bigger pot. It's almost as if the rays of sun that are no longer blocked by blinds and shades are causing me to flourish and grow, too. I mean, only a few short weeks ago was I completely stumped as to how to make my mom's secret cheese blend. And now, I've got one bowl of goat cheese and ricotta, and another of mozzarella and parmesan, both waiting in the wings for their turn to be layered into tonight's feast.

While the meat sauce bubbles away for forty-five minutes, I walk to my laptop to solve the next problem in my quest to return to Italy: narrowing down my lodging options. Once I'd sent in a written application to the bank requesting access to the frozen account along with identification credentials, enrolling at CII was a breeze. And I even transferred the balance to my own bank, consolidating everything into one tidy account. Apparently, all year the bank had attempted contacting me multiple times about the lack of activity, but with no luck: a clerical mix-up caused them to reach me at my mom's old phone number and address. Thank God they didn't charge dormancy fees. The bank and enrollment were all officially squared away as of last week. I'd sent a text to Gio. It was late, and in my excitement, I'd completely forgotten about the time difference.

"I am officially enrolled at CII! Maybe in between pasta parties you'll have time to give me another Vespa tour? Or another moonlight stroll?"

Now that I'm officially enrolled, I need to find a place

to stay. I shove over a notebook covered in mostly illegible chicken scratch with the names of various places to look up. Pre-Italy April would have given up by now, finding these obstacles the perfect excuse to stay put. But Post-Italy April sees this as an opportunity. I'm on a mission, and I not only feel Mama Pasta rooting me on, but Mama Appleby, too. Finding availability for an entire month—one that kicks off the tourism season—is proving to be challenging, however, especially since student housing filled up ages ago.

Option one, the bed and breakfast category of away-from-home lodging, is the most appealing to me, mostly because of the guaranteed fresh complimentary *cornetti* every morning. It's not, however, the most financially lucrative option. I'd surely deplete not only what's left of my mom's bequest, but rack up a serious credit balance as well. My next option, hotels, offers more places to stay with cheaper price tags, but I can't help but feel like I'd be missing out on rustic Italian charm. Option three seems like the most authentic—and affordable—choice, but the catch is that it's complicated and time-consuming: renting an apartment for a month. How would I even begin that process as a foreigner? Would I need some sort of visa? What's the application process? I can see myself being crushed underneath a stack of legal contracts, paper cuts from every page slowly slicing away my will to live. And even if I do figure out all the details, would renting a place for the relatively short duration of a month be possible? And could I really get all that squared away by the time I land in Rome five short months from now? Option four is starting to look a lot more appealing than it sounds: pitching a tent among well-hidden ancient ruins. A fifth offer hangs in the balance, but pride—or maybe shyness—is preventing me from seriously considering it.

My phone dings. *"Aprile, sorry I am late to reply. I have been working at the museum and pizzeria for two weeks. I am so happy you return to* Roma. *Now you can see our beaches. Bring a swimsuit. Or not."* The winky emoji tells me the rest.

The timer on the microwave buzzes: it's time to cook the pasta. While the lasagna sheets submerge under the boiling water, I mix in some basil and honey with the ricotta cheese and goat cheese. Then, after I mix in some parsley into the mozzarella and parmesan mixture, I bring a teaspoon to my lips to taste test the cheeses. "Mom would be proud," I discern, licking up the rest of what's on the spoon.

Building the lasagna becomes a dance, every layer spread over the pan to the music of Dean Martin's Christmas album, his holiday cheer my own secret ingredient added to the dish. With a final sprinkle of parmesan cheese on top, I then don an oven mitt that kicks my outfit up several notches, and place the pan on the middle rack. The aroma of tomatoes and cheese awakens the memory of the meals I enjoyed in Italy, the place I'll return to in the spring with an openness to learn, and a readiness to connect with my mother through her—our—love of cooking.

A quick photo of the lasagna in the oven sends off to Greg. "Sixty minutes 'til Santa arrives. Get your jingle bells over here."

⌁

The pan feels warm through the oven mitt as a blast of heat grazes my face.

"You're starting to spoil me," Greg says from the table.

"Five dinners so far this month? Maybe you *should* be my girlfriend. Italy definitely rubbed off on you."

"I hope you're not sick of Italian," I say, closing the oven door shut with my knee as I place the pan of lasagna on top of the stove. "But I suddenly have superfluous amounts of basil now." I throw him some side-eye. "And I've been so excited to finally have the right sauce!" I'd incorporated my mom's pasta sauce not only into spaghetti, but also pizza, meatballs, and now the lasagna—it originally called for a much simpler tomato sauce, but the thrill of finding her recipe book overcame me; I've been using her pasta sauce for all kinds of dishes, modifying with reckless abandon when the mood strikes.

I pour us each a glass of hot apple cider and sit across from Greg, the side of his face illuminated by the Christmas lights in my window. "We have to wait fifteen minutes before slicing and dicing."

"Oh my God, that's torture. Even Tot wants in on this." Sitting in the middle of the kitchen, looking up at the stove, Tater Tot sits patiently, her fluffy tail whipping to and fro every so often.

"Pretty sure she doesn't recognize me now that I actually spend time in the kitchen."

"Oh! I almost forgot." He gets up and grabs a foil-covered tray that he had set on the buffet. "Room in your fridge for this?"

"Ooh, what have we here?" I take it from him and find a spot on the top shelf.

"It's a surprise." He lifts an eyebrow, and when I sit back down, he leans closer to me and says, "So, what are we going to wear to this shindig?" The eagerness in his voice is topped with a pinch of mischief.

"Well, it's a wedding," I say taking a sip of cider. Steam rises from the mug, slightly fogging my glasses. "Something, you know, formal?"

"Even for your ex?"

"Yes. Even for my ex. No Crocs. I can't be that mad at him anymore; he gave me my mom's recipes." When Ian dropped off that box, a sadness I wasn't prepared for filled me. It was an ordinary cardboard box, with the extraordinary purpose of filling in the missing puzzle piece of our long and arduous breakup. It carried so much emotional baggage that it no longer was just a box, but The Box. When he handed me a pile of my belongings, it felt like he was erasing any imprint that my love left on his heart.

But then, finding those cookbooks with my mom's notes jotted down all over the pages, that box was suddenly a gift. A gift that only could have come from someone who knew my heart and soul intimately. At one point, Ian's and my lives overlapped, and in that space were, among other things, the recipes that my mom tweaked much to my appetite's delight for so many years.

"Did you guys ever use them when you lived together?"

"No, we never even opened them. All my mom's stuff went into boxes and I couldn't open anything without bawling. He was the one who cooked. His own recipes—if you can call throwing steak on a grill a recipe." The timer on my phone goes off, and I head for the stove. "I have more of her stuff in my storage unit. I found some of her old clothes that fit me! And some photo albums, too." For too long, I feared her old belongings would only remind me of losing her, but now they make me feel closer to her, like a small part of her has returned to me.

The spatula slices into the lasagna gently, carving out two healthy sized squares. I set one in front of Greg, and he eyes his plate greedily.

I bite my lip and look up at him, not ready to pierce my fork into my own slice. "Are you ready?"

"Are *you* ready?"

I nod, picking up my fork and slicing off a corner. "Cheers."

Every layer is in harmony. From the sauce, to the tender beef, to the soft cheeses blending together beautifully, it tastes wonderful. I finally did it.

He washes down his last bite with a swig of cider. "Please tell me I won't have to wait a whole year to have this again." He flashes a mischievous smile.

"We'll see." I take my final bite, ecstatic that the flavors are in order. "Or maybe I'll add my own flair to it next time. I might pick up some tricks in Rome."

We both agree that the pasta program will be full of inspiration to find my flair. But until then, I still have to figure out where the heck I'll be staying. Which, as Greg so eloquently points out, is "absolutely insane. Who flies to another country without any plans for where to sleep?"

The CD loops back to the first track, and Dean Martin carols about a white Christmas.

"A wise friend once reassured me that details have a way of working themselves out."

❧

Underneath the foil lies a cheesecake. It's unassumingly plain, yet overwhelmingly enticing. Like when Audrey Hepburn wore a little black dress—it was the simplicity that made it beautiful.

"Oh my God." My smile is uncontrollable, pushing my cheeks up so high that they block the bottoms of my eyes. "Don't tell me you made this."

"I didn't make it. Your mom did."

I nearly spill the hot chocolate over the side of our matching snowman mugs that we got at the Christkindlmarket downtown a few years back. "You're gonna need to explain that one."

"You were so obsessed with the Italian cookbook that you didn't even notice the dessert one. I took the liberty of snapping a pic of the cheesecake recipe. *Voila*." He points to the cheesecake.

"Wait, I looked at that one after you left. There was no cheesecake recipe listed."

"Did you flip to the back? There's, like, five pages of notes."

I set down my snowman and immediately yank the recipe book in question from my kitchen drawer, flipping to the back where I indeed find pages of handwritten recipes that all appear to be my mom's creation. After scanning the cheesecake-less table of contents the other night, I'd stuffed the book in the drawer with a resigned sigh. "The red velvet cupcakes! Simon loved these! And there it is; there's the cheesecake, clear as day. Shortbread cookie crust and everything. It *was* almond extract!" I think back to the honey almond gelato from *Della Palma*, how it perfectly complimented the cheesecake flavor scooped beside it. "I was actually on the verge of figuring this one out."

"So, you don't want to try my cheesecake then?" he sasses me.

"Oh, I absolutely want to try it. But maybe I've had a little of my mom's culinary intuition in me all along and I was just too scared to trust it."

While I slice each of us a generous portion, Greg reaches into his bag and presents a jar of cherry pie filling, a bag of chocolate chips, and a Tupperware container of sliced almonds. "Take your pick: it's time to put your own twist on your mom's cheesecake."

Opting to top our slices with the cherries, we take our cake and hot chocolate into the living room, my tree proudly twinkling before the window for the city to see.

Greg scans the coffee table. "You've lived here half a decade and you still don't have coasters?"

Remembering my novelty coasters in the kitchen made from old records, I run back to grab them, nearly tripping over my winter boots sitting haphazardly by the door. "It's a Christmas miracle," I say, setting one before him. "I cook. I *coast*. I'm a new woman!"

"Speaking of new," Greg says, dipping a forkful of cheesecake into his hot chocolate—God, he can be brilliant sometimes— "when are we recording the new podcast episode? You said you have a bunch of reviews from your trip, and I haven't even seen 'em."

Between the bank headache, playing with my mom's old recipes, and now trying to find lodging for when I return to Italy, I've been too busy to even think about my Rome restaurant reviews.

"Let's do it today." I grab my *Order Up* notebook, flip it to the first review, and hand it to him.

He looks pleased, and flips through the rest. "April." He looks up at me. "These are all four-apple reviews."

"Actually, one got four apples plus an orange. What, you didn't expect me to dish out any cores in Italy, did you?"

"No, not cores, but maybe slice an apple in half or something. You didn't find even one thing wrong with these places?"

Shaking my head, I say, "Have you listened to our show? We're not exactly harsh food critics. I wanted to give bonuses to a few more, but that seemed excessive even for me." I stand, making my way back to the kitchen for another slice of cheesecake. The perfect cheesecake.

I pass the photo of me, my grandma, and my mom, and I can feel their spirit—her spirit—brightening up the holiday. It was a moment years ago, but it's also right there in front of me in the here and now. She's a part of my history, and a part of my present, living inside this wooden frame, in cheesecake batter and spaghetti sauce, in my dreams, memories, and forever in my heart.

EPILOGUE

The words leave my lips while my eyes remain shut, my head still cradled by the soft pillow.

He waits to respond until I look at him. "That phrase not on the flash cards, *Aprile.*"

I pull the covers farther up to block the burning sunrise, nestling myself in Gio's dangerously comfortable bed. "It's not. I've been using an app before class when you're at work."

He gasps, putting his hand over where his heart lies beneath his bare chest. "You study without me?"

"Mostly for verb conjugations."

He gently pulls the covers back from my face just a smidge, ignoring my protests. "The sun… it paints your hair gold in the morning." He tucks a few strands behind my ear.

I smirk, trying to play it cool, but the fire on my cheeks paints them pink.

He asks if I was merely practicing verb conjugations now, or if I was really asking the question. "Is today finally beach day?" Hope sparkles in his gray irises, almost looking as blue as the sea we'll be splashing in today. I pause before answering, taking a mental photo of the scene: the two of us, in his warm bed, beams of an orange sun setting the room on fire with a vivacious warmth. After three weeks of waking up next to Gio, I'm kicking myself for almost turning down his offer to let me stay with him, but I had no other options. I guess this was one time desperation worked in my favor. With only one week left in the pasta program, I'm savoring every second until I return home. The smell of raw dough, flour wedged under my fingernails, the Italian spring air filling my lungs, Giovanni's open heart melting mine with every beautiful word he says.

"*Oggi é il giorno.*" Today is the day.

He smiles and leans over, pulling the covers all the way over our heads. His rough stubble tickles my cheek as he kisses my ear, and his hands don't neglect a single inch of my body, as they travel from my cheeks, my collarbone, to my tummy, grumbling with a hunger for one of his spectacular breakfasts that will have to wait a little longer.

✍

He glances back at me while standing at the kitchen sink, his eyes smiling at me while the water rinses the *cornetti* crumbs from our plates.

"*Grazie per la colazione.*" It's the first time I've thanked him for breakfast in Italian, and his silence can only mean one thing. "Crap." In the center of the small kitchen table sits a pot of bright pink azaleas, and their petals jiggle as I lean against the table, defeated. Flustered, I snap my fingers while my brain scrambles to find the right Italian words. "Uh, *capisci?* Did I say it wrong? Is my accent atrocious?"

"*Hai capito*," he corrects me. "But, no, you sound *perfetta*." He turns the water off and walks over to me, scooping me up into his arms. "I was thinking of which beach to visit. There is one—beautiful views—but it is near *Napoli*. Far drive. Or there is one closer… with a castle." He arches one eyebrow, setting free a twinkle in his eye that seems to already know my answer.

"I didn't pack my suit of armor. Will that be a problem?"

He lets go of me after kissing both my cheeks and waves his hand as he walks toward the bathroom. "*Nessun problema.* Bring clothes for over your swimsuit. We can walk through the castle this evening."

While Gio shaves away his dark stubble, I rummage through my suitcase for my swimsuit, tags still dangling from the straps. It's balled up underneath a shirt that's covered in flour residue. I had brought a bag of flour back to his apartment after class a couple weeks ago, eager for Gio to show me some kneading and rolling techniques he'd promised me. But I'd grabbed the bag of flour by the wrong end, completely whitewashing his kitchen tile.

"Oh, God, butterfinger alert." I knelt down, desperately grabbing fistfuls of flour and throwing them in the sink, clouds of dust trailing behind like the smoke of miniature jets taking flight. "Do you have a mop? Or a shovel? Geez." I coughed, inhaling some of the powder. I worried when he didn't answer. He must regret opening his apartment to me, I'd thought. But when I looked up, he was doubled over, shoulders shaking with quiet laughter. He reached down and grabbed a fistful of flour, launching it directly at my shirt.

"I need that for my *tagliatelle*! How dare you deplete my

ingredients!" My smile gave away my happiness though; I'd finally gotten floured by an Italian cook.

You can't use this now, he'd protested. "Now, it is for play." He flung another handful at me.

"This is war."

His kitchen was unrecognizable after five minutes.

When we called a truce and felt it was time to change clothes, he began peeling off his shirt right there in the kitchen. Changing clothes suddenly fell to the back burner while better activities presented themselves.

I sigh at the memory, at how easy time seems to pass with Gio by my side. I carefully take my top from the suitcase, folding it inward so as not to leave a trace of powder in his bedroom—not so much because he'd need to clean the rug, but because I know he'd wash my shirt, wondering why I hadn't done so yet. Sure, it would be a charming sight, my top hanging delicately from the clothesline out of a Roman apartment, but I'd rather not wash away such a fond memory yet.

The Santa Severa Castle brings major fourteenth century medieval vibes to the shores of a wide, peaceful beach. That's one of the most miraculous things about Italy: its past isn't buried or stashed away in a moth-eaten box, but it's alive and well, mingling with the present like an old friend.

It's easily the hottest day of the month so far, with temperatures flirting with eighty underneath a sweltering sun. All of Rome seems to be ready to welcome summer, half naked people taking up nearly every inch of sand. Gio and I share an oversized beach towel close to the water. He hands me a lemonade from the bar, and I can't tell which is sweating more: the glass or his chest. Better look at his chest a little longer to be certain. The patch of dark hair in the center ruffles in the breeze. It feels soft between my fingertips.

"You decide what to cook for your final?" He props himself up on an elbow.

Another of Italy's magical powers is that time passes faster here. In less than a week, I'll already be preparing my own pasta dish for the final exam at CII. The parameters are rather loose; as long as we prepare any of the pastas we've studied in class, we're encouraged to use our own intuition to create an original dish. Sauces, cheeses, garnishes… all up to us. Six months of following the recipes in my mom's old books without ruining them stroked my ego, but I wasn't in the driver's seat then. Now, I need to become a pasta architect, designing my own signature dish tasty enough to stand up to scrutiny.

"I'm thinking about doing a twist on spaghetti. At first, I was thinking about making some type of citrusy lemon sauce, but I think I'm going to go in a totally different direction." I push my sunglasses up on my head. My pupils contract in the sun, and I look Gio right in the eyes, lowering my head and leaning in as if I'm about to reveal a juicy secret. "Spaghetti pie." A gulp of cold lemonade trickles down my throat, the sugary citrus dancing on my tongue while teenagers dance where the sand meets the water, their footprints lasting seconds before washing away.

"A dessert pasta? You love *la dolce vita* too much, *bella*. The teachers… they faint!" As if the unobstructed ball of fire in the sky isn't melting me enough, he flashes a charming smile that threatens to turn me into a puddle.

"Not a dessert; it'll be a savory pie. Light on sauce—which will be based on my mom's, of course. I'll toss some meat in there—I'm thinking a sausage of some sort—and eggs and cheese to keep it all together. Garnish it with fresh basil. What do you think? Have I lost my mind?" I clasp my hands together in a gesture of hope.

He tilts his head, his eyes inquisitive. "*Una frittata?*"

I clap twice. "Yes! But fewer eggs and more spaghetti. It's all the joys of regular spaghetti without the need to twirl a fork."

"It is a trick to cut the pasta!" He pinches my chin and kisses me on the cheek. "I think it is probably delicious. You should do it." The teenagers move farther into the water, splashing each other and laughing. Gio nods toward the sea. "Ready to get wet?"

We split what's left of my lemonade, and walk along the shore away from the castle to a spot that's less crowded. The rush of the water drowns away the noise of people anticipating a new season. The waves constantly shift shape as they cascade barreling toward the shore, leaving their past behind them without so much as a glance, before crashing into oblivion at our feet. I see my life reflected on the white tips of the waves, my past simultaneously behind me, yet also a part of my present, planted in my core as my future blooms around it. Gio holds out his hand and I take it. As we walk into the Tyrrhenian Sea, I embrace the impermanence of everything, the clear blue water a peaceful reminder that everything carries with it the things that are no longer here. All we ever really have is the moment we're in. It was bittersweet landing at Fiumicino three weeks ago, the hands on the clock already ticking the month away. How could Gio and I possibly go back to nightly video chats with an ocean separating us again? But learning to let go is freeing. Accepting the impermanence of everything—and everyone—refines our ability to appreciate them, highlighting the value they add to our lives.

"She would be proud of you." Gio pulls me toward him, the water nearly up to our shoulders. After a beat he adds, "I'm proud of you. Three weeks ago—" under the water, he takes my hands in his "—these hands did not know how to knead dough." His laugh is light and joyous, and it lifts me up to the skies. It's a sound that may be absent from my future, but it can never be erased from my present. And that's enough. Because as long as we carry those who were important to us in our hearts, they never really leave us.

"Well, your one-on-one instruction has been quite thorough." I grin at him while raising an eyebrow. The heat on my skin isn't from the sun. The wind kicks up a spray of salt right as our lips meet, and it's a treat for the senses sweeter than any Italian dessert.

Our moment in the sea is subjected to Italy's unpredictable passage of time. Minutes—hours? —later, Gio says, "*Il castello ci aspetta.*"

"As much as I'm enjoying this," I gesture to the surrounding waters, the sparkling white tips of the waves, "I don't want to keep the castle waiting any longer. It's already been there for hundreds of years. The least we can do is be on time for our tour."

"After, I show you the beach on the other side. The sand is black."

I laugh, tossing my head back, my hair dipping into the sea.

"Oh, I promise, it is no joke."

"No, I know, it's just… there's surprises on every corner here. A beach with a castle, black sand… Italy's always got something up its sleeve, doesn't it?"

"There is always a secret Rome waits to share. You just need to be willing to look."

RECIPES

APRIL'S SPAGHETTI PIE

3 tablespoons olive oil

2 cloves garlic,
  chopped finely

Half an onion,
  chopped finely

1 large carrot, chopped
  and blended in
  food processor

6 ounces Italian sausage,
  peeled and crumbled

1 fifteen ounce can
  tomato sauce

10 ounces spaghetti

4 eggs

1 cup shredded mozzarella

1 tablespoon sugar

1 teaspoon honey

A few fresh basil leaves,
  chopped

A few sprigs of fresh parsley

Heat olive oil in large frying pan, and add onions and garlic. Stir occasionally for about five minutes.

Add sausage and stir for another five minutes.

Add tomato sauce, blended carrot, sugar, basil, and honey, and cook over medium heat for another ten minutes.

In the meantime, cook spaghetti in a pot of boiling water until al dente. Drain and add cooked pasta to the frying pan, mixing it with the sauce.

Preheat oven to 350 degrees and grease an 11-inch cake pan.

Add eggs and mozzarella to the saucy pasta and mix well.

Transfer pasta to cake pan and cook in the oven's middle rack for 20 minutes.

Let it set for another five minutes before slicing. Garnish with fresh basil or parsley and enjoy!

TURKEY MEATBALLS IN THE FAMOUS APPLEBY TOMATO SAUCE

For the sauce:

18 oz. tomato paste

30 oz. water

1 Tbs fresh chopped basil

1 Tbs sugar

1 Tbs honey

3 Tbs olive oil

3 cloves garlic, crushed

a pinch of salt & pepper

half an onion, diced

4 oz. goat cheese

For the meatballs:

1 lb ground turkey

4 cloves garlic, diced

2 ½ cups bread crumbs

½ cup parmesan cheese

1 egg

1 tsp parsley

1 tsp red pepper flakes

dash of salt and pepper

Mix all the meat ingredients in a large bowl with clean hands, and shape into balls. Place on a plate and chill in fridge while preparing sauce.

In a large sauce pan over medium heat, add garlic and onions in the olive oil for few minutes, then add tomato paste, water, honey, sugar, salt, and pepper. Then stir in the goat cheese until melted.

In a frying pan over medium heat, brown the meatballs in olive oil for about 15 - 20 minutes, or until browned on all sides.

Then place balls in sauce, and let simmer on low heat for one hour, adding basil toward the end. Stir occasionally.

Serve on top of spaghetti, with garlic bread or *bruschetta*, on a bed of rice, or just eat them on their own! Sprinkle a bit more parmesan and enjoy! Serves six.

EASY CHEESY SPINACH LASAGNA WITH THE SPECIAL APPLEBY CHEESE BLEND

8 oz. goat cheese

15 oz. ricotta cheese

1 ½ cups parmesan cheese

2 cups shredded mozzarella cheese

24 oz. tomato sauce

16 oz. lasagna sheets

2 ½ oz. baby spinach

1 ½ tsp basil

1 tsp parsley

Squirt of honey

Nonstick cooking spray

Pinch of salt

Boil lasagna sheets in plenty of salted boiling water. While pasta cooks, prepare cheese blend. Mix goat cheese, ricotta cheese, 1 tsp basil, and honey into one bowl. Mix 1 cup parmesan cheese, mozzarella cheese, and parsley in another bowl.

Spray a pan with cooking spray.

Spread one-third of the sauce on the bottom, followed by a third of the spinach, then a third of the parmesan/mozzarella mixture. Then add a layer of cooked lasagna sheets, followed by one-third of the goat cheese/ricotta mixture. Repeat those layers twice more.

Top with ½ cup parmesan and ½ tsp of basil. Bake at 375 degrees for 35 minutes, then let sit for fifteen minutes. Serve with bread and a salad, and enjoy!

GIO'S ITALIAN HOT CHOCOLATE

2 cups milk

6 oz. dark chocolate chips

4 Tbs sugar

4 Tbs cocoa powder

2 Tbs Nutella

1 tsp cinnamon

Pour milk in saucepan over medium heat until warm.

Add chocolate chips and stir until melted.

Add cocoa powder, sugar, cinnamon, and Nutella. Stir until smooth.

Drink out of your favorite holiday mugs and enjoy! Or serve with cookies, marshmallows, or fresh fruit. It should be thick enough to dip, like fondue! Makes about 4 servings.

APRIL'S CHEESECAKE SNOWBALLS

8 oz. cream cheese, softened
1 cup powdered sugar
4 Tbs butter, melted
1 tsp almond extract
pinch of nutmeg
6 oz. biscotti cookies, crumbled

Mix cream cheese, butter, almond extract, and nutmeg in a bowl. Then stir in the sugar.

Crumble cookies in another bowl, and sprinkle a layer of crumbs onto a large plate or tray.

Scoop cheese batter into balls and drop them onto the layer of crumbs. (They will be too goopy to form into perfect balls right now, but that's okay!)

Use a spoon to sprinkle more cookie crumbs on top of the cheese globs, and set the tray in freezer for at least an hour.

After chilling, grab the globs and roll each in the bowl with the remaining cookie crumbs. They should be firm enough to mold into balls now.

Sprinkle with more powdered sugar, and enjoy! Makes about two dozen snowballs.

ACKNOWLEDGMENTS

This book has been my world for the past three and half years. Each chapter, each character, each scene an ingredient adding its own flavor to complete *A Recipe from Rome*. This story wouldn't have been nearly as tasty without help from the following people:

Gratitude to my editor Vivien Williams of Blackwater Press. From your assessment of an early version of the manuscript to the final edits of the book, your professional eye and creative suggestions helped to reframe the story in a much stronger way taking it to new heights. April and Simon benefitted greatly from your stellar editing and keen knowledge of Italian culture. Any remaining errors are mine and mine alone. Thank you. Or should I say *grazie mille*?

Gratitude to Elizabeth Ford of Blackwater Press. The feedback from your assessment of an early version of the manuscript gave me clarity on the big picture and helped me strengthen the narrative. Thank you.

Kim Bookless, your wealth of knowledge about the literary and publishing world helped to steer me in the right direction when I wasn't sure what the next step was. Thank you for being so generous with your time and resources.

Amy Austin, thank you for taking the time to read an early version of the manuscript and sharing your honest opinion.

To the supportive online "bookstagram" community, you are the best damn cheerleaders an author could ever ask for. Thank you for your encouragement and virtual high fives.

Readers, thank you for flipping through these pages and taking a chance on a first-time author—it means more to me than you could possibly know. I hope this story transported you to Italy.

To my friend who took me on a trip to Rome, which inspired this book. You know who you are. Thank you for sharing this fascinating city with me, and for giving me all your bread.

Last, but never least, thank you to my mother for literally everything I am blessed with in my life. I don't know where I'd be without you. Or your mini cheesecakes.

ABOUT THE AUTHOR

Laura Botten is a voice actor and radio producer based in the Chicago area. Her work has been published in the online literary magazine *10th Ward Lit*, and she writes regularly on her blog. When she's not writing, she's daydreaming, reading, playing with her cat, singing along off-key to seventies rock, and over-indulging in cupcakes. This is her first book.

You can keep up with her online at her website *www. LauraBotten.com* or on Instagram @laura.botten

If you enjoyed this book, please tell your friends, or consider leaving a review online to help other readers find it.